# *Faultless* LOVE

## KG Fletcher

VINCI
BOOKS

## By KG Fletcher

The Bennetts of Langston Falls

*Faultless Love*

*Shameless Love*

*Breathless Love*

*Reckless Love*

*Fearless Love*

The Stardust Duet

*Love's Refrain*

*Love's Reverie*

*For my mother, Patricia,*
*who raised all five of us in a home filled with love.*
*So much love.*

Vinci Books

vinci-books.com

Published by Vinci Books Ltd in 2026

1

The publisher and the author have made every effort to obtain permissions for any third party material used in this book and to comply with copyright law. Any queries in this respect should be brought to the attention of the publisher and any omissions will be corrected in future editions.

A CIP catalogue record for this book is available from the British Library.

Paperback ISBN: 9781036708160

The EU GPSR authorised representative is Logos Europe, 9 rue Nicolas Poussion, 17000 La Rochelle, France contact@logoseurope.eu

# Chapter One

## TED BENNETT

Ted Bennett walked in a single file line behind the row of inmates toward the steel door leading to the common area outside. The men jostled for their first taste of fresh air in twenty-four hours, and most ignored a torn and tattered colorful motivational poster taped to the cinder block walls while en route. The guys liked to make fun of the optimistic prison chaplain responsible for putting the poster up. He was known for his intentional inspirations that peppered the dark, dank prison, this particular poster reading; "Freedom is nothing but a chance to be better."

Passing this poster day in and day out, most of the guys only had one thing on their mind: sunlight, and a few precious minutes of clean air. But for Ted Bennett, it was different. He read the saying every day for five long years and swore to himself he'd live by those words when he was finally set free. The phrase motivated his exemplary behavior, his romantic notions of hope turning the page to the latest chapter in his life. No matter how many times he looked at the razor-topped fence line, he had no idea how good it would feel to walk through the yard toward the gate to freedom. And now, finally, he was given an opportunity to prove himself to the outside world.

The warmth from the late summer sun penetrated the bus window as a beam of iridescence peeked through the clouds and landed on Ted's bare arm. He blinked against the ray of bright light, eyes hidden behind a pair of scratched sunglasses that had seen better days. Hours earlier, his former roommate, a big lug-of-a-man aptly named Rocky, had tossed the glasses to him on his way out of the halfway house in Blue Ridge.

"Make good choices, Teddy Bear," Rocky teased with a smirk.

The look on his grizzled face emoted joy, or maybe it was jealousy. Ted would never know because he wasn't looking back. Today, he was a free man. Well, technically, he was in phase three of his split sentence. For the next twelve months of his life, he'd be supervised by his new parole officer, who was waiting for him at the next stop of his journey —home.

An elderly woman sitting across the bus aisle bit down on an apple, the crunch causing Ted to look her way. His mouth watered just thinking about the sweet fruit, his last meal hours ago.

"You want one?" Her gray eyes crinkled in a polite smile as she pulled another ripe apple from a bag resting on her lap. Thrusting her hand across the aisle, she offered it to him. "Go on. I got plenty."

Ted hesitated and stared at her gnarled fingers surrounding the fruit's red skin. When their eyes met, his lips twitched into a genuine smile, her random act of kindness catching him off guard.

"Thank you, ma'am." Taking the apple from her hand, he eagerly took a large bite.

The woman chewed while watching him, as if giving him the onceover. His shoulder-length sandy brown hair was tied back at the nape of his neck, and his sharp jaw was covered with a well-groomed beard. Gone was the clean-cut, guy-next-door version of his former self, the years in prison morphing him into a harder, and more cautious man. The thick rope of muscles rising from his arms, back, and across his chest were formidable and impressive, his t-shirt taut with ripples of strength thwarting off any trouble.

"You visiting out here?" she asked with boldness. Her confidence in chatting with a guy three times her size was beguiling, most folks erring on the side of caution when he was in their vicinity.

Ted shook his head, wiping his lips with the back of his hand. "No ma'am. I'm... on my way home."

"What were you up to?"

Adjusting the bent frames of his sunglasses, Ted exhaled a long breath and clenched his jaw. He knew she was only trying to make small talk and didn't want to come across as rude, especially after sharing her apples. Pondering what to say, he glanced out the window. The late-summer scenery in Georgia's northeast corner whizzed by him in hues of faded forest green and sky blue, freedom a pinprick on the horizon.

"I was, uh... visiting an old friend." He shifted in his seat to where he looked right at her. "He needed me."

"Was your friend sick? Of course, it's none of my business." She looked away, as if embarrassed by her question.

Ted cleared his throat. "He was... in prison."

Her thin eyebrows raised in surprise.

"It was a horrible place and... and almost broke him,"

he continued. "My friend was convicted of a crime he didn't commit."

Ted's nostrils flared thinking about the day the unfortunate verdict was handed down to him. He was nothing more than an innocent bystander during a prank gone wrong—a joke that changed so many lives in a single moment. Unfortunately, the jury determined he was an accessory to the crime. The judge handed down the harshest penalty possible, making an example out of him. The cruel sentence changed the course of his life forever.

The elderly woman stared back at him. "That's terrible. Couldn't your friend get an appeal?"

Ted shook his head. He wasn't threatened by the woman or her questions in the least, and it felt good to talk to someone outside the constraints of his former life behind bars.

"He tried, numerous times. His appeals were always denied."

"Well, how did he do it being locked up for so long, especially as an innocent man? I can't even imagine."

Looking at the apple in his hand, Ted sighed. "He lived day by day, hour by hour... second by second. He toughed it out until the very end."

The woman nodded. "He sounds like a very courageous man."

Ted eyed her again and gulped down his emotions threatening to surface. His voice hushed. "He thinks he's a coward."

"A coward? No. Not an innocent man like him."

The bus wheels hummed across the highway, the quite chatter of other passengers nothing but background noise. The two of them quietly ate their apples for a few minutes before her next question caught him off guard.

4

"How long were you in there?"

His head jerked to find her leaned against her seatback staring at him, the smile on her face emoting empathy and understanding. She'd figured him out.

Clenching his jaw, he nodded. He wasn't going to continue lying to her, his longing for authentic communication and genuine interaction put to the test.

"Too long." He bowed his head in shame. "Five years in the state penitentiary, twelve months in a half-way house, and now... three hundred and sixty-five days of parole ahead of me."

His eyes glistened from behind his sunglasses as he ran a fist under his nose. He was more than ready to get back to his family in Langston Falls. Back to his father, brothers, and sister who ran the family business. But his sentence was far from over. He had hundreds of community service hours to complete, monthly interaction with his new parole officer for the next year, and numerous fences to mend among the people in the small town where he grew up.

Eyeing the woman again, he offered her a big grin. "I appreciate the apple, ma'am. I didn't realize how hungry I was."

She nodded, both of them saluting their apples in the air. As he took his last bite, he was startled when she reached across the aisle and placed her hand on his shoulder.

"You've got this." Her encouragement meant the world to him.

A half hour later, the bus made a wide turn into the Langston Falls station on the outskirts of town near the railroad tracks. Right away, Ted noticed his father standing near the liftgate of his old pick-up truck. The family's patriarch was larger than life, his imposing figure reminding Ted of a black bear standing on his hind legs. But looking at him through the bus window, Ted noticed his father's dark hair peppered with more silver since the last time he saw him, and his shoulders slumped ever-so-slightly. His father must've been working too hard, and Ted vowed to take some of the pressure off now that he was back. Peeling red letters spelling "Bennett Christmas Tree Farm & Winery" on his dad's truck made his lip twitch with a smile, the rolling vineyards and evergreen blanket of trees across two-hundred acres of family land coming to mind.

He was almost there.

Filing out of the bus among the crowd, Ted bid the elderly woman farewell. Stepping off the last stair, his pace quickened as he walked across the hot asphalt toward his father. Roy looked on, his mouth high-jacked into a fatherly grin as he rested his hands on his denim-clad hips.

"Hey, Dad," Ted said, his voice faltering with profound melancholy. He stopped mere feet in front of his father, the veins in his hand noticeable as he clutched a beat-up leather bag strap in a death-grip, the satchel holding only a few things leftover from his incarcerated life.

"Teddy," Roy's baritone voice rumbled. "Let me get a good look at you, son."

Ted lifted his chin and stood a little taller.

Roy nodded, pressing his lips into a thin line, his eyes raking up and down Ted's looming six-foot frame. Finally, his dad closed the gap between them, wrapping his arms around him in a firm hug. The tender gesture surprised Ted, and he dropped his bag, gripping his dad's back.

"Welcome home, Teddy. Welcome home." Roy's voice was raspy with emotion—the emotions Ted couldn't seem to express buried deep in a hardened heart begging to be set free. His father's sentimental display was unusual for a man who was all ease: constant chuckles, friendly winks, and a total comfort in his farm-tanned skin. But Father Time had definitely taken a toll on Father Bennett.

"Thanks, Dad." Ted pressed his eyes shut. Breathing in his father's familiar scent, the fleeting essence of pine trees and winery grapes were a heady combination.

They lingered in the hug until Roy broke their connection and sheepishly pulled a bandanna from his pocket, scrubbing the fabric across his wrinkled eyes. "Well, that's enough of that," he announced. He picked up Ted's bag and headed toward the truck, efficiently tossing it into the empty bed, his feelings once again in check.

"Becky's got your room all ready for ya, and she's been cooking up a storm since we finally learned when you were coming home. I'm willing to bet she made all your favorites."

Ted went around to the passenger side and slid across the worn upholstery. The mere mention of his baby sister conjured up all kinds of brotherly sentiments. The last time he'd laid eyes on her, she was a freshman in high school, a pretty little girl with a heart-melting smile.

"How is Becks, Dad?"

Roy turned the key in the ignition, and the truck motor groaned to life. Backing out of the space, Roy kept the conversation positive. "She's doing fine. Keeps the hired guns well-fed and has come a long way with some great event planning."

"Event planning? Becky?"

"Yep. Thanks to your baby sister, we've got a few annual festivals on the calendar now. The tourists love it and believe it or not, these events have tripled our income in the last two years. But she'll tell ya all about it when we get home."

"You never mentioned this to me before."

"Well, I didn't want to overwhelm you with all the changes while you were away."

"Please, Dad. Tell me about it now. Becks can fill me in with more details later."

Roy paused for a beat before he offered a quick nod. "Well, we got the Harvest Hoedown coming up next month. There's already a billboard up on the Blue Ridge Parkway advertising it. And then we got the Christmas Tree Festival in December, the Grape Stomp, Honeybee Festival…."

"Wait a minute," Ted interrupted. "How can you run all these new festivals and still have time to run the Christmas tree farm *and* the winery?" He was wide-eyed with genuine concern, eyes glued to his father, who chuckled in response. No wonder his dad looked tired.

"Now, don't you worry about a thing, Teddy. A lot has changed over the years, and we've hired quite a few more folks to get things done. It was always your mama's idea to incorporate some fun celebrations into the farm. I guess you could say your little sister made a promise to her and has followed through with flying colors. It's a real family affair with your brothers helping out, too. And now that you're home, you'll fit right into the mix. I know your mama would be proud having all her children working together. It's what she always wanted."

Ted blinked back a sudden surge of emotions, the mention of his sweet mother causing his heart to gallop like a racehorse. Thoughts of her often comforted him while he was in prison: her deep laughter and kind eyes. The feel of her strong arms wrapped around his neck in a motherly hug. Her soft voice telling him everything would work out how it was supposed to.

When the warden delivered the news Lillian Bennett

had succumbed to her long battle with cancer, the only thing Ted wanted was to see his mama one last time. But there wasn't a goddamn thing he could do about it. Adding more salt to his wounds, he wasn't even allowed to pay his final respects at her funeral on the family land, confined like an animal in his cell and left alone to grieve her death between the cold concrete walls. He would never forgive himself for not being there for her in her last days. Ever.

Roy reached over and squeezed Ted on the shoulder as if he understood. "She loved you very much, Teddy. I like to think she's your guardian angel now, looking out for you."

Ted didn't dare look at his father for fear he might lose control and fall completely apart. What was up with all the angst and melancholy bubbling up since he left the halfway house? He was stronger than this—he had to be.

Nodding, he gritted his teeth and turned his attention to the forest wall lining the two-lane highway, the dizzying colors of nature whizzing by much like the painful memories of the last six years of his life. He felt sick to his stomach, the onslaught of recollections he'd kept tucked away filling his mind. His case manager warned him he might find himself on an emotional roller coaster once he was back home and advised him to carefully navigate his feelings, or he might implode and get into more trouble. Boy, he wasn't kidding.

"Lookie over there, Teddy. Fred Wagner changed out his fence a few months ago. Kind of girlie lookin' if you ask me." Leave it to his father to change the subject with an added injection of humor.

Ted looked past his father out the window at their neighbor's pristine white picket fence line with a subtle scalloped edge. The faded pasture beyond the posts was dotted with a few grazing horses. A long time ago, he'd ridden a horse or two on the Wagner property with his girlfriend, Robyn Morgan, by his side.

Robyn. Sweet, beautiful, blameless Robyn, the only girl he ever loved.

She was his high school and college sweetheart, the one he was sure he'd spend the rest of his life with. They'd gone through most of their young adult lives together, their youth and virility blazing with certain promise. She'd just started law school when everything came crashing down, her goal to become an attorney like her father. Everything came to a screeching halt during the trials, Robyn putting her schooling on hold, faithful as she stood by him until the very end. Her tear-stained face was seared into his memory on the fateful day when he was taken away in handcuffs and sent to hell. Even her father, who'd represented him in court, couldn't save him from the life-altering sentence, his plea deal accepted with the pounding resonance of the gavel, sealing his fate, and setting her free.

Ted pinched his lower lip between his fingers and pushed down his tender feelings. He'd cut off all communication with Robyn while he was behind bars, claiming it was for the best. A strong, intelligent woman like her didn't need to be tied down to a convicted felon like him. But now that he was out on probation, he knew the time would come to revisit Robyn sooner rather than later and tell her face to face how sorry he was for what he'd put her through. He'd rehearsed the moment over and over in his head for years. Would she accept his apology? Or would she look at him with disdain and remorse, the years they'd shared nothing but a distant memory she'd rather forget?

Once upon a time, his entire life was a large canvas dotted with colorful dreams and aspirations with his forever girl grinning by his side. But those days were long gone, Robyn's smile nothing more than a faded image on a few photographs he carried close to his heart. And Ted was a different person now—a harder, unforgiving man with a lot of baggage to unpack and sift through.

"Wagner's fence line is very girlie, Dad," he finally agreed. Roy's shoulders shook as he chuckled with mirth, the sound a healing balm to Ted's wounded spirit.

A few minutes later, the truck slowed, and the entrance of the family homestead greeted him with gratifying grandeur. His heart swelled with pride as they drove under the curve of the custom, heavy-gauge steel letters spelling out "Bennett Farms." Perfectly trimmed gardenia bushes dotted with withering white flowers, and a few tall Georgia pines flanked the entry, the visual stunning Ted with legitimate homesickness.

Roy bypassed the drive leading to the main house and took a detour down a long, graveled road dead-ending at a storage facility on the outskirts of the farm.

"We're not meeting my parole officer at home?" Ted asked, confusion mounting his expression.

"We thought it'd be best to get this initial meeting over with away from everybody else, and then we can celebrate with your siblings who are waitin' for ya at the main house, okay?" Roy glanced at Ted with a furrowed brow.

"Sounds good, Dad."

His case manager at the halfway house explained his new parole officer, Sam McNeil would be waiting for him when he arrived. Ted noticed a car already parked by an open garage which housed some of the equipment used on the farm.

"Hopefully, Mr. McNeil isn't a complete asshole who wants to make my life a living hell for the next year."

Roy cocked his head with a harrumph. "Well, here's the funny part, son. Sam McNeil isn't what you're expecting."

Ted frowned. "I'm not following you, Dad."

The moment the driver's side door of the car opened, he understood. *She* wasn't what he was expecting at all.

# Chapter Two

## TEDDY

Ted's boots crunched along the gravel as he approached his parole officer with curiosity. Sam McNeil held her chin high with a look of expectation, her smile causing him to instinctively smile back. Even with her dark hair pulled back into a tight bun, black-rimmed glasses covering her brown eyes, and dressed in modest business attire with sensible shoes, Ted could tell she was a looker.

"Mrs. McNeil. Hi." He awkwardly shoved his hand out and was surprised by her firm and steady shake.

"Theodore Bennett. Welcome home."

"Please, call me Ted or Teddy. That's what everyone else calls me around here. Theodore is my birth name and a little too formal if you ask me." Shifting his weight back and forth, he averted her imposing gaze as if he might have already crossed a line talking to an officer of the law in such a friendly manner.

"I mean, you can call me whatever you want, ma'am."

"How about I call you Ted, and you can call me Miss

McNeil. Once we get to know each other a little better, I might even let you call me Sam. Deal?"

Ted's eyes shot to her face as she continued to smile back at him. Nodding, he casually peeked at her left hand and confirmed she wasn't a Mrs. at all—no wedding ring.

"Um, sure, Miss McNeil. You're the boss."

Roy came up and palmed Ted's shoulder. "Miss McNeil has already scoped out your living quarters at the house and chatted with some of your siblings about what's expected in this next phase of your sentencing. Two thumbs up from the get-go, right chief?"

"That's right," she grinned, nonplussed by his father's use of the nickname, "chief." "My goal today is to make sure you arrived safe and sound. I also need you to sign off on some official paperwork, get a urine sample, and I need to look through any personal items you might have brought home with you from the halfway house. Other than that, we'll schedule our next meeting a week from today to see how you're adapting and to give you a chance to set up your community service hours."

"Okay," Ted agreed. "All I brought from the halfway house is in one duffle bag. It's just some clothes, my Bible, and a few photos. The bag is in the truck bed."

"Great." Miss McNeil pulled a small plastic bag from the purse dangling over her arm. Inside was an obvious specimen cup with a yellow lid. Ted's credentials were clearly marked on the bag and the cup.

"Why don't we get this part over with." She turned to Roy. "Is there a facility nearby where Ted and I can go?"

"Uh, sure thing. He knows where it is in the back of the first garage."

Ted scowled as Miss McNeil handed the bag off to him. "I don't understand."

Sam cocked a perfect eyebrow, her position as his appointed parole officer on full display. "As an offender under parole, the court has set certain conditions that should be strictly followed. These include adherence to curfews, non-possession of firearms, employment, and non-intake of alcoholic beverages and drugs. Random testing is a preventative tactic against any violations while granted parole." Her response was a memorized speech hitting all the bullet points of his new reality.

With her hands on her hips, she eyed Ted inquisitively. "I want you to succeed, Ted. And testing is one way to help achieve our goal and maintain compliance within the corrections system. Now, I know your farm includes a popular winery. I've already spoken to your father about keeping your employment away from the blended grapes so you're not tempted to indulge. Just stick to the Christmas tree side of things, and you'll be fine. Do you think you can handle it? Or do we need to come up with a plan B, off property?"

Ted swallowed hard, the tone of Miss McNeil's voice professional and firm. This lady meant business.

"I was, uh, already planning to work on the Christmas tree farm."

"Good," she grinned, waving her arm out in front of her. "Shall we, then?"

"Excuse me?"

"I need a urine sample to take back to town for analysis. Is there a problem?"

"You're going to... watch me piss?" Ted thought his days of humiliating public exposure in the penitentiary were long behind him.

"Yes, Ted. I'm required to watch the urine flow leave your body and go into this little cup. Your 'piss,' as you called it, is evidence. Believe me, this is not one of the perks of my job."

"Get it over with, son," Roy encouraged. His cheeks were flushed a rosy red as if embarrassed for him.

"Fine."

Ted walked through the open garage, passing several tractors and bailers stored for the Christmas tree season. He could play by the court's rules, even if it meant exposing the family jewels in front of Sam. When he approached the bathroom door at the back of the building, he inhaled a deep breath and gripped the knob, forcing it open on squeaky hinges. The smell of bleach hit his senses as if the toilet had recently been cleaned, although the dingy builder-grade tile still held definite grunge throughout the grout in the floor space, dirty footprints of the hired help evident.

Of course, it was just his luck to be assigned a female probation officer. Tension mounted in his rigid stance, knowing what he was about to do in front of her. If the probation officer was a guy, he'd have no problem whipping out his dick and pissing on command. But having a petite, no-nonsense, *attractive* female watching his every move made him hesitate. His fingers fumbled as he unzipped his jeans, the presence of Sam and the invasion of her female hormones in the tiny space making his feral mind run wild. He hadn't been this close to the opposite sex in years, most of the officers he'd reported to of the male species.

"Here, let me help." She grabbed the clear bag and took out the cup. With a quick twist of her delicate wrist, she unscrewed the yellow top and handed the cup to him.

Ted muttered a polite "thanks" and nervously pulled out his penis. The damn thing was starting to get hard in his hand as Miss McNeil's gaze took in his length.

"So," she started. There wasn't a hint of shyness or discomfort in her tone. "Are you glad to be home, Ted? Are you looking forward to seeing the rest of your family and some of your friends?"

"Um, yeah. Sure." Ted blew out a long breath, silently begging his dick to cooperate under the circumstances.

*Langston Falls. Water. Waterfalls. Raindrops keep falling on my head...* he thought to himself.

How was he ever going to piss when the appendage in his hand was turning rock-hard? A tiny trickle of urine finally sputtered from his tip, and he willed himself to relax. As if satisfied by what she witnessed, Miss McNeil politely turned away, giving him the privacy he needed to finish the job.

"Well, you have a lovely family. I hope we can get through your probation period without any mishaps. I'm only a phone call away if you have any problems or concerns."

Ted managed to screw the lid on the cup, sheepishly handing it off to Miss McNeil before he shook his dick, tucked it back into his jeans, and zipped them up. Turning toward the small sink mounted on the wall, he quickly washed his hands. The worst was over, for now.

"I can assure you, there won't be any problems, Miss McNeil."

"Great!" She turned and nonchalantly walked out of the bathroom carrying his urine sample safely deposited into the clear bag. She made it seem like it was something she did every day.

Back at the truck, Sam looked through his bag with efficiency and nodded. "You're good to go, Ted." She pulled a card from the breast pocket of her summer blazer. "Here's my number and the info regarding our meeting next week. I'm always on time, and I expect you to be as well."

Ted eyed the card with Miss McNeil's credentials. "Of course."

Turning toward his father, Sam nodded curtly. "Mr. Bennett, it was a pleasure meeting you. I look forward to a positive outcome in your son's case."

"Absolutely. You have my word."

"Thanks. I'll be on my way so Ted can get back to his homecoming. Enjoy." She offered one last professional smile before she got in her car and drove away in a puff of gravel dust.

Roy rubbed the back of his neck and chuckled. "Well, I'm glad that's over with. I hope it wasn't too awkward for you."

Ted tugged at his beard, aware of a certain appendage still tingling in his pants. He'd have to tend to his needs later, in the privacy of his bedroom. "After what I've been through, it wasn't awkward at all, Dad."

"What do you say we go on up to the main house now? You must be hungry after such a long bus drive. And your brothers and sister are probably wonderin' what's taking us so long. You ready for some home-cookin'?"

Ted cocked his head, the tension lifting from his shoulders after his first successful meeting with his parole officer. He was more than ready.

"You better believe it, Dad."

# Chapter Three

## TEDDY

Right away, Ted spotted several people hanging out on the huge wraparound front porch of the family farmhouse through the truck window. Heads turned as his father sped up the hill, and two giant dogs bounded across the yard toward the vehicle, barking with fervor.

"Labradors?" Ted asked. He was trying to hold it together, knowing he was about to be reunited with his family.

"Yep. The yellow lab is Delia. The black lab is Jaxson. We've had them for about four or five years now. I think you'll enjoy having them around." Roy put the truck in park and paused. "You ready?"

All Ted could do was nod, his eyes transfixed on his three brothers and sister trotting toward them across the grassy knoll in front of the house. Their faces said it all; they were excited to welcome him home.

James, who was a year and a half younger, opened the passenger side door with a wide grin, his dark head shaking from side to side. "Teddy!" He grabbed him and pulled him out of the truck cab with force, Ted stumbling right into his brother's arms. "Oh, my God! You're here. You're finally here!"

"Hey, Jimmy."

James slapped him on the back, the two dogs underfoot sniffing and pawing at Ted's jeans. "Get back, D! Give the man some room, Jaxson." James grabbed the dog's collars and pulled them away, the alpha of the family giving Ted room so the rest of his siblings could greet him.

"Ted, my man!" his baby brother, Hank, shouted, coming in for a landing with a bear hug of his own. His youthful, smiling eyes held adoration and what looked like relief.

Ted staggered backward from the force, holding on to Hank for a few seconds. He was amazed at how grown-up and strong his little brother was since the last time he saw him in the courtroom. His sharp jawline held a smattering of scruff, and his brown hair was tousled, curling over his ears. Hank looked every bit like a country music artist with his black tee tucked into his faded jeans and worn cowboy boots on his feet. Ted was anxious to hear all about his brother's band and hear his music, some of the tunes their father touted as "sure-fire-hits."

Walt was next, peeling Ted out of Hank's arms and into his own. "Welcome home, Teddy," he mumbled into his ear. They were four years apart, often sparring in their youth. Between the testosterone and their combined competitive nature in sports, they were a handful for their parents while growing up.

When Walt pulled back from the hug, he held Ted's head between his large hands and gave him the once-over.

"You look mean, bro. I like this new look you got going on here. It's totally badass. I'm willing to bet you're covered in prison tattoos, too. Am I right?"

"That's enough, Walter," their father admonished.

"Do you mind if I have a turn?" A sweet voice cut through the chaos of dogs barking and brotherly teasing.

Walt stepped aside, and all eyes landed on Rebecca, who remained a few feet away from Ted. The hem of her colorful sundress fluttered in the breeze, and a few wisps of golden hair escaping from her high ponytail skated across her flushed cheeks. She was the youngest in the family, an "oops" baby coming into the world when Ted was almost ten years old. Her big, brown eyes fixated on his, and she slowly approached him, her expression giving nothing away.

Ted held his breath, mesmerized by the grown-up version of his little sister. The dappled light of the yellow sun through the trees highlighted her femininity and made her look like a watercolor painting. Rebecca Bennett was all grown up, morphed into a gorgeous woman.

"Hey, big brother." Her slender neck tilted as she looked up at him, and her eyes misted with sentiment.

"Hey, yourself, Becks." There was a lump in his throat the size of a wine barrel.

Wrapping her arms around his middle, she pressed her head against his chest. "I'm so glad to see you."

"I'm glad to see you, too." He was tender with his touch, taking his time with their reunion.

The two of them remained in an embrace for several seconds, Ted holding on for dear life. He'd dreamt of this moment for years—finally home and surrounded by the people he loved most in the world. He willed himself to memorize everything as a substantial silence settled over the lawn, a completeness transitioning in his body. Even the dogs were quiet, sitting obediently at Jimmy's feet.

Becky shifted in his arms as he tried to remember every detail: her hair's golden highlights and citrusy scent. The freckles on her nose and how she grinned with her eyes pressed shut. He was safe, and dare he say, happy for the first time since his life careened off course.

Ted felt Becky's body rise as she inhaled a deep breath. Tilting her head back again, she opened her eyes and rested her chin on his chest, her sweet smile causing his heart to swell.

"You hungry?"

Ted affectionately swept an errant wisp of her hair behind her ear, enthralled by her grown-up beauty.

"Starving."

"Well, come on then." Grasping his hand, she pulled him toward the house. "I made your favorite, chicken parmesan."

Ted's mouth immediately watered. It'd been a long time since he'd had a home-cooked meal, the mere mention of his favorite childhood dish causing his stomach to rumble with pleasure. Leave it to his little sister to remember. Clambering up the worn porch stairs with the big dogs afoot with tails wagging and male voices rumbling in a bass line of excitement, Becky let go of Ted's hand, the immediate, profound absence making him wince.

Late at night in his jail cell, he often wondered what his reunion with his family would be like, hoping it wasn't awkward or uncomfortable. But James, Hank, Walter, and Rebecca welcomed him home with open arms, the deep love he felt for each of them filling him with unfathomable joy. This reunion was everything he could have ever hoped for—and more.

Upon entering the home, Ted noticed the large farmhouse table already set with familiar heirloom china, the open dining room connected to the kitchen filled with delicious food aromas. Jaxson and Delia settled onto two large dog beds in a corner near the mammoth stone fireplace, their submission impressive as they looked on with panting muzzles.

"You need a minute to freshen up?" Roy asked, handing Ted his duffle bag.

"That'd be good."

Hank eagerly swiped the bag from Ted's grasp. "Let me show you to your room while Becks and the others get dinner on the table."

"Don't be too long, Teddy. Everything is practically ready," Becky chimed in.

"Okay," he called back to her.

Ted followed his baby brother through a narrow hallway and up a wooden staircase. The Bennett home had been in the family for generations, the occasional upgrades turning the farmhouse into a modern-day, comfortable homestead. His old room was on the backside of the house with two long windows looking out over the expanse of land with a view of the ancient red barn and vineyard. Jimmy and Walt were roommates in the revamped carriage house on the property, Hank and Becks still living with their father in the main house, their rooms across the hall from Ted's.

As he entered his old bedroom, he was overcome with a strange feeling of familiarity, the air thick with gratitude and excitement, nerves and elation. Between his family's exuberant welcome and the pounding of his heart, he was feeling it all.

Hank tossed the duffle bag onto the queen-sized bed made neatly with a blue and red patchwork quilt among a bevy of fluffy pillows. Sitting next to the bag, his brother's youthful face appeared animated with happiness.

"Becky stocked your bathroom with all kinds of toiletries. And she washed and folded your old clothes and put them away nice and neat in the drawers and closet. Although, I doubt you'll fit into any of them because now you're so buff."

Ted stood still in the middle of the room, taking in his surroundings. He'd barely spent any time at home before his incarceration except to work on the farm, most nights spent with Robyn at her house. They were living together since college graduation while she started law school, his boyhood bedroom nothing more than a landing pad of sorts where he kept extra clothes and would often shower after a long day of work on the farm before he'd head over to her place.

Now, looking around, he was amazed by the colors and details he never seemed to notice before: the blue walls and high ceilings. The antique glass of the windows near his great grandfather's roll-top desk. The quilt's crisp red and denim patches covering the inviting bed made up just for him. Had his life always been so muted when he was on the family farm? Was his attention to detail faded because of the intenseness of his relationship with Robyn?

"Did you hear me, bro?" Hank asked, interrupting his thoughts.

"Say again?" Ted approached the dresser opposite the bed and opened a drawer, amazed at the neatly stacked t-shirts lined up inside.

"How'd you get so muscular? Did you work out every day in prison? I mean, there was probably nothing else to do. Have you been taking enhancements or drinking muscle milk or something?" Leave it to his little brother to ask a string of questions in one breath.

Ted stripped off the shirt he'd been wearing all day and tossed it onto a nearby chair. Facing Hank, his brother whistled.

"Dang, man! Look at you. You're a modern-day Hulk." His eyebrows arched above his wide eyes. "Walt's gonna be so disappointed you don't have any prison tattoos."

Chuckling, Ted unzipped his duffle bag and pulled out a deodorant stick, swiping it under his arms. "No tattoos and I've kept in shape working for the past eleven months at a warehouse unloading trucks. Oh, and since I've been out of prison and at the halfway house, I've been able to eat way better, too."

Hank hung onto his every word, nodding as if he understood. "Good for you, man. Folks in Langston Falls aren't going to recognize you. In fact, you might scare the crap out of some of them with your bulging biceps and all that hair." He laughed, the joyful sound pinging the air.

Ted grinned, shrugging on a clean shirt accentuating his imposing figure. "Well, I don't plan on cavorting with the townspeople any time soon."

Hank nodded again, his smile fading, and his expression turned pensive. "Dad didn't want me bringing this up on your first day back home, but I feel like you should know."

"Oh?" Ted stilled. "Know what?"

Hank inhaled a deep breath. "For what it's worth, everyone in these parts was stunned by your sentencing and didn't think it was fair." Standing, he hung his head and gripped the back of his neck. "You were robbed, Teddy. Everyone knows it. When you were sent away, I felt so... helpless, unable to do anything. I should've been there for you. You're my brother." When he looked up, his brown eyes filled with tears. "I don't know how you did it all those years, Teddy. I would've fucking died."

Ted tossed the deodorant on the bed and approached his brother, palming his shoulders. "The worst is behind me, Hank. I'm sorry you felt helpless. I didn't mean to make you feel that way."

Hank nodded. "I know you didn't. But how did you survive?"

Ted exhaled a quick breath out of his nose, averting his brother's intense gaze. "I had power over nothing, but I knew I needed to stay positive like mom always taught us. I knew someday I'd be released, and I could move on with my life."

"But how? Tell me *how* you did it?" Hank swiped a tear from his cheek, his brow furrowed with concentration.

Ted swallowed hard, not sure how to explain. Ambling over to the window, he looked outside at the stretch of family land. "I had to keep breathing. I had to feed my body, sleep when I was tired. Get through each day under the radar. So that's what I did. I kept breathing, and I stayed alive." He turned to face Hank. "And now, here I am. I'm back home in my bedroom talking to you, my favorite little musician brother."

Hank offered a weak grin, nodding as if he finally understood. "Dammit, Ted, I'm so glad you're finally home."

"Me, too, buddy. Me, too." Ted opened his arms wide, and Hank shuffled into his embrace, slapping him on the back.

"God, Teddy! You're a *beast*!"

Ted laughed, the sound coming out of his mouth peculiar yet freeing. "I want to hear some of your songs later, okay?"

"Sure."

"I'm proud of you, Hank-ster."

Now it was Hank's turn to laugh out loud. "You're the only one who's ever called me by that nickname. I used to hate it, but now...," he paused, his lips turned up into a wide smile. "Now, it's the best name in the whole world."

# Chapter Four

## TEDDY

Ted was silent throughout the meal, taking in the domestic scene all around him. Listening to the pleasant conversations between his father, brothers, and sister, they mainly discussed work on the farm and the upcoming Harvest Hoedown. Ted was thrilled to learn Hank's band was scheduled to perform during the event, the group a fan-favorite in these parts and sure to bring in a lively crowd.

As Ted finished every last morsel of chicken parmesan off his heaping plate, he reminded himself things on the farm were different from what they used to be. His siblings were all grown up, and he would have to navigate his new role cautiously, careful not to step on any toes. What his new role entailed, he wasn't sure.

"You want seconds?" Becky asked from across the table. "I've got plenty, but you might want to leave room for dessert. I made another one of your favorites—peanut butter cookies."

All eyes landed on him, forks and knives stilled as they waited for him to say something—anything.

Pressing a fabric napkin to his lips, Ted shook his head. "I'm pretty full, Becks. Your chicken parmesan is the best meal I've had in years. Thank you for this and the cookies. I'll have a couple later if you don't mind."

Becky's eyes glimmered with adoration, and her cheeks held a rosy hue. "Anything for you, Teddy."

Ted offered his sister a genuine smile and tossed the napkin on his empty plate he'd practically licked clean. "Can I help you with the dishes?" The entire table erupted in a banter of noise as tableware was gathered, everyone insisting Ted relax and enjoy his first night home.

"Why don't you go on out back and sit in one of the rockers. The sunsets have been beautiful lately. It might do you some good to catch your breath and take in the scenery." His dad patted Ted's hand resting on the table.

James poured the remnants of a bottle of wine into his short glass, the familiar label showcasing the family farm logo in red and green colors. "Come on, Teddy. We can watch the sunset and let the dogs roll around in the grass."

The legs of Ted's chair scraped loudly against the wooden floor as he stood and grabbed his plate, stacking his brother's on top.

"Teddy! Leave the dishes and go outside with Jimmy. We've got this," Becky insisted.

Sighing, Ted handed the dishes off to his sister. "Alright. But tomorrow night, I'm on KP duty. It's only fair."

"Fine," she giggled, shooing him away.

James was already outside and threw a worn tennis ball across the expanse of the lawn. The big dogs scampered wildly after it, reminding Ted of him and his competitive brother, Walt, in their younger days.

"Ten bucks says Jaxson gets to it first," James challenged.

Ted stuffed his hands into his jean pockets and shrugged. "I wouldn't know."

They watched the dogs run to the edge of the tree line where the ball landed. Sure enough, Jaxson clamped down on the ball first and galloped toward them in a flash of sable fur, ready to do it all over again.

"I have to give Delia a fair chance, or she pouts," James explained, gripping the black lab by the collar and tossing another ball into the yard for Delia.

"Reminds me of Walt and me when we'd play kickball or basketball back in the day. I'd have to give him a fair shot, or he'd pout, too," Ted teased.

"You'll still run circles around him, especially with your imposing physique. But I'll bet he won't give up and fight you to the death, just like old times."

*Old times.*

Ted leaned against a porch post, smiling with ease, thinking about his youth. He was content to breathe in the fresh air and watch the animals, safe from the government organization that once held complete control over his life. Behind bars, he had power over nothing, including when he ate, slept, showered, or saw his father once a quarter behind a sheet of bullet-proof glass in the visitor's area. He'd much rather be with his real brothers than Big Brother.

After a few more rounds of ball throwing, James sat back in a rocker and picked up his glass of wine, sipping from the rim. "You must have a million questions running through your mind," he started.

Ted sat in the vacant rocker next to him and leaned back. The sky was turning shades of sherbet, the orange and raspberry colors sweeping near the edge of twilight. "They can wait."

"You sure about that?"

Delia sat on her haunches near Ted. He reached over and stroked the animal's coarse, yellow fur. "Well, you probably already know the only question on my mind." Turning to look at his brother, he allowed the words to finally roll off his tongue. "How's Robyn?"

James averted his gaze, throwing back the last dregs of merlot. He rocked for a few beats before answering. "I don't know how to say this to you, Teddy. Robyn had to let you go. She wanted to be a part of your homecoming—I mean, we invited her. But after thinking it through, we all thought it best if she stayed away. This has been very hard for everyone." He turned and looked Ted right in the eye, his brow creased with compassion. "I can't even imagine how hard it's been for you."

Ted continued to stroke Delia, his jaw clenched to keep his simmering emotions at bay. The sweet pooch licked his hand as if sensing his inner turmoil.

"Teddy, it's confusing and emotional for Robyn. She's sort of... lost."

"Lost?" Ted whipped his head to glare at his brother. "Really, Jimmy? Robyn is *lost*? Come on, man. She's gotta be living the highlife in Atlanta as a lawyer by now. How can she be lost when she was able to attain what she set out to do in her life with no one holding her back? I'm nothing but a sad memory."

"No, Teddy. You got it all wrong. Robyn finished law school after you were sentenced, but she never took the bar exam. She never made it out of Langston Falls."

"*What?*" Ted was shocked. "You mean, she's still here? Living in her grandmother's cottage?" His thoughts were all jumbled, and he couldn't quite compute this new information. "If she didn't take the bar exam, what in the hell has she been doing, Jimmy?"

James pressed his lips together as if unsure he should give Ted any more information.

Gripping the arms of the rocker, Ted pleaded. "Come on, man. Please, tell me."

James rose from his seat, his empty glass in one hand and a tennis ball in the other. The black and yellow labs wagged their tails with eagerness as they anticipated the throw.

"She's still living in the little house y'all shared on her family's property. Her grandmother passed away while you were in prison and her father has renters living in the main house now. Robyn works at a local shop in town. Becky often hires her to help with some of the festivals. She's got a real knack for party planning." His arm jerked as he threw the ball with the force of a major league pitcher, sending the dogs galloping across the grass.

"*Party planning?*"

Ted was stunned, the thought of Robyn being anything other than a successful, kick-ass lawyer hard to imagine. Before he could delve any further, Becky pushed open the back door. She carried a tray holding a plate of cookies and several glasses of milk. His father, Walt, and Hank brought up the rear.

"Here you go, Teddy. Cookies and milk, just like the old days." Becky set the tray on a nearby table before offering him a glass and a cookie. His brothers milled about the table, noshing as if the cookies were the only scrap of food they'd had in days. Standing near his rocker, she seemed expectant.

"What?" he snapped, looking up at her from his seat.

Becky seemed taken aback by the crude tone of his one-word question, and she blinked several times. Everyone was silent and turned to look at him. Ted counted to three in an effort to remain calm. He was still reeling from Jimmy's announcement regarding Robyn's life demoted to a party planner.

"I'm, uh, sorry, Becks. I didn't mean to raise my voice at you."

Becky nodded with a restored smile. "I understand. You don't have to eat cookies if you don't want to—"

"Believe me, I want to," he interrupted, standing tall and taking a huge bite. The cookie melted in his mouth, the peanut butter and brown sugar flavors invading his senses with flashbacks of his youth. Taking a swig of cold milk, he swallowed. "You make the best goddamn cookies of anyone on the planet, Becks."

"Right?" Walt chimed in, coming up alongside him and slapping his shoulder. Cookie crumbs dusted his upper lip.

"Language, Teddy," his father admonished.

"Sorry, Dad. Sorry, Becks." Ted turned toward the table to grab another cookie and was disappointed by the empty plate.

"Don't worry, there's plenty more." Becky hurried inside.

Swiping his hand across his beard, Ted eyed Jimmy, who seemed to nod with understanding.

The news regarding Robyn didn't sit well with him, and he'd be damned if he let her off the hook. But now wasn't the time to dwell. He needed to languish in a few more cookies and shower his little sister with appreciation. He half-heartedly laughed at a joke Hank told before noticing the moon rising into the stratosphere in a hazy orb—the same moon hanging over the cottage he once shared with Robyn three miles down the road.

Later in the night, Ted lay in bed and stared out the windows of his boyhood bedroom at the starry sky above the vineyard. Propped upright against a pillow, he held an old photo, his eyes scrolling the image. It was the same photo he'd kept close to his heart while he was incarcerated. He stared at Robyn's adoring expression frozen in time. She'd somehow slipped the picture between the pages of his Bible before he was sent to prison. The leather-bound book he'd received as a child during a summer church camp was one of the only worldly possessions he was allowed to take into his cell.

As a young man, Ted never really gave his faith much thought. Sure, he believed in a higher power—how could he not being surrounded by the beauty and majesty of the North Georgia Mountains? But he wasn't a practicing man of faith, only gracing the inside of a church during Easter or maybe Christmas Eve.

But after wallowing in self-pity those first agonizing weeks behind bars, he finally relented and opened his Bible looking for answers. He searched for a verse to calm his wounded spirit, praying God would send him a sign and give him the strength he needed to get through his sentence.

When Robyn's picture slipped from the pages of the Bible and fluttered into his lap, he was astounded. The small gift from the heavens filled him with hope in an instant. Kneeling at his bedside with the photo clutched between his fingers, he wept for hours and thanked God for answering his prayer. He knew right then he could get through anything, including this new hell. And he did…

The old farmhouse was silent in the night, the bedside lamp throwing slants of soft light across Ted's body. His weary eyes traced the outline of Robyn's captured smile, her innocence and love in the photo apparent. He was so sad he didn't have Robyn in his life anymore. But he was grateful she was in that cell with him for all those years.

And he knew what he had to do. He had to continue feeding his body when he was hungry and sleeping when he was tired. He had to keep breathing and stay alive. Because he knew without a doubt, the sun would rise above the land tomorrow. And there was no telling what the new day might bring.

# Chapter Five

## ROBYN MORGAN

For the one-hundredth time that day, Robyn picked her phone up and stared at the simple text she'd received from Becky Bennett the night before.

*He's back.*

Robyn cupped her forehead with her hand, her elbow leaned on the desk. Try as she might, she couldn't finish the simple task of filling out the work order, something she'd been doing for years. Her thoughts were scattered, her mood tense. Eyeing the rather large empty coffee cup wrapped in a cardboard sleeve among the paperwork clutter, she thought maybe she shouldn't have drunk the entire latte with a double shot of espresso she'd picked up from the local café. Or better yet, perhaps she shouldn't have polished off an entire bottle of Bennett Farms Merlot the night before? If she'd foregone the wine and just gone to bed, she wouldn't have woken up with a raging hangover which caused her to buy the decadent latte on her way into work in the first place.

Tossing her pen across the desktop, she folded her arms

against her chest and sulked. Maybe she wouldn't be in this predicament if she'd moved far away from Langston Falls and started a new life before it was too late—before Ted Bennett returned home.

Glancing at the text again, the short message was like a tiny pebble tossed onto the glassy surface of her grandmother's pond, the ripple effect causing a cacophony of emotions to come ashore. Teddy was back, his harsh prison sentence finally over and done.

Robyn always knew this day would come. At one point, she thought it might come sooner as Roy told her his son was an excellent inmate, never causing any trouble and up for a potential early release because of his good behavior. But the parole board and the dickhead judge who sentenced him put a stop to that. They wanted to make an example out of Teddy, keeping him behind bars, the cruel and unusual punishment undeserved.

And completely, one hundred percent, her fault.

"I'm off on my lunch break. You want anything?" Charlotte Ross, the flower shop owner of Langston Petals, stood in the office's doorway.

Robyn looked up and shook her head. "No, I'm good."

Charlotte frowned. "You okay today? You look a little pale."

"It's probably because I overindulged last night, and now I'm paying the price adding an overloaded coffee to the mix." Robyn held up the empty paper cup in a toast before tossing it in the wastebasket near the desk.

"That'll do it," Charlotte laughed. "Were you with Anderson last night?"

Robyn pressed her lips together and shook her head again. "Nope. Just me. Anderson's on a work trip in California."

"Hmmm." Charlotte continued to give her the once-over. "You know I'm here for you if you need to talk, right?"

"I know. I'm fine, really."

Charlotte nodded. "Okay. I'll be back in an hour. Keep an eye out front for any customers."

"Will do."

Robyn remained seated and watched her boss exit the office, the heaviness in her spirit remaining. Her boyfriend, Anderson, was away on a business trip in California for the next week, his expertise in the world of negotiation needed for his company specializing in acquisitions.

After receiving the text from Becky and polishing off the bottle of wine the night before, she Face-timed Anderson in her inebriated state, needy for some undivided attention. She was hoping for whispers of sweet nothings in her ear. But when her phone screen illuminated Anderson's handsome face at a club in downtown LA, she knew he didn't have time for her moment of weakness. The thumping music and loud guffaws of laughter were one thing, but his loosened tie, wet whiskey lips, and animated expression left her disillusioned. He panned his camera around the table to say hi to the group of employees he was entertaining, most of which were gorgeous west coast women.

Seriously?

Even in her tipsy state, Robyn noticed the coy smiles and prominent cleavage in their tight club dresses as they lifted slim cocktail glasses in a greeting. Yeah, they weren't trying too hard.

Why was it okay for Anderson to hang out with the opposite sex, dancing and drinking the night away while on a business trip, but he'd shoot her down in a millisecond when she brought up Ted or his family? Their call was short-lived and left Robyn with a bad taste in her mouth—

or maybe it was the lingering affects of fermented merlot grapes?

With a heavy sigh, she wearily stood and tossed her phone onto the desk, the anticipation of a daytime call from Anderson put on the back burner. Gone were the days when she pushed through her angst, studying day in and day out for law school, her work ethic admirable. Her classmates deemed her most likely to succeed. Too bad she didn't have it in her to finish what she started. If they could see her now, hung-over and depressed, working in a tiny flower shop in downtown Langston Falls, they'd strip her of the title for sure. And don't forget, she was still living on her grandmother's property on the outskirts of town, not in Atlanta near her lawyer-father. Her future as an attorney was nothing more than a fading dream.

Anderson teased her mercilessly, challenging her to get off her butt and carry through with her plans. But truth be told, she didn't have it in her anymore. In fact, she much preferred the slower pace of her flower shop job. And she loved living in the pretty cottage near the pond, the breathtaking view of the North Georgia Mountains hard to replace. She'd lost her edge and passion for law when Teddy was sentenced, only going through the motions to get her degree so she'd be distracted for the first few years. The fire she once had in her belly simply fizzled out, and she didn't know how to get it back, knowing there was no justice in law.

One of the perks of the pleasant atmosphere of Langston Petals was the sweet aroma of flowers. Her daily employment inside the four walls of the shop was also a feast for the eyes. Display cases held a variety of cut bouquets wrapped in cellophane and buckets of single flowers for those customers who wanted to create their own arrangement. The wide assortment was a glorious rainbow of colors and scents. The shop also offered potted plants and the wares of some of the local businesses and artists on display tables throughout. There was even a live fir tree in the corner, decorated with twinkle lights and Christmas ornaments advertising the Bennett Christmas Tree Farm year-round.

Robyn approached the tree and fingered the needle-like branches, the sweet pine smell constantly reminding her of Teddy. Her eyes traced the tree's height, and she wondered what he was doing at that moment. Did he wake up in his childhood bedroom with the blue walls? Was he relieved to be back on the farm with his loving family? Were there any moments when he thought about... her?

Bending low, she felt the dry soil in the sawed-off wine barrel the tree was planted in and decided to grab the watering can. The shop was empty, the only sounds coming from a small display fountain in the corner. The peaceful, bubbling resonance was comforting in her jittery, caffeinated state.

Taking her time, she went to the workroom beyond the cash register area and grabbed the watering can off the counter where Charlotte had been working on a large floral arrangement. Leftover snippets of rose thorns and green leaves were scattered among the workspace. Robyn eyed her boss's latest creation and smiled, the layered and lush piece capturing nature's beauty. Charlotte was well-known for keeping her elements local and seasonal. Today, she worked with a garden-inspired, monochromatic color palette using white hydrangeas, sweet peas, jasmine vine, and Playa Blanca roses. The dramatic centerpiece was for a customer's upcoming dinner party, Charlotte's talent apparent.

Breathing in the exotic and intoxicating sweet scent of

jasmine, Robyn closed her eyes. The small, white flowers were one of her favorites. Charlotte once explained in Hindu traditions, jasmine was considered the flower of love, and the rich floral aroma was an aphrodisiac. Inhaling deeply, Robyn wondered if that's why she was so drawn to the scent, her heart aching for her true love—her heart aching for Teddy.

Placing the empty watering can in the work sink, she turned on the faucet. When the automatic doorbell sounded, alerting her to a customer, she quickly turned off the water and carried the half-full can into the showroom. A tall man admired the Christmas tree in the corner with his back turned. His shoulders were broad, and a ponytail hung through the back of his ball cap.

"Are you picking up today? Or just looking around?" she asked in a pleasant tone.

The man's shoulders lifted as if he'd taken a deep breath, and he slowly turned. Robyn locked eyes with his before her entire world went into slow motion.

Standing rigid between a tropical Anthurium and the butterfly-shaped petals of an orchid display, Teddy Bennett stood taller than she remembered, broader as well, at least in the shoulders. Gripping the watering can handle until it hurt, she took in his muscular frame. His presence filled the room with heat and testosterone; his looks changed over the years. Gone was his youthful exterior, his hardened jawline covered with a thick beard, his dark eyes piercing her with a look she knew well—one part heartbreak, one part fearless. Taking a step in her direction, everything from hope to desperation flooded her. He was crossing the shop, coming toward her like a twister, inescapable and downright dangerous.

With each step, Robyn could feel her strength waning,

her grip on the handle slipping. With nowhere to hide, Teddy's intense focus seemed to undress her. She held her breath, her vision blurred in a shimmer of tears.

The up-close version of Teddy was alarming, his once sweet disposition and charming smile replaced with an intense glare. Even though they grew up together and loved each other hard for most of their young adult lives, she realized this was someone she didn't know anymore.

"*Robyn?*"

The gentle sound of her name across his lips was the tipping point. Her knees went weak, and she felt herself crumble before him, completely losing her grip on the watering can handle altogether. The spout hit the floor with a metal clang, sending a shower of water arcing across her body and spilling all over the linoleum. She collapsed on the wet floor, her head throbbing with intensity.

Teddy knelt in front of her, his strong hand gripping her by the forearm. "*Jesus*, Robyn? Are you okay?"

Her breathing staggered, and her neck wobbled in a half-hearted nod. She didn't dare open her eyes to look at him for fear she might pass out altogether.

"Careful in those sandals. I don't want you to slip on this water." He continued to help her up, the warmth of his touch zapping her with an electrical current. He guided her to a stool behind the checkout counter and helped her sit.

"You sure you're alright?" The low timbre of his voice held genuine concern.

Robyn finally allowed herself to stare at Teddy up close. "Yes, I'm… fine," she managed to say, her voice cracking with emotion. "Hi."

"Hi." A slight smile played on his full lips. She immediately noticed his wet jeans where he'd knelt to help her.

"I'm so sorry about the water. Let me get you a towel."

She started for the workshop, her body humming with newfound energy. "You want coffee? We've got a machine back here. I can make some. I've got skim milk in the fridge but not any vanilla creamer, and that's what you like."

Teddy leaned his impressive physique against the doorframe, watching her every move. "You're not a lawyer?" he asked.

Robyn handed him a clean towel and exhaled loudly. "Huh... everything got put on hold during your trial. I did finish law school but I... haven't taken the bar exam yet. I think about taking it. I don't know." Teddy approached her and gently pressed the towel against her cheek. She hadn't even noticed the water droplets dripping down her face. "What are you doing here, Teddy? Did Becky tell you this is where I work?"

"No." His baseball cap caused a shadow over his eyes. "I didn't know. I came into town to pick up some flowers."

"Oh." There was a hint of disappointment in her response. "Who's the lucky lady?" She demurely angled her face and waited with bated breath.

Teddy clenched his jaw and took off his baseball cap. Running his hands through his golden-toned sandy hair, he looked at her with an expression of sadness clouding his undeniably masculine features.

"Mom."

# Chapter Six

## TEDDY

Robyn didn't mention her presence at the funeral to Teddy, her smile sweet and accommodating as she continued to look up at him. "I've got the perfect bouquet of yellow roses. I remember those were her favorite."

Ted was on an errand at the shop to buy flowers to place on his mother's grave at the family farm, something denied to him while he was locked up. He remembered every detail regarding the funeral, his father filling him in during a prison visit when it was all over. The entire town of Langston Falls paid their last respects at the wake, including Robyn. Each member of the Bennett family spoke, the family patriarch reading a penned statement from Teddy in his absence. It was the most genuine and heartbreaking letter he'd ever written.

Floored by Robyn's awareness of his mother's favorite flower, he followed her into the showroom where she opened the heavy glass door of a display case and retrieved a golden bunch of roses. As she turned to pass them off she said, "The letter... the one you wrote for the funeral, well it was…" But she couldn't seem to find the right words. He could sense her pain, and the loss of a woman who'd been a mother to her as well was something he hadn't thought of before. But there was more to it, the hurt between them evident.

He gripped her by the wrist, not letting go.

"What are you doing?" Her expression was marred with alarm, her brow furrowed. Seeing the fear in her eyes he loosened his grip, sliding his hand lower to hold hers.

"I never should've taken you to that party."

Robyn swallowed hard, her glimmering emerald eyes staring back at him, leaving him bereft. How many days and nights had he pined for this woman? He'd tried in vain to remember the touch of her skin. And now, here she was, flesh and bone standing right in front of him. He was perplexed when she seemed to relax beneath his grip and offered a broad smile. She tugged on his hand.

"Come on. I want to show you something." She pulled him toward the exit at the far end of the building. Shoving open the door to the alley where the large dumpsters were located, the late-summer sun was intense in the heat of the day.

Blinking against the glare, Teddy looked around and gasped when he realized what was parked in front of him. He let go of her hand, dumbfounded by the brightness highlighting the recently washed Jeep.

"My car," he announced, looking right at her, the yellow roses still clutched in his grip. "You kept my car."

He continued to circle the vehicle in awe, aware of the ridiculous smirk on his face. She watched him, her gorgeous smile and presence reminding him of the girl he once loved so long ago. Who was he kidding? He still loved her.

"Okay, this is wild," he chuckled. "Can I get in it? For old time's sake?"

"Of course. It's your car." Digging into her pocket, she pulled out her keys, taking the Jeep key off the ring.

Teddy traded the roses for the key and opened the driver's side door, climbing inside. He rolled down the window before he started the engine. Leaning his muscular arm on the sill, he nodded with glee at the sound, revving the engine a few times. "Good car. Lots of memories."

Robyn's dark brows drew together as she held the roses in front of her. Slowly, she approached the window, the wish in her voice noticeable. "What now?"

He knew the simple question held a hundred broken dreams. "I honestly don't know."

The engine's rumble filled the silence between them before he finally turned the engine off and climbed out. He handed off the key with chagrin, and she passed him the flowers.

"My dad drove me into town. I, uh, don't have my driver's license anymore because it expired. I'd love to take the Jeep for a spin on the back roads when I'm legal again. Would that be okay?"

Robyn shaded her eyes with her hand to fend off the glaring sun. "Of course."

He nodded toward the cellophane-wrapped roses, the happy yellow color a reminder of what he'd come into town for. "How much do I owe you for these?"

"On the house," she replied in a whisper.

"Thanks, Robyn." He motioned with his free hand for her to walk ahead of him into the shop.

The hush between them was deafening, and as they neared the store's front entrance, she stopped in her tracks, blocking the exit with her back toward him.

"You didn't have to sacrifice yourself for me." When she turned around, Teddy noticed her eyes bright with tears. "It wasn't your fault."

His heart ached at the pitiful sight of her pained expression, knowing he was the one who caused her angst. "It was the only way. Even your dad knew that."

She nodded as a tear slipped down her cheek. "I know. I can never repay you."

Teddy set the roses on a nearby table and moved closer to her. "You owe me nothing but your happiness. Really Robyn, be okay. Be all you wanted to be. Please."

He opened his arms wide, offering her a hug. She nodded and stepped into his embrace. They clung to each other amid the sound of the water fountain and the scent of sweet flowers. For a moment, they were just a boy and a girl, their bodies pressed warmly together in melancholy closeness. He memorized every touch and feel, her presence saturating his being.

His hands roamed up her back and neck, and he paused to hold her face, his thumbs caressing her damp cheeks. Something intense and sincere overtook them as tension swelled, the silence stretching on. Her breathing turned shallow, her body language begging him to cross a line.

As he tentatively captured her lips in a tender kiss, her luscious mouth poured heat into him, and he thought he'd died and gone to heaven. But the kiss was short-lived, the pain in her voice hard not to notice when she pulled back. Her lashes were wet with emotion.

"I always knew you'd come home. But everybody said I had to stop waiting for you because we were no good for each other... that I had to let you go."

"I wanted you to. You needed to move on from me. You deserve the best... everything your heart desires. That's all I ever wanted for you." Teddy clutched her hand directly over his heart but then pulled away when the doorbell rang, like he was doing something wrong.

Robyn tensed and moved a few steps away from him as two elderly women entered the shop in a gaggle of laughter. Quickly, she swiped her hands across her tear-stained face.

"Careful, ladies. There's a puddle of spilled water by the checkout counter. I was just about to clean it up." Her voice lilted in a high pitch as she went into business mode.

Teddy slipped his baseball cap over his head to remain incognito, keeping his focus on Robyn and following her toward the watery mess.

"Can I see you again?"

Robyn picked up the wayward watering can, carefully stepping over the puddle in her sandals. "I'm not sure," she whispered. Grabbing a roll of paper towels near the cash register, she ripped off long sheets and layered them over the puddle. "I'm kind of dating someone right now."

Teddy pressed his teeth into his lower lip, aware of the immediate surge of jealousy coursing through his hot blood. "Is it serious?"

"I... I don't know." She busied herself wiping up the water. "He's quite a catch, though. And I'm... happy. Really."

Her response surprised him. She looked about as happy as a fish on a hook. But he knew their first meeting after all these years might be awkward and couldn't blame her for the remorseful vibe in the room.

"Well, I'd still like to go for a ride in the Jeep with you sometime... that is if your boyfriend wouldn't mind you hanging out with an ex-con."

Robyn glanced over at the ladies peering at some of the framed artwork on the wall before leaning back on her heels and looking up at him. She studied him for a few more seconds, looking so pretty it hurt.

"I'd love to, Teddy."

Her positive response prevented his heart from fracturing into a million tiny pieces.

---

Ted was quiet on the ride back to the farm, the yellow roses resting on his lap. Lost in thought, he rolled his lower lip between two fingers and didn't realize his father had asked him a question until he felt a firm hand grip his shoulder.

"You okay, Teddy?"

Swallowing hard, he breathed in a deep intake of air through his nose. "Yeah, Dad. Just thinking about Mom."

Roy seemed to understand. "I know it was hard for you not being at her funeral. And I know you want to pay your respects."

The truck stopped near a large meadow half a mile from the Bennett compound. A lone, one-hundred-year-old oak tree stood prominent among the faded grass. Ted looked out across the stretch of land, knowing his mother's grave was somewhere under the gnarled branches of the magnificent tree.

"I'll leave you to it, then."

Ted nodded. "Thanks, Dad. I'll be up in a little while."

"Take your time, son."

The cellophane wrapper surrounding the flowers crinkled in his hands as he got out of the truck and shut the door. His father drove off, the vehicle picking up dust in its wake. Stepping off the graveled road onto the grass, Ted approached a rusted gate in the fence line, the hinges squeaking with age as he walked through.

Warm air skirted across his face, and dappled light showed through the branches of the mighty oak, highlighting the fading summer leaves. Ted focused on the tree, the whooshing sound from the fluttering foliage comforting in his bereaved state. As he came closer to the family plot of headstones covered in lichen and moss, he removed his baseball cap and looked for his mother's marker. The stone wasn't hard to find, the white marble decorated with a wreath of wilted daisies, probably left behind by his sister, Rebecca. He remembered his mother and Becks often creating the intertwined flowers on lazy summer afternoons, wearing them around their necks and in their hair. The thought made him smile, his longing for those innocent moments of days gone by coming at him full force.

"Hey, Mama," he started. Kneeling to the ground, he palmed the dry grass and gently rested the yellow roses in front of the marble slab. "These are for you." He tenderly ran the tips of his fingers across the words etched into the stone, "Beloved mother, wife, and friend."

A gust of air blew his long hair back from his face, and he sat on his rear, resting his arms on his bent knees. He breathed in the lingering scent of summer, the woodsy musk of the outdoors and ancient farmland mysterious and primitive. His eyes traced the area where his mother was laid to rest, the beauty surrounding him evoking a kind of serenity in his spirit.

Unrestrained in the great outdoors had an effect on him. Or maybe it was an intuition his mother was nearby. He lay back with his head leaned against his entwined fingers and looked up at the bright blue sky through the tree branches. Puffy clouds floated above him, and he was content to lavish in the freedom of his mother's divine presence.

"I'll never forgive myself for not allowing you to visit me while I was locked up." Tears pricked the edges of his eyes, his voice gravelly with emotion. "I didn't want you to see me in there. I didn't want to break your heart all over again."

Ted willed himself to keep it together, like those times behind bars when he didn't think he could make it another day. He concentrated on each intake of air, in and out—in and out.

"You died on a Sunday morning," he spoke out loud. "While we were growing up, Dad always told us dying was part of life. We learned about death at a young age with all the animals on the farm, and especially when Granny Bennett and Papaw passed on." He paused, wiping the back of his hand across his face.

"I thought for sure I'd die in prison. It was definitely hell on earth. But I'm out on parole now, Mama. I'm home again, just like you promised I'd be. I should've never doubted you." He blew out a long breath.

"And... and when I went into town today to pick up your flowers, guess who I saw, Mama?" He paused, the air filled with the caw of a nearby crow.

"*Robyn*. Can you believe it? She works in a flower shop now. She's the one who suggested I get you the yellow roses... because... they were always your favorite." A hiccup sob escaped his mouth as he shut his eyes, causing a torrent of tears to sluice down his cheeks and into his beard. Shaking his head, he sat up and sniffled, embarrassed by his behavior.

"I miss you, Mama. I promise I'm gonna work hard on the farm and help Dad, Becks, and the boys with whatever they need. I want to make you proud."

Standing on wobbly legs, Ted ran his hands across his

jeans, his voice turned quiet. "I'm so sorry I wasn't there for you. But I'm home now, and I'll be nearby from now on."

Leaves rustled in the tree. Ted looked up half expecting to see his mother in angel form sitting on a branch, her warm, motherly smile imprinted in his memory.

"I love you, Mama."

Shoving his baseball cap back over his head, he took in the headstone one last time before he turned and trudged through the tall grasses toward the main house in the distance. A flock of birds flapped overhead, the squeaks and squawks a welcome sound in the silence of his grief. He continued across the rolling hill and was greeted by Delia, the yellow lab coming right up next to him, happily wagging her tail.

"Hey, girl," he muttered, thankful for her presence.

Delia licked his hand, the animal's unconditional love easing the painful void in his heart. But the feeling didn't last very long. In the distance, he could see his father on the front porch waiting for him, the prodigal son returning home.

Ted was suddenly propelled forward with exhilaration and the powerful feeling of being alive. He wasn't about to waste another minute now that he was free. Not one damned one.

# Chapter Seven

## ROBYN

"I can't wait to show Becky Bennett what you came up with for the festival. These table arrangements are romantic yet rustic. Charlotte, you're brilliant," Robyn gushed. She held a sturdy mason jar filled with sumptuous white hydrangeas interspersed with tall sprigs of lovely lavender and sunflowers. The rim of the vase opening was tied off with a simple burlap bow.

"How many tables did she say again?" Charlotte asked.

"Thirty. About ten of them are long picnic tables, so we might want to put two of these on those. Fifteen are the café tables they use for the winery tastings. Becky listed an extra five tables so she could have extra flowers for the food and wine stations."

Charlotte nodded. "Makes sense. I'm hoping we can get Becky to come over here tomorrow or the next day to take a look at my creation. I want to make sure we're both on the same page."

An idea struck Robyn, the perfect scenario for her to

accidentally run into Teddy again. "If you want, I can swing by Bennett Farms and show her myself."

Charlotte's hands stilled, her eyebrows raised. "Really? You sure you don't mind?"

Robyn felt heat snake up the back of her neck, the thought of seeing Teddy again a heady possibility. "I don't mind at all."

"Well then, we'll be ahead of the game for once. Let me know what she thinks. And if she wants to add anything or make them larger, we've still got time to put in another flower order."

Robyn grinned from ear to ear, holding the jar filled with flowers, the creation exuding an aroma of smoky notes from the sweet lavender. "I'll take it over when I get off work today."

A few hours later, with the floral creation tucked safely in the cup holder of the Jeep, Robyn sped through town, anxious to lay eyes on Ted Bennett again. Unlike the first time she saw Teddy when she was hung-over wearing no makeup and with her hair in a messy bun, this time her hair was down, spilling over her shoulders in long, beachy waves, and she wore a pretty peasant blouse paired with her favorite jeans. She was intentional with her appearance now, hoping he might wander into the flower shop again. Before she locked up, she darted into the ladies' room and refreshed her simple makeup, her pretty features enhanced with rosy cheeks, mascara, and lip gloss.

The drive was familiar, one she'd navigated a thousand times before. She knew she was close when she passed Fred Wagoner's fence line. The borderline of his property had changed over the years, the swooped style picket fence decorative and giving off a feminine vibe. She wondered what

Ted might think about it, probably making fun of Fred for his choices.

The big arched sign of Bennett Farms loomed ahead, and Robyn slowed the car down. A sudden flood of insecurity infiltrated her system, and she seriously thought about turning around. With her heart beating madly, the thought of laying eyes on Teddy again urged her forward. Her bosom arose in a deep breath.

"You got this," she said to herself, checking her face in the vanity mirror again.

The terrain was bumpy in the Jeep, her hair bouncing against her shoulders. Gripping the steering wheel tighter, her eyes grew wide when she spotted one of Teddy's brothers on the front porch. She couldn't tell which brother it was until she was nearly parked, James waving a hand in greeting. Two big dogs panted by his feet, the country farm setting pristine with the majestic mountains in the background.

"Hey, Jimmy," she said through the rolled-down window. She wasn't about to get out of the car unless she was sure Becky was home. "Is your sister around? I've got some flowers to show her for the Harvest Hoedown."

James grinned, his handsome features eerily similar to his brother Ted. He came right up to the car and gripped the window ledge. "She's inside getting supper on the table. How are you doing, Robyn? It's been a while. I haven't seen you since the last festival."

Disappointment flushed her features, knowing she was imposing during the dinner hour. "Yeah, I know. I'm doing alright. How are you?"

James tucked one hand into the front pocket of his blue jeans and used the other to open her door. "Where are my manners? Come on inside and join us. I know everyone would love to see you, especially Ted, if you're up to it."

Robyn swallowed. "You sure?"

"Of course. Come on in." He egged her on, swiping his arm in a grand gesture for her to lead the way.

"Okay," she squeaked, grabbing the vase of flowers and scurrying to his side. The big dogs came right up to her, giving her the once-over with playful licks and sniffs. "I'm sorry, I forgot your dog's names."

"The yellow lab is Delia," he said as he ruffled the older dog's head. "And the black one is Jaxson." The lab ran in circles around them not unlike the way this now grown man used to run after his big brother.

"Cute. Excitable. I guess Cooper's not around anymore, huh?" For many years, Cooper was the Bennett family's golden retriever, a familiar canine when Robyn and Ted were in high school and college.

"Sadly, he's somewhere over the rainbow bridge. He was a good dog."

"Yes, he was."

They ambled up the front steps, Robyn pausing with second thoughts. "You know, I forgot... I have plans tonight. Maybe I should..."

"—Robyn!" Becky interrupted, squealing with delight. She held the door open with her backside, a colorful apron tied around her feminine figure. "What brings you to Bennett Farms today? We weren't supposed to start the festival prep till next week."

Robyn remained on the porch and presented the mason jar of flowers with two hands. "Charlotte wanted your take on this flower design for the tables. Said we could add to it if you're not satisfied, but we'd need to put in an order soon if you want something different. Instead of you having to come all the way into town to sign off on it, I volunteered to stop by and… show you myself."

A sly smile burgeoned across Becky's lips. "Well, I'm glad you did. This little arrangement is perfect for the Hoedown. And the lavender smells divine." She took the jar from Robyn and looped her free arm through hers. "Supper's almost ready. Now that you're here, I insist you stay and eat with us."

"Oh, no. I couldn't. I don't want to impose," she balked.

"Nonsense. I won't take no for an answer," Becky maintained.

Robyn eyed James for help. He shrugged. "Looks like you're staying for supper, Robyn."

The interior of the Bennett farmhouse was precisely how she remembered, the mammoth stone fireplace and long kitchen table inciting a rush of fond memories. Robyn looked about the room nervously, her eyes tracing the room for Teddy, but he was nowhere to be found.

"Go on and wash up. I've got stuffed shells on the menu tonight. It's no meat Monday, so I made a ton." Becky flitted about the kitchen like she owned the place.

"Can I help you with anything?" The table was already set, and she watched Becky place the mason jar of fresh flowers on a lazy-Susan in the middle of the table next to the salt and pepper. Her warm smile indicated she was pleased.

"No. Everything is practically ready. I'll add another place setting and call the boys while you wash up."

"Okay."

Robyn walked through a narrow hallway, passing the staircase. She paused, knowing Teddy's childhood bedroom was on the second floor. Was he up there now, showering after a long day on the farm? The thought of hot water and steam surrounding his muscled body sent a shiver up her spine. Her face flushed, and she forced herself toward the half bath, shutting herself inside.

"Dinner with the Bennetts," she mumbled, peering at her reflection in the oval mirror above the sink. She vigorously soaped up her hands. "I can do this. I can act natural around him."

Her eyes were wide and dark as if sensing Teddy's presence. Licking her lips, she tried to steady her erratic breathing. Perhaps coming over here wasn't such a good idea after all?

Gripping the antique knob of the door, she flicked off the lights and nearly collided with a large Bennett on the other side.

"*Whoa!*"

She knew the timbre of that voice anywhere. "Sorry, Teddy."

He gripped her by the shoulders, giving her the once-over. Shock flashed across his features, morphing into something more lighthearted. Was he glad to see her?

"What are you doing here?" he asked.

"I, uh… I dropped off a flower arrangement for your sister. She invited me to stay for supper. I hope it's okay." She was mesmerized by the thick whiskers surrounding Ted's lips, his manly pheromones tickling her senses being so near.

"Of course it's okay. I'm glad you're here." They hugged awkwardly in the middle of the dim hallway, Robyn's entire body buzzing with energy. "After you." Ted motioned for her to walk in front of him toward the kitchen, the sounds of the gathering Bennett family happy and energetic.

"Robyn! What a pleasant surprise." Roy Bennett hugged her hard.

"Thanks for having me," she stuttered.

Walter offered a polite nod in her direction before Hank swooped in and swung her around in a circle. "You're a sight for sore eyes. How are ya?"

Robyn was breathless and palmed her tummy when he set her back on the floor. "I'm... dizzy," she laughed. Ted looked on with absolute pleasure.

Dinner was delicious, Becky outdoing herself with pasta shells oozing with a creamy cheese filling, a crisp salad with homegrown heritage tomatoes, and homemade garlic rolls dripping with real butter. Wine bottles were uncorked, and the meal turned into a sweet assembly of toasts and memories. Teddy sat next to Robyn, and more than once, his foot accidently brushed against her ankle, causing a rush of thrilling shivers down her spine. Or maybe it wasn't an accident? Careful with her reactions, she demurely eyed him with a sweet smile every time.

"The flowers are perfect, Robyn. Tell Charlotte I approve," Becky stated, passing a large salad bowl across the table to her.

"You don't want to add anything?"

"No. It's perfect; shabby chic, country-style. Just make sure y'all order enough sunflowers for the hay bale arrangements by the barn doors."

"And cornstalks," Robyn added.

"Yes, and cornstalks. And boys?" she announced. "This year we're adding square dancing, so I expect all of you to participate with a lovely lady. This'll be a real hoot and holler of an evening," Becky grinned.

The brothers groaned as Teddy cleared his throat. "I don't know about the square dancing, Becks, but I'm looking forward to seeing Hank-ster in the spotlight performing with his band."

Robyn rested her fork on her plate. "That's right. You've never seen him sing in public, have you?"

A flash of sadness swept across Ted's expression as he shook his head. "Not yet."

"Have you got the setlist nailed down, Hank?" James asked.

"Yup. We've been rehearsing for weeks. I've got some new songs I can't wait to share with y'all." His eyes crinkled against his boyish grin.

The family voiced how excited they were for the upcoming Harvest Hoedown—everyone except Walt. He leaned back in his chair, twirling his wine glass in his hand, taking it all in. He hadn't said two words since Robyn joined them at the dinner table, his menacing looks and glances her way hard not to notice. She always knew he was the broody, competitive brother, but his intentional disregard for her was concerning.

After a simple dessert of vanilla ice cream topped with chocolate sauce served in Ted's great-grandmother's dessert bowls, Robyn ambled out onto the back porch to view the sunset beyond the mountain range. Roy insisted she sit in one of the rocking chairs and relax, his southern charm and manners hard to say no to. Teddy leaned against a porch post with his hands tucked into the front pockets of his jeans. It was nice to see him relaxed among his family. He was one of them—always had been and always would be. No one brought up anything about his jail time or the hearings while she was there, and Robyn was thankful.

One by one, the Bennetts said goodnight, leaving Robyn and Ted alone in the twilight. She knew they were being polite, giving them space to talk quietly alone. Sighing, she angled her head to get a good look at him.

"Are you tired?"

"A little bit."

"Me, too. It was good to see you tonight. And Becky outdid herself with dinner." She stood. "I need to get home. I've got work tomorrow."

"I'll walk you out."

Their feet crunched along the pebbled path as they made their way around the ancient farmhouse. Standing next to the Jeep, Robyn jokingly stuck her hand out for a shake. "Well, goodnight, Teddy."

He chuckled, his warm fingers surrounding hers in a squeeze. "Goodnight, Robyn."

They lingered in the shake until Ted pulled her forward, wrapping his arms around her in a hug. It was a natural response, hugging him back, her fingers roaming his broad shoulders. Her insides pulsed with longing as she inhaled his intoxicating scent of manhood and pine, and she thought she might combust with wanton energy.

"I'll see you around," she mumbled near his ear.

His whiskers tickled her cheek as she pulled back, anxious to get out of there before doing something foolish —like jumping into his arms and straddling his waist, suckling his lips, and pummeling his mouth with her tongue. Her exhale of hot breath was shaky, her panties damp thinking about the possibilities.

"See you around, Robyn."

The way he looked at her with all the tenderness of a former lover left her scrambling, her movements awkward and geeky as she climbed into the Jeep to go home. The car jerked when she accelerated a little too hard, and when she looked in the rearview mirror, her heart ached seeing Teddy's shadowed figure waving goodbye.

# Chapter Eight

TEDDY

Being back on the farm agreed with Ted, his quiet mornings starting at the butt-crack of dawn. Even the big dogs acted like it was too early, lifting their heads and lazily blinking against the kitchen lights as they lay on their doggie beds and watched him fix his coffee in a to-go cup. He preferred the early hour, when the world was still asleep, the hush and rolling fog across the mountaintops almost spiritual as he welcomed each new day as a free man.

Robyn was never far from his mind. He kept her picture safely tucked away in the bedside table drawer, only taking it out if he had a fitful night's sleep. Her serene smile seemed to calm him, just like all those years behind bars. She was still with him in spirit, and he often wondered when he might see her again. There was still so much to say. But the ball was in her court, especially with a boyfriend in the picture. Even though Ted wanted her with every fiber of his being, he wasn't about to wreck her life all over again. He'd done it once, and once was plenty enough.

The Christmas tree season would kick into high gear in

less than three months, and Ted was more than prepared. His Papaw Bennett planted his first crop of Fraser Fir trees in 1952. Most people thought he was crazy, but now there were hundreds of thousands of trees in production, the working farm the livelihood for his entire family. His father's passion for cultivating and harvesting trees paved the way for him to do the same with his vineyard, the winery business better than anyone ever imagined. Now, Roy Bennett passed on his legacy to his kids, all while sharing the love of growing beautiful Christmas trees, hard work, and good wine with those around him.

During his first week back, Ted took stock of the land, steering clear of the vineyards per his probation officer's request. He was impressed by the trees in the ground, and he already knew how to monitor and control insects and weeds, the insecticide sprayers and tractors coming in handy for his daily work. But many of the two and four-year-old pine and fir species required pruning and shearing to maintain the classic Christmas tree shape their farm was known for. Using large shaper sheers, the work was grueling and arduous, the long hours of manual labor in the late-summer sun leaving him exhausted by the end of the day. Still, he was thankful for the new rhythm, his heart pulsing with freedom and gratitude surrounded by family and nature.

"What in the hell is that?" Ted stopped in his tracks after entering through the backdoor of the kitchen. In the middle of cooking something, Becky looked up, the pervasive scent of garlic hitting his senses.

"What?" she smiled. "You seemed to enjoy my garlic rolls the other night when Robyn was over for supper." She continued to stir a wooden spoon in a small saucepan on the stove.

Ted wasn't about to take his sister's bait. He approached

the large farmhouse sink and washed his hands. He was taking a break; he and his brother James sidelined after the main tractor they worked on experienced engine failure.

"Where's Jimmy?" she asked.

"He's waiting on the mechanic. Told me to take a quick break."

"I'm glad." Becky continued to stir. "You've been working way too hard if you ask me. I hope you're staying hydrated."

"I am." He used a paper towel to dry his hands before swiping it across his sweaty brow. "What is that?"

"It's melted butter and garlic. I have to keep stirring it so the butter won't scorch."

"No, not what's in the pot. What's the funny-looking round light shining on you?" He motioned to a large circular bulb clamped to a tripod. "And why are you so dolled up?"

Becky laid the spoon in a metal rest nearby, her glossed lips glinting in the bright light. Wiping her hands on a frilly apron, she reached for the tripod and clicked the light off.

"It's my ring light."

"Ring light?"

"Yes, I use it when I'm filming my weekly blog post for my YouTube channel."

"Your what post? And you have a... a YouTube channel?" Ted didn't mean to repeat everything she said, but he wasn't entirely tracking with her.

"Yes, silly. I have a pretty popular blog people follow. It's called, *The Farmer's Daughter*. I post mostly recipes I make every week for our family and workers here on the farm. It's like some of the food shows on TV but on a much smaller scale. Here, take a look." She handed him her cell phone. "*The Farmer's Daughter* has become popular over the last couple of years, especially with all the annual events we now host at the winery. I like to take pictures and post them on my social media, too. My followers really love them."

Ted squinted at the small screen and scrolled through her social media. Numerous familiar pictures of the farm popped to life in a thread, the snapshots impressive. Interspersed in the stream were several videos and candid shots of Becky holding a plate of something yummy with a link to the recipe underneath. His little sister was always smiling, the soft ambiance from the ring light accentuating her rosy cheeks and cupid lips.

His eyes widened as he read her profile. "You have... *fifty-thousand* followers?"

"Yup," she casually replied.

Ted's mouth gaped as he turned and watched her chop a healthy bunch of parsley. "This is incredible, Becks. You're a star! What does Dad think about all of this? What do our *brothers* think about it?"

Becky continued to chop, the large knife thumping against the wooden cutting board. "They think it's great. And get this, every time I post a picture or video with one of them in it, their followers increase too, especially Hank's. He's walked through the kitchen a few times playing his guitar and singing while I've been filming. I swear, every time I introduce him, I get tons of requests from women who want to meet him." She laughed. "You should hear the song he wrote called, *I Love Chicken*, to commemorate Granny Bennett's fried chicken recipe. It's hysterical and a fan favorite."

Ted couldn't quite fathom the amount of exposure his siblings had on the internet. No wonder their family farm was a tourist attraction. That had to be better than all of the news coverage when he was on trial. Back then, his family and friends were bombarded with newspaper and television hounds sniffing out the worst. His story even made national headlines, the paparazzi deeming him an all-American disappointment. Surely Becky's fan base didn't know anything about her oldest brother's ugly past. What if he ruined what his sister had going for her? The thought sickened him.

"I'll, uh, be sure to stay out of your way while you're filming. I don't want to mess up what you've got going on with this." He opened the refrigerator and grabbed a water bottle, averting her reaction.

"Hey." She grabbed him by the wrist.

Ted kept his head bowed, wishing he could forget the past six years of his life, wishing none of it ever happened. The fridge closed with a soft thump.

"You're my big brother, and I love you with all my heart. Do you believe me?"

Glancing at Becky, Ted felt his cheeks heat with embarrassment. How often had his little sister stuck up for him during the trial? During the hearings, she was a freshman in high school, her loyalty and love helping him through the worst days of his life. How could he ever forgive himself for missing out on watching her grow up and blossom into the successful young woman and entrepreneur she was today while he was locked up in hell?

"I do believe you. And I love you, too, Becks."

"Good. Now give me one of your big ol' Teddy bear hugs. You still owe me about a million of them."

"Awe, Becks. I'm sweaty and gross. I don't want to mess up your pretty apron."

"I don't care." She bullied her way into his arms.

Ted closed his eyes while holding his sister. He was so damn proud of her. She was a shining star in the family, strong and independent, the similarities between her and their mother striking. When his mama was alive, she was a hugger too; the endearing trait passed down to his little sister. He'd be fine making up a million hugs for her.

They were interrupted by a woman's voice clearing her throat. "Excuse me."

Ted let go of his sister and turned to see Sam McNeil standing by the backdoor. She smiled warmly and nodded. "I had a feeling being back home would agree with you, Ted. You look good." She shifted her focus to Becky. "Hey, Becky. How are you?"

"Hi, Miss McNeil. I'm fine. Come on in. I'm filming my blog post."

"What's on the menu today?" she asked with pleasure.

"Homemade garlic rolls."

"Mmm, so that's what I smell in here. Lots of real garlic, I assume."

"You got that right," Becky giggled. "May I get you something to drink?"

"No, thank you. I'm just here to see Ted."

Feeling awkward, Ted set his bottled water on the counter and shoved his hands into his back pockets. "I'm sorry, Ms. McNeil. Did I miss an appointment with you? I thought we weren't meeting again until next week?"

"Well, here's the thing, Ted. Sometimes, when you least expect it, I might decide to make a house call out of the blue to see how you're doing in real-time." Sam cocked an eyebrow as if gauging his reaction.

Becky immediately came to the rescue, gripping Ted by the bicep. "Miss McNeil, I can assure you, my big brother has been working way too hard on the farm. I only see him during meals. And he's like an old man going to bed by eight o'clock every night and getting up before sunrise every morning. The only time he's left the farm since he came home was to go into town to buy some flowers for our mother's grave—and my daddy drove him. He's an outstanding parolee; you have my word."

Sam seemed amused by Becky's defense. "I'm glad to hear this. I wish I had a brother or a sister like you who was invested in my life." She turned to look at Ted. "I'm happy to see you doing so well."

As she started to dig into her purse, Ted felt heat flare up the back of his neck. God, what if she needed another urine sample? How embarrassing, especially in front of his little sister. When Sam pulled out her cell phone, he sighed with relief.

"I've still got you down for next week. But don't be surprised if I make another house call. It's what I'm known for."

"That's fine, Miss McNeil. You're welcome anytime."

Sam nodded. "Okay. I'll be seeing you. And Becky?"

"Yes, ma'am?"

"I'll be sure to check out your recipe on the blog today. It smells delicious in here."

"Thanks, Miss McNeil."

Ted and Becky waited until Sam exited before they looked at each other. His sister's eyes were wide with trepidation.

"My heart's pounding, Teddy. Weren't you scared?"

Ted plucked his bottled water off the counter and twisted off the top. "No. Why should I be scared?"

"Because she could send you back to prison. I mean, one little mistake, and you're gone."

Ted swallowed a gulp of water and wiped his lips with the back of his hand. "I'm not gonna mess this up, Becks.

Don't worry about me, okay? I'm safe here on the farm. Nothing is going to happen to me here."

"If you say so."

The sound of a woman squealing outside diverted their attention. And then they heard James' booming voice. "Down, boy! *Down!*"

"What in the world?" Becky's voice lilted.

They rushed out the back door to find Sam flat on her ass in the grass with Jaxson on top of her, licking her face. The parole officer laughed and allowed the big dog to paw all over her.

"It's okay. I'm okay!" she reassured.

James wasn't convinced and forcefully grabbed the dog by the collar, getting him off her. "Shit, I'm so sorry about that. Jax is still a puppy at heart, especially around the pretty ladies." He offered Sam his free hand. "Here, let me help you up."

Ted scrambled down the small wooden stairs and took over, holding Jax back as Delia cowered near the bushes lining the porch. "You sure you're okay, Miss McNeil?" He gritted his teeth and hoped this wouldn't cause a ding on his record.

"Yes, I'm fine."

James pulled her by the hand to her feet. "Easy does it. You're sure?"

When she stood in front of his brother, their eyes met, and her cheeks flushed. Wiping off a few wayward pieces of grass from her pants, she batted her lashes at him. "Mighty fine. Thank you."

"You're welcome."

Ted glanced at his sister, who pressed her lips together to thwart a grin. Were these two flirting with each other?

"I'm Samantha McNeil, your brother's parole officer.

But you can call me Sam." She held her hand out, and they shook. "I didn't have the pleasure of meeting you last time I was here."

James continued to pump Sam's hand, staring at her like a star-struck teen. "The pleasure's all mine, Samantha... I mean, Sam," he stuttered.

Jaxson whined, tugging against Ted's grip on his collar. This was one for the books—his brother smitten by his parole officer. But he couldn't be, could he? She was off limits. If they dated, she'd be violating her oath to serve while assigned to Ted.

Still, it was fun to see his brother acting like an idiot.

# Chapter Nine

## ROBYN

Robyn's bare feet thumped back and forth against the boards of the screened-in porch floor, the rhythmic pulsing of the antique metal glider she sat on moving at a slow pace. The air was muggy, the humidity causing a layer of sweat to glisten her face. Staring out the screen at the small pond in the distance, she contemplated a quick dip, the vacant dock beckoning her to strip and jump off with a splash.

Using her hand to fan herself lazily, she sighed. Her thoughts reverted to those days long ago when it was just her and Teddy skinny dipping without a care in the world. This September was one of the hottest on record, her core temperature spiking with memories, the heat pooling in her belly. Planting her feet on the floor, she stopped the glider and decided to tamper her heated skin by taking a dip in the private pond.

The screen door squeaked as she pushed through, pulling her t-shirt up and over her head. Tilting her head back, she squinted in the bright sunshine and considered sunscreen in the day's heat. But she'd only be a few minutes, languishing in the coolness of the water. The dock was weathered and gray, the bottoms of her feet growing hotter with each step on the sun-drenched boards. Oh, how she longed for the cooler days and nippy autumn nights, the lingering high temperatures of Indian summer holding on until the bitter end.

Stripping off her frayed jean shorts, Robyn stood on the dock in nothing but her bra and panties. She shielded her eyes from the diamond glimmers off the pond's surface and scoped the private area. A hot breeze caused the leaves in the trees to whoosh, the air feathering its way across her exposed skin. Sweat pooled between her breasts, saturating the underwire of her bra. Reaching around her back, she unhooked the garment and tossed it onto her shorts.

A wide smile donned her features as she took a running leap and cannon-balled into the water. The relief from the heat was immediate, and as she rose to the surface, she flung her head back Little Mermaid style, whipping her long hair with a slap against her bare back. She tread water, kicking her legs beneath the surface, the refreshing coolness against her nipples causing them to pebble into hard nubs. Back-floating, she relished the slight breeze across her bare chest pointed toward the heavens.

This is what she needed—a moment of calm serenity in the privacy of her ten-acre backyard. It was just her and nature, thoughts of Teddy momentarily put on the back burner. Her part-time boyfriend, Anderson, was back in Atlanta for the week stuck in meetings. They hardly saw each other as of late, his career keeping them in the long-distance relationship category. The man had a comfortable condo in Midtown and tried more than once to convince Robyn to move in with him and become a city girl. But she wasn't ready for that kind of a commitment—not prepared to give up the peace and tranquility of her home in Langston Falls and all the memories she kept close to her heart. And now that Teddy was home, how could she leave?

Robyn couldn't imagine being in Atlanta during this time of year, the traffic and temperature amped up during the heat wave a horrific byproduct among the cityscape. She'd much rather be floating in a pond near the mountains, the shrill grate and tempo of urban life non-existent in what Anderson called her redneck world.

He'd called earlier, asking her to visit him in Atlanta. While he finished the workday, he proposed she stop by her dad's law office and say hi, shop at one of the big malls, or take in a matinee movie in the air conditioning. She was tempted when he suggested they end the day at the fancy Sun Dial restaurant downtown, the romantic notion of watching the sunset against the backdrop of the city, something she used to enjoy.

But truth be told, she wasn't in the mood to hang out with Anderson. It wouldn't feel the same. She knew it was because of Teddy. Thinking about running in to him again was the only thing these days that got her heart racing. Her mind wandered as she floated, conjuring up a slew of instances where she could make that happen with the best chance being at the Harvest Hoedown. She'd be on the Bennett farm for several days helping Becky with the setup, and there was no way she wouldn't see him, hopefully with his shirt off and as sweaty as she'd been five minutes ago.

Relaxed, Robyn continued floating on her back, her fingers conducting a symphony of sorts back and forth across the water's surface. A flash of red through the tall grasses at the pond's edge garnered her attention in her peripheral vision, and she tensed. Her arms flailed in a splash as she ducked her exposed chest under the water, one arm instinctively covering her breasts.

"*Who's there?*" she yelled, bobbing up and down.

Her question was met with another rustling of leaves as the breeze blew through the muggy air. Careful, she glided through the pond toward the swimmer's ladder attached to the edge of the dock, her eyes tracing the embankment. Ripples lapped against the earthy shoreline, and she was startled again when she saw the distinct figure of a person huddled behind the tall, longleaf grasses. Narrow blades of the woodoats cascaded over the pond, the ordinarily green shades starting to turn tan in the late season. The red ball cap was prominent, the person hiding easy to spot.

"This is private property, and you're trespassing. *Please leave now!*" she shouted.

Her long legs propelled her forward as she sliced through the water, anxious to put her clothes back on. Her cell phone was back in the screened-in porch, and the family renting her late grandmother's house was out of town—not that her screams could be heard from half a mile away on the property they shared.

"I'm warning you."

She shivered and gripped the ladder, hoping whoever was hiding in the grass was a worker her renter might have hired and not some murderous felon who stumbled upon her oasis. When the red cap arose from the thick patch of grass, Robyn's breath hitched, the figure another felon she knew personally.

"*Teddy?*"

Ted Bennett stood tall, like a Phoenix rising from the ashes. Taking off his ball cap, his hair blew back from his face, his dark eyes focused on hers for a beat before he gallantly turned away as if to give her privacy.

"I'm sorry, Robyn. I didn't think you'd be here in the middle of the day."

"Wha… what are you doing here?" Water droplets dripped from her eyelashes, and she blinked several times.

Ted seemed nervous, twisting the ball cap in his hands. "It's hot as hell, and I had the urge to dip my feet in your pond. Seriously, I didn't think anyone would be around. You must've had the same idea. Great minds think alike," he chuckled before he sheepishly glanced in her direction again. The skin above his beard was red from heat exhaustion. Or maybe it was embarrassment?

Robyn felt her pulse tick, the very thought of Teddy joining her in the water a giddy consideration.

"I'm sorry I disturbed you, Robyn. I'll be on my way so you can enjoy your swim in privacy." He shoved the cap on his head and turned to leave.

"*Wait!*" she pleaded.

Teddy stopped and slowly turned around, his eyes flicking to hers. The sight of him gazing at her half-naked in the water was almost too much to handle. Her vision blurred, and she struggled for her next breath. The audacity of what she was about to do sent a thrill down her spine.

"I don't mind you being here," she started.

Pushing off the dock, she swam toward him, her feet sinking into the silt and oozing between her toes as she entered a shallow area near the shore. Crouched in the pond, a dragonfly whizzed by her wet head, and she made a split decision that felt natural, like breathing in and out. She blamed her actions on the heat sizzling any semblance of her brain, her entire body having a mind of its own as she slowly stood tall. Water sluiced off her skin, her slick breasts bare and on full display.

A pained expression crossed Ted's face, and Robyn

wondered if she'd gone too far. He scrubbed a hand across his bearded jaw as if contemplating his next move. The air seemed to still, and Robyn waited, holding her breath. When he didn't budge, she held her hand out, reaching for him, the need to touch him filling her with desperation.

"Please, Teddy." Her voice scratched with longing, her fingers trembling with possibility.

Ted licked his lips with a decision before he flung his hat off and lifted the edges of his tee up and over the hard muscles of his body.

Robyn's voice squeaked in her throat, taking in the swell of his hardened physique. His long hair floated in the breeze as he took it a step further and shucked off his boots and shimmied out of his jeans, leaving him standing there in nothing but his boxers.

"You sure about this, Robyn?"

She swallowed hard, her head bobbing with a definitive nod.

Ted splashed his way into the pond, reaching for her hand. When their fingers entangled, his firm grip pulled her forward to where she was pressed firmly against his sweltering chest. As they eased into the water, visceral memories assaulted her senses, her body brought back to life from skin-on-skin touch. Her wandering fingers marveled at the feel of his strength flexing beneath the water. Dropping his forehead against hers, she felt tendrils of heat from his raspy exhale skate across her skin before he palmed her cheeks and captured her mouth in a deep kiss. Her nipples turned into tingling peaks rubbing against the hard planes of his chest, the sunbeams a kaleidoscope of bright light surrounding them.

"I missed you so much," he mumbled into her mouth.

Robyn was lost in the kiss, nipping and licking his lips.

Tasting. Exploring. The feel of his hands on her naked body was pure bliss, the sensations rocking her core. His hairy face skirted her collar bone, tender kisses peppering her skin. In one fluid motion, she stood, and he captured a pebbled nipple between his lips, anchoring her waist in his large hands. Her head tilted looking down at him, taking in his gorgeous presence, filling her with love again.

"God, Teddy…," she exhaled. "You ever wonder what would've happened if—"

"Don't," he interrupted, easing back.

"Don't, what?" she asked, tucking his damp hair over his ear. Water surged all around them as Teddy arose, his imposing figure towering above her. His eyes traced her body, and she felt a slight tinge of self-consciousness.

"You're so goddamn beautiful, Robyn." He closed the gap between them with a hug. "I don't know what you're thinking asking me to skinny dip with you."

Robyn giggled. "We're not skinny-dipping, silly. We still have our underwear on." Pulling back, she reached for both of his hands and pressed them against her breasts.

"Robyn…"

"What? Don't you feel it? Don't you want me?"

"Of course I want you." He trailed a finger between her breasts only stopping when he reached the lace of her panties. "But you told me you met someone, and you're happy. I'd never forgive myself if I caused you any more pain."

"I don't love him," she interjected. Her heart galloped. "I love you, Teddy. You're the love of my life." She watched his Adam's apple bob in his throat.

"I… I love you, too, Robyn. More than you'll ever know."

A wide grin unfurled from her lips, and she blinked back

the onset of hot tears. "Come on." Taking his hand, she started up the shore. "Let's rinse and towel off. Then we can catch up like we used to, curled up on the glider in the screened porch. Unless you want to swim some more."

Ted palmed the silk panties covering her round cheeks, giving her one last push up the side of the pond.

"I've got a better idea."

# Chapter Ten

## TEDDY

Ted stood in the grass, boots in one hand and his clothes clutched in the other. He watched Robyn trot across the dock and retrieve her discarded clothing, disappointed when she pressed the fabric against her chest, hiding her alluring bosom.

"You still got the outdoor shower area?" he asked. They walked side by side like they had for years, the air pulsing with possibility.

"Yes. I was about to put away the hose for the season but knew better. This heat wave is the worst," she lamented.

"I know. I sweat so much out on the farm, and the sap from the pine trees turns gooey like tar."

Robyn laughed and it sent a shot of adrenaline through him. To make her laugh, to make her happy was all he'd ever wanted to do. But was there any way this could turn out well?

The entire Morgan compound looked exactly the same; Robyn's tiny house near the pond painted the same Tiffany-blue with white shutters. The screened-in porch looked out over an open meadow and the pond, her late grandmother's farmhouse a tiny blip in the distance.

"You still have renters in the main house?" Ted asked

"Yes. It's the same family, only the kids have grown up, and the couple got divorced. I don't see much of them anymore. But the rent gets paid, and the yard is maintained."

"That's good. You ever think about moving in?"

"Into that big ol' house? I don't know. I like the cottage. It's perfect for me. It's home." She placed her clothing items on the back stoop and confidently walked bare-chested right past him toward the outdoor shower area. Flicking on the hose, she said, "This water will be cold but refreshing."

Licking his lips, Ted watched her with unbridled fascination, her lush curves under the waterfall of fresh water causing a certain appendage to tent his soaked boxers. This unexpected afternoon with Robyn was a gift, pure and simple. He had no idea she'd be home when he decided to walk the three miles in the sweltering sun to take a swim in her pond. Sure, he hoped he might run into her, but not half-naked and looking more tempting than ever.

He used to know every outline of her curves—the subtle dip between her ample breasts. The soft spot below her ear where he liked to nuzzle. The curvature of her middle, right before the swell of her womanly hips. The taste of her on his tongue…

"You ready?"

Ted startled out of his daydream, his cheeks heated with awkwardness. Robyn was wrapped in a towel, holding the running hose for him to take over.

"Yeah. Sure." He walked toward her and was blindsided when she pressed her thumb over the nozzle and sprayed him down with a blast of cold water.

"*Ahhh!*" he bellowed.

"I told you it's cold!" She laughed.

"You're gonna be sorry, young lady."

Robyn dropped the running hose and took off. Ted shook his drenched head and turned the water off before he was hot on her tail. They ran around the house like two little kids, squealing and panting with laughter, Ted gaining on her. As she pulled open the screened porch door, he caught the edge of her towel and ripped it off.

"Teddy!" She collapsed half-naked on the glider, palming her chest rising and falling in deep pants. Her eyes were wide looking up at him as if waiting for him to make the next move.

Careful, Ted kneeled in front of her and edged his way between her bent knees.

"What… what are you doing, Teddy?"

"Shhh. Lean back and relax." Looping his fingers through the elastic of her panties, he pulled them down, the fabric curling in on itself.

"Teddy?" She palmed the cushion on either side of her body, rigid with uncertainty.

Ted looped her panties over her legs and feet before flinging them to the side. Pressing his hands against her inner thighs, he marveled at her soft mound presented in her wide seated stance. He was tender in his actions, pressing feather-light kisses along her skin, slow in his efforts. His mouth watered to taste her, his dick hot and solid between his legs.

"Oh, God," she whispered.

"Relax, Robyn," he mumbled against her fevered skin. "I've dreamt of this moment for years."

Her fingers found their way into his wet locks, and she leaned back, opening her legs wider for him. Ted grunted and moved forward with purpose, his wet tongue eagerly tracing her hot seam. Gripping her by the thighs, he feasted, lapping her tangy well like a starved man eager to squelch his hunger. The overhead ceiling fan gave off a slight breeze as sweat dribbled down his neck and back, Robyn's moans of ecstasy urging him on.

Lifting his head from between her heated legs, he caught a glimpse of her beautiful face. Her eyes were closed, her brow furrowed, and her luscious mouth gaped in ecstasy. He slid two fingers deep inside her folds and watched her breath hitch.

"That's it. I want to watch you come undone." Her eyes blinked open, and he smiled at her. "Just like old times."

She nodded aggressively, yanking him by the hair and urging him forward.

"Oh, you want more of this, huh?"

"Yes, Teddy." She hissed. "Don't stop."

"Oh, I'll never stop." He latched on to her clit and sucked hard, Robyn's high-pitched moans climbing higher and higher as she came closer to orgasm.

"*Teddy*!" Her body turned stiff as her sweet juice flooded his tongue before she collapsed against the seatback.

He lay there with his bearded cheek pressed against her leg, the utter contentment he felt worth every single second he was behind bars. He'd do it all over if it meant he could have this moment again.

"Make love to me, Teddy," he heard her say.

Lifting his sweaty head, their eyes locked. Robyn traced his lips with the tip of her finger. "I don't have to be anywhere today. It's my day off."

"I don't have to go back to the farm. I can stay."

The immediate smile she offered made him want to weep with joy.

"How did you get here? Did your dad drop you off?"

"No. I walked."

She seemed surprised. "Three miles? In this heat?"

"I don't mind the heat, especially coming over here. I picked the perfect day."

"I'll say." The look of love on her face was noticeable. "Why don't you rinse off in my shower inside? I'll throw your boxers in the dryer so you can have them for later when I drive you home."

Ted paused, the word "home" a contradiction of sorts. Bennett Farms was his birth home, but this was his true home—right here, with Robyn. He'd never felt more at home in his entire life.

Ted stood and stepped out of his wet boxers, handing them to her.

"What are you doing?" she giggled, gripping the edge of the glider.

"Giving you my boxers so you can throw them in the dryer."

Robyn pressed her teeth into her lower lip, her gaze dragging down his rock-hard length mere inches in front of her. "Wait," she said. "Take one step closer to me, lover-boy."

Ted smirked and did as he was told, the anticipation of her lush mouth closing over the tender skin of his dick making him harder. Her eyes flicked to his, her grin naughty before she opened her mouth wide and closed her eyes.

"Oh, fuuuck…" Ted planted his bare feet in a broad stance on the floorboards, cupping the back of Robyn's head. The feel of her wet tongue and full lips was pure rapture. He followed her rhythm and rocked his hips with pleasure.

"You need to... slow down," he panted. "I want to be inside you."

Robyn kept going, his mischievous little minx tempting him to explode in her mouth.

"Robyn!" He yelped, jerking himself free. Sweat poured from his body. The look on her face said it all; she was still his girl, the love of his life.

"I'm sorry." Her big eyes held apology and mirth, sexual innuendos, and loyalty. The atmosphere sizzled with unrepentant love.

"No, you're not," he chuckled.

Reaching for her hand, he helped her up. Her naked body held faint tan lines from the summer, her skin glistening with perspiration. Sliding his fingers across her blushing cheek, he marveled at the softness of her skin.

"I want you to get in the shower and I'll join you after I make a quick call to my dad," he advised. It took everything in his power to break apart their connection, but he knew he had to.

"Why do you need to call your dad?"

It was a fair question he hoped he could explain without coming across as a complete delinquent. But there were rules he had to follow if he were to get through this last year of parole unscathed.

Ted continued stroking her cheek. "He's my supervisor while I'm out on parole. Sometimes my parole officer shows up unannounced, so I need to keep him in the loop."

"Are you going to tell him you and your ex-girlfriend just had oral sex?" Her eyes glimmered with amusement as she lightly ran her hands down his exposed chest.

Ted shook his head. "I'm not that transparent with him. I'll think of something."

Robyn rose on her tiptoes and pressed her lips against his mouth. "Don't be too long. I'll be waiting for you."

He watched her trot into the house, her magnificent backside sending a surge of heat to his raging boner. Taking a deep breath, Ted willed himself to settle down, sure his dad would catch wind of his naughty escapades if he wasn't careful.

Sitting buck-naked on the glider, he grabbed his wayward jeans and fished his phone out of the pocket. As he dialed his father, the aroma of Robyn's secret garden permeated his fingers, curling around his nostrils.

"Where ya at, son? I hope you found yourself a shady spot to wait out the heat of this day." His dad's voice was casual, full of unconditional love.

Ted cleared his throat. "I'm, uh, at the Morgan pond. Thought I'd take a swim in the pond and cool off."

There was silence on the other end of the line for a beat. "Are you with Robyn?"

Shaking his head, Ted gripped the back of his neck. "No, sir. I'm enjoying the peace and quiet. It's just like I remembered." That was the understatement of the year.

"Well, be careful. You're technically trespassing on the Morgan property if you're unsupervised. I don't want you to get into any trouble."

"Don't worry, Dad. I wanted to cool off and clear my mind. This place was once a sanctuary to me. I don't think Robyn would mind."

Roy grunted. "I know she wouldn't mind. It's her city-slicker boyfriend I'd be worried about."

"I'll be careful."

"Alright then. I'll see ya at suppertime."

"Bye, Dad."

Ted felt a twinge of guilt for lying to his father, but only for a minute. Grabbing his pile of clothes and boots, he entered the home he once shared with Robyn, overcome with déjà vu. Everything was exactly how he remembered. Pausing to take it all in, his senses averted when he heard his name being called from the bathroom.

"Teddy? I'm waiting for you."

His chest rose in a deep breath, the magnetic pull she had on him luring him down the hallway. "I'm on my way."

# Chapter Eleven

## ROBYN

Robyn lay in her bed with one hand draped dramatically above her head. A single tear made a path down her cheek, her heart already grieving the absence of Teddy. They spent the entire afternoon wrapped up in each other's arms, making love several times and declaring their devotion in whispered tones of sweet nothings. They were ravenous for each other, not able to get enough.

"Do you understand how much I love you? How much I need you?" Ted cried out earlier, his formidable figure looming above her naked body as he pumped her tirelessly.

"I know," she soothed. "I know, Teddy."

They came together, the passion off-the-charts in an explosion of colorful adoration. She needed Teddy, too, and couldn't imagine another day without him in her life, the long drought finally over.

Robyn begged him to stay for dinner, desperate for him to spend the night. But she understood the rules he needed to adhere to. He had to go home to Bennett Farms, and when she offered to give him a ride, he insisted he walk home so he could stretch out their perfect day before he returned to reality.

Teddy forlornly told her how guilty he felt, blaming himself for smashing her dreams of becoming an attorney and following her career path in law like her father. Those dreams came to an abrupt halt when he was sentenced to years in jail, the plea bargain he agreed to one she begged him not to take. But that was water under the bridge, and he swore he'd make it up to her, even if it took him the rest of his life. Ted Bennett vowed he would never go another day without telling her how much she was loved and appreciated.

They'd figure it out somehow. But for now, they needed to lie low, especially since her current boyfriend was still in the picture, even if it was long-distance. The heady feeling of being safe in Teddy's arms was one she coveted for years, her overwhelming sensitivity hard to compare being with Anderson.

Sighing in the aftermath of tousled sheets damp with sweat and Teddy's lingering essence, Robyn sat up. Just the thought of his charming grin and captivating eyes made her swoon for more. Oh, how she prayed for a reunion with Teddy Bennett, and how they'd pick up where they left off, the love between them unscathed and more powerful than ever after all these years. What was she thinking continuing to date Anderson when she knew Ted was back in town? She was weak when it came to Teddy. And now that they had rekindled their unrestrained passion, she owed it to Anderson to come clean.

Her cell phone rang. Glancing at the lit-up receiver on the nightstand, she was disappointed it was Anderson calling and not Teddy. She hesitated. She didn't want to end things with him over a phone call. No. She needed to do it in person and as soon as possible.

"Hello, Robyn."

"Hey, Anderson," she nervously greeted. Shifting on the bed, she pulled the sheet up to cover her bare breasts. "Did you, um, have a good day?"

"It would've been better if you were in town."

"I'm sorry. I … needed a day off, you know?" Could he hear the guilt in her tone?

"I get it. I couldn't have gone out to dinner with you anyway."

"Oh? Why not?"

"I have to catch a redeye out of town tonight back to LA. We're putting this deal to bed, baby!"

Robyn eyed her own bed, annihilated from her earlier sexual escapades with Teddy. If Anderson only knew.

"That's great."

"We'll celebrate when I get back next week."

"Next week?" Robyn's brow furrowed. "Why so long?"

"There's a lot to sign off on, and I want to celebrate with my colleagues. I heard Devon say the owner might even charter a yacht out of Santa Monica for a couple of days. This is huge!"

Robyn half-expected Anderson to invite her to the festivities, but he was quick to dismiss her in his usual crass way. "I'll be back for that Hoedown thing. Then we need to seriously talk about you relocating to Atlanta. I miss you, babe."

Robyn froze when she heard a female voice in the background. The phone turned muffled for a beat before Anderson returned to the line.

"Sorry about that."

"Are you… with someone?" she dared to ask. Not that it

mattered. In fact, she hoped she caught him red-handed. This wasn't the first time she suspected he was cheating on her, nor the last. But wasn't she doing the exact same thing to him? Cheating with Teddy?

"Alice brought me some paperwork. I'm at the office, Robyn. Don't get your panties in a wad."

Robyn shifted her naked ass under the covers, her panties tossed somewhere in the vicinity.

"I'll be out of commission for several days, so don't freak out if you can't get in touch with me, okay?"

Robyn nodded.

"You there?"

"I was nodding."

Anderson chuckled. "Okay. I'll see you next week, and we'll celebrate—just you and me."

Before she could say another word, the line went dead. Robyn stared at her phone. Her screen saver was a shot of the red barn on Bennett Farms, decorated for Christmas with a massive wreath her boss created hanging from the ancient wood loft. Sliding her photos open, she found her secret file and pressed it. Hundreds of pictures of her and Teddy filled the screen, her lips turning up into a melancholy smile. She would never get over him. He was the love of her life—her soul mate.

Knowing she had to string Anderson along before she saw him again left a bitter taste in her mouth. But she'd get over it. He was probably already popping open a bottle of champagne, pouring the bubbly into his assistant's mouth as he straddled her across his desk. Robyn wasn't naïve. Anderson and Alice often openly flirted right in front of her when she visited Atlanta. The man was a hound dog. He was also a diversion until the man of her dreams came back home.

Flinging the sheet off her body, Robyn decided to compartmentalize Anderson until their breakup was official. They weren't engaged, and they'd never even come close to uttering the words, "I love you." They dated, so what? Anderson had to know her whole heart belonged to Teddy. Wasn't it obvious?

Robyn ran her hands through her disheveled hair in front of the bathroom mirror. Her eyes were bright, and her cheeks flushed. And was that a *hickey* on her neck? Pressing her lips together to stifle a giggle, she fingered the love bite as heat pooled between her legs. God, she already missed Teddy. She was a goner, hook, line, and sinker.

Later in the evening, after one too many glasses of Bennett Farms wine, Robyn turned out the lights and closed her eyes. She'd kept the sheets on her bed, pressing her face into Teddy's loitering scent. She longed for the day when he wouldn't have to leave her again. As she drifted off into sweet, sublime slumber, a strange noise brought her back to full consciousness. Sitting up, she listened intently to what sounded like pennies being thrown at the glass pane of her window.

Robyn was suddenly transported back to those dreamy days of high school when Teddy Bennett would sneak out of his house and come calling in the middle of the night. Giggling, she flung the covers back and trotted to the window, unclasping the hinge, knowing he was on the other side.

"You don't have your key anymore?" she teased, helping him through the small opening.

"I thought this would be more romantic."

His foot caught the edge of the sill, and he fell forward into Robyn's belly. She caught him before he dropped to the floor. "Damn, I'm not as young as I used to be making a late-night house call." He stood tall in her bedroom, the moonlight casting shadows across his hairy face.

"Hi." He cupped her cheek, and she leaned into his touch.

"Hi." Her face ached with a broad reciprocal smile. Knowing he felt compelled to walk back to her house in the middle of the night left her deeply contented.

"I need you naked and back in bed."

"Yes, sir."

Lifting her nightgown up and over her head, she flung it to the side, anticipating Teddy's touch. She watched him pull a silver packet from his pocket. He struggled to get out of his jeans, his commando composition making her giggle with pleasure.

"I love that sound," he chuckled. In one fell swoop, he scooped her up into his arms and brought her to the edge of the mattress. "I couldn't stand being away from you for another second, not after today."

"What did you tell your father?"

"I didn't tell him anything. I snuck out."

"You… what?" Robyn couldn't believe he was throwing caution to the wind. "Teddy, we're not in high school anymore. This is serious. I don't want you to get in any trouble."

"I won't. I'll get back to the farm before the sun rises. I need you, Robyn. After today, I don't think I can be away from you for another night again. Are you okay with that?"

Robyn felt her eyes ping with tears. "More than okay."

Gently, Teddy pushed her onto the bed and climbed across her body, flinging the foil packet near her head. When his fingers pressed against the apex of her thighs, she inhaled sharply, her center already wet and throbbing with desire.

"Did I do this to you?"

"You know it." Her hands traced his rippling abs, snaking their way down to his penis. He was rock-hard. "Did I do this to you?" She teased right back, cupping his balls.

"Hell, yeah."

Teddy leaned back on his haunches and took matters into his own hands, ripping the foil and sliding the condom on his length. He tested her readiness with his thick fingers before sliding home, easing into her, and filling her completely. Moonlight kissed his skin as their bodies became one. She was overcome with primal need and tried to convey what she was feeling in the moment.

"You're the first boy I ever kissed, Teddy," she whispered, nipping at his skin. "… and I want you to be the last."

His hot breath floated across her collarbone as he nodded into his favorite spot in the crevice of her neck. "You're the one, Robyn. You're the only one for me."

# Chapter Twelve

## TEDDY

Ted blinked against the morning light coming in through the window, his body aching nicely from overindulging in pleasure. Robyn lay asleep, cocooned in the nook of his arm, her face pressed against his chest. Looking down at her beauty, he was undeniably grateful she wasn't married and living somewhere else far from the memories they created together in Langston Falls.

"Mmmm," she stirred.

Ted's face twitched with a slight smile. "Morning."

"Good morning." Her long lashes fluttered as she opened her eyes, her lazy smile leaving him gobsmacked with love. Sitting up in the bed, her pretty brow morphed with apparent worry. "The sun is already up. I thought you had to get home before sunrise, before your dad would notice."

Ted shook his head. "As long as I'm back by seven, I'll be fine."

"You sure?"

"Positive. I'm a grown-ass man, Robyn. I think I'm

allowed to spend time with the woman I love after being away from her for so long."

Robyn averted his gaze and looked down at her hands.

"What is it?"

"It's... nothing."

"Tell me."

Her features softened. "I'm... so glad you're home, Teddy. I can't believe we made it through this." Her eyes were shimmering emerald pools as she looked at him. "I can't believe you still want me after all these years."

Ted pulled her into his arms and pressed a light kiss on her head. "Believe it or not, you were with me in that jail cell the entire time. You're the one who kept me going, every single day, every hour, every minute. I never stopped thinking about coming home to you."

"I thought about you, too," she whimpered. "All the time."

Relief swept through him as he pulled back from her, their eyes locking. "I love you, Robyn."

"You have no idea, Teddy, no idea how much I love you."

"I think I do."

The moment lingered as they stared at each other, the love between them permeating the room. There was no other place he'd rather be than holding Robyn Morgan in his arms.

———

A half-hour later, Robyn parked in a graveled space near the Bennett farmhouse. The big dogs barked a greeting, prompting the rest of Ted's family to come out onto the front porch to investigate. He knew he'd have to explain his absence and hoped his family, especially his father, would understand.

Robyn turned to him, her features wrinkled with worry. "I'll tell them this was my fault. I'll explain I needed you last night."

Ted entwined his fingers with hers, bringing her hand to his mouth and kissing her skin. "You don't have to explain anything. Everything is going to be fine. Please, don't worry." He opened the passenger door and climbed out. Pausing for a beat, he peered into the Jeep interior. "You coming?"

Robyn seemed surprised and mumbled a quick reply. "Of course." Her attire was sweatpants, flip-flops, and a wrinkled tee, her golden hair piled on top of her head in a quick bun. There wasn't a stitch of makeup on her face, yet she was still the most beautiful woman Ted had ever laid eyes on.

They held hands, their feet crunching along the pebbled path as Jaxson and Delia greeted them with wagging, happy tails. He felt Robyn squeeze his fingers as they eyed his family. They were all lined up on the porch like the Von Trapp family singers, eagerly awaiting an explanation for his absence.

His sister, Rebecca, held a checkered tea-towel in her hand, and he was sure she had a breakfast spread already laid out for his family and the day workers inside. James leaned against a porch post with his arms crossed, the scowl on his face indicating trouble. Walt sipped from a mug of coffee, the gleam in his eye apparent as if anticipating the inevitable intense lecture from their father. Hank offered a faint smile and rubbed the back of his neck, his youthful good looks giving nothing away. Roy Bennett stood tall, the expression on his face pensive.

"Good morning, Robyn. How are ya, darlin'?" The family patriarch came down the steps and opened his arms for a hug.

Robyn glanced at Ted before letting go of his hand, she and his father hugging affectionately.

"Good morning, Mr. Bennett. I'm good, thank you."

"Well… why don't you go inside and get yourself a cup of coffee and some breakfast? Becky made monkey bread this morning. The whole house smells like cinnamon."

Robyn looked over at Ted again with uncertainty.

"Go on," he reassured. "I'll be inside in a minute."

Robyn nodded and started up the stairs. Rebecca and Hank greeted her with fondness and escorted her inside. Ted kicked at a piece of gravel with the tip of his boot.

"Well, let's get on with it. Go ahead and read me my rights, Dad. You already know where I was. I was at Robyn's house, a home we used to share. I was with the woman I love… "

"Stop it, Ted," Roy interrupted.

"What?"

The apples of Roy's cheek turned red, indicating he was none too pleased. "Your parole officer, Ms. McNeil, made it very clear you were to remain on the farm property unless you made arrangements with her to travel elsewhere."

"Travel elsewhere? Come on, Dad. I was three miles down the road. I hardly call that traveling elsewhere."

"Geez, Teddy. You know the rules," James chimed in, coming up alongside their father. "You're supposed to be at work or at home unless accompanied by Dad into town. That means your butt belongs here, on the farm."

"I'm well aware of where my fucking butt belongs, Jimmy. But I hardly call three miles down the road breaking my parole. I wasn't doing anything illegal. I wasn't drinking.

I wasn't doing drugs. I wasn't gambling. *Fuck*! I'm a grown man, for Christ's sake!" Ted seethed. "That woman in there is the only reason I'm alive today." He pointed aggressively toward the front door. "And I'll be *damned* if I allow anyone to keep me away from her ever again!"

The tension was thick, and Ted noticed Walt, who'd been watching them intently, slink inside without saying a word.

"Take the dogs in the house, Jimmy, and give me and your brother a few minutes alone, please."

"Yes, sir." James whistled for the animals and disappeared into the farmhouse, leaving Roy and Ted alone.

"Walk with me, son."

Ted was obedient and walked beside his father around the side of the house. He did his best to tamper his pent-up rage with deep intakes of air through his nose. They were silent and walked for several minutes before Roy came to a halt. The North Georgia Mountains and the family land spread out before them in morning splendor.

"I know what it's like to pine for your woman... "

"Dad," Ted interrupted. His shoulders sagged, his heart breaking for his father, knowing he missed his bride.

"Please, let me finish. I want you to hear this."

Ted nodded with a clenched jaw, shoving his hands into his jean pockets.

Roy looked toward the mountains rising up from the foggy land, his voice wistful and full of longing. "Your mother meant everything to me. For forty years, we were out of our minds in love." He walked forward a few feet, lost in thought.

Ted watched the larger-than-life man place his hands on his hips and bow his head. "Dad?" He frowned, his concern growing.

Roy whipped his head around to look at Ted, his face pinched with sorrow. "I want you to know I love you with everything I have."

"Daddy—"

"No, goddamnit," Roy interrupted. "I want you to hear me. I love you, Teddy. I do."

"I know, Daddy. I know. I love you, too."

"Your mother and I wanted nothing more than to see you thrive in your life and succeed. To make something of yourself. You still have it in you, Teddy. You do. It's not too late."

"You're the best father a son could ever ask for. You've always been there for me. You've always believed in me." Ted took a step closer, alarmed by his father's emotional outburst and the tears streaming down his weathered face. This wasn't like him.

"But Dad, aren't you tired of worrying about me all these years? Aren't you sick of me and what I've put you through? What I've put this entire family through?"

"You stop it right there," Roy growled. "I am your father, and I'm entitled to worry about you for the rest of your life. You don't have a say in that."

Ted swallowed hard, his own emotions threatening to surface. "I'm sorry, Dad. I'm sorry I've let you down yet again." With his head bowed, his long hair hung limply around his face. He startled when he felt his father's hand clamp down on his shoulder.

"There is nothing you can say or do to stop me from loving you. Do you hear me?"

"Yes, sir." His voice was barely a whisper being in such close proximity to the man who continued to show him unconditional love.

Roy patted his shoulder before he resumed his position

staring at the mountains. "Now, I understand you and Robyn want to be together, I do. I know what it feels like to want nothing more than to be with the woman you love. And that's why I'm proposing something."

"What, Dad?"

"I want you to invite Robyn to stay here with us on the farm anytime your heart desires. It's a safe place for you and her to rekindle your relationship—a place lining up with your new house rules implemented by the court. Of course, you'll have to run it by Ms. McNeil first, especially for any, uh… sleepovers."

Ted's eyes grew large as he came up beside his dad, his proposition a deliberate means to an end.

"Heaven knows I don't want to put Robyn in a compromising situation. But it would sure make things a hell of a lot easier around here knowing you're safe and following the rules." Roy ran his hand under his nose before looking directly into Ted's face. "Does the idea even appeal to you at all?"

Ted closed the gap between them and wrapped his arms around his father in a bear hug. Slapping him on the back, he chuckled with gladness. "Of course, the idea appeals to me. You always have the best ideas, Dad."

The two men pulled back from each other, Roy nodding with relief. "Then it's settled."

Ted continued to chuckle. "I'll definitely ask her, and I'll run it by Ms. McNeil first thing. And Dad?"

"Yes, Teddy?"

His tone turned serious. "I won't let you down again. I promise."

Roy laughed out loud, swiping at his tear-stained face. "We'll see about that."

# Chapter Thirteen

## ROBYN

Robyn listened intently to the Bennett brothers jabbering away about their upcoming day, their plans to set up the stage for Hank's band on a flatbed trailer near the barn, a source of contention for Walt.

"Why can't you set up on the ground? Why do we have to back the big rig down the hill close to the barn and use the trailer? You know how precarious the space can be, especially with the drop off of the hill." Walt lamented.

Hank shook his unruly wavy hair, inexorable in his position on the matter. The youngest Bennett son wasn't taking no for an answer. "Because it's the perfect *stage*, Walt. Why can't you understand this? We need a stage so everyone can see us."

Robyn sipped her coffee and stared at the half-eaten piece of monkey bread on her plate, listening to the conversation. She wished she could disappear. The morning treat was delicious, but her stomach was in knots thinking about Teddy and his father arguing outside.

Becky pulled out the chair next to Robyn and sat, her cheery disposition a pleasant diversion. "Not hungry?"

"Oh, it's delicious, Becky. I'm just—"

"Nervous?" she interrupted.

Robyn nodded, her cheeks flaming with embarrassment. She leaned in closer to Becky to explain. "Teddy and I... we just happened. He thought I was working yesterday and walked over to my place to swim in the pond."

Becky nodded. "Sounds like Teddy. The end of the summer work getting the tree farm ready for Christmas sales is grueling and hot as Hades." She glanced at her brothers, still immersed in their heated conversation about stages and the hoedown setup. She leaned closer to Robyn's ear so only she could hear. "So, you were home, and y'all picked up where you left off?"

Robyn averted her eyes and smiled. "Kind of," she whispered, not wanting the boys to overhear. "One thing led to another, and we couldn't stand the thought of being away from each other ever again." She squeezed Becky's wrist resting on the table. "He snuck out last night and threw pebbles at my window. He used to do that when we were in high school."

"How romantic," Becky blurted a little too loudly. All three Bennett brothers turned silent and looked at the pair of women sitting at the kitchen table. Becky grimaced and offered Robyn an apology. "Sorry."

James pulled out the kitchen chair across from Robyn and sat, interlocking his fingers together. He reminded her of a prosecutor in a courtroom. "You know this is serious, don't you?"

"Jimmy, stop it. Robyn did nothing wrong," Becky interjected.

"Yeah, but moving forward, she can help Ted do what is right, so they don't send his ass back to jail again. All it takes is one mistake, one little slip-up, and he's gone again." His tone turned serious, his eyes blazing with fire. "You wouldn't want that to happen, would you, Robyn?"

"Knock it off, Jimmy," Hank said, coming to her defense.

"Listen, fellas. I understand what's at stake here; truly, I do," Robyn appeased. "You have to know I would never do anything intentionally to mess up Ted's life."

"Like going on a beer run with his low-life friends?" Walt's voice was low and sinister, all heads swinging to look in his direction.

"*Walter*!" Becky's eyes were wide, and she immediately clutched Robyn's hand. "He didn't mean it, Robyn. We're all a little on edge figuring out Teddy's parole."

"Yes, I do. I mean every single word." Walt approached the table and crossed his arms in front of his burly chest. "If you hadn't begged Ted to go on a beer run so your popular friends could continue to party, none of this bullshit would've happened. In fact, you and Ted would probably be married by now living the highlife in Atlanta. Do you ever think about that, Robyn? Does it ever cross your mind your actions have consequences when it comes to Teddy?"

"That's enough, Walt. Leave the lady alone." Hank's expression twisted with concern, his face sagging with a frown.

"Fuck you, Robyn Morgan. *Fuck all of you!*" Walt grabbed a kitchen chair and shoved it as he exited the kitchen. The wood clattered to the floor, leaving everyone speechless in his wake.

Becky shook her head. "He's a ticking time bomb with

all his pent-up anger. I'm so sorry he decided to take it out on you."

Robyn inhaled a deep breath and looked around at the Bennett clan. "But why is he so angry? I thought he'd be happy having his brother home."

"This whole... transition has been difficult to navigate," James explained. "When Teddy was behind bars or at the halfway house, we all knew he had to follow the rules if he was ever going to get out of there. In a weird sense, he was... safe. But here? All bets are off."

"What do you mean?" Robyn continued to grip Becky's hand, the thought of Teddy not safe on his own home turf disconcerting.

"Ted has tasted freedom again. But he's *not* free—not for another year. He still has rules to follow and things he has to do before truly being on his own. Can he do it by himself?" James' tone was even and tempered.

Hank chimed in. "We're his guardrails, you know, like on a highway, so he doesn't wreck. We have to keep a close eye on him and make sure he succeeds. God knows none of us wants to lose him again, especially Walter."

"*Walter?*" Robyn asked. "Since when are Ted and Walt close? They fought all the time growing up, you know that."

Becky squeezed Robyn's hand. "Walter loves Teddy more than any of us realized. He had a real hard time those first few years without him. Daddy even had a family counselor come over and chat with him for a few months. Having Teddy home means the world to him."

Robyn's mouth gaped. She had no idea. "Wow. I'm so sorry. I... I didn't know."

"That explains his angry behavior," Hank added. "We all love you, Robyn. But we need you to keep a better eye on our big brother. Please, don't let him mess this up, even if we all know you two belong together."

All eyes stared at Robyn, making her shift in her seat. Since Teddy came home, she finally recognized what was at stake for the first time. "I understand."

The big dogs scrambled to their feet as the screened door squeaked open, Roy entering the kitchen entrance with Ted lagging behind.

"How about some of that monkey bread, Becky? My mouth's been watering all morning smelling it baking in the oven." Roy seemed energetic and happy, a far cry from his earlier disposition on the front lawn.

"Coming right up, Daddy." Becky squeezed Robyn's hand one last time before she rose from the kitchen table.

Robyn felt another hand squeeze her shoulder, the immediate surge of electricity rocking her to her core. She flicked her eyes up to Teddy's.

"Can I talk to you in private for a minute?" His low voice was husky as he offered her his hand.

"Sure."

No one said a word as Teddy pulled her through the kitchen and into the hallway, leading her up the stairs. When they were behind the closed door of his childhood bedroom, he wrapped his arms around her, hugging her close.

"Is… everything alright?" she mumbled, pressing her cheek against his chest.

"Mmm-hmmm," he replied. He continued to hug her. "I hope my family wasn't too hard on you while I was outside."

"Nope," she lied. "All good."

They disengaged, and he pulled her to the bed and sat,

patting the space next to him. She hesitated before she eased herself onto the mattress.

"Being with you over the last twenty-four hours, I've felt a spark of magic again. I know you've felt it, too."

Robyn nodded, clutching her hands together in her lap.

"I put you in a precarious position overnight, and I want to apologize."

"I'm the one who should be apologizing, Teddy. I didn't know about all the rules you had to follow during your parole."

Tucking a stray piece of hair over her ear, he smiled. "How could you have known? I never explained the conditions of my parole to you."

"No, you didn't."

Placing his hand over hers, he squeezed. "My dad has a solution, something adhering to the rules."

"Oh?" Her heart blipped.

"He gave me permission to ask you to stay with us, anytime. Well, with me, him, Hank, and Becky. Walt and Jimmy have their own place in the carriage house. I have to run it by my parole officer, but I'm sure she'll give us the green light."

Something warm spilled into Robyn's chest, diffusing and spreading over her. Knowing Roy always had his son's best interests at heart filled her with love.

"You see, I can't move back in with you like it was before. Not until this last part of my sentencing is officially over or until I make arrangements with my parole officer." The look on Ted's face was imploring, his dark eyes bright with hope. "Until I can do that, can you at least think about staying here more? Please?"

Robyn swallowed, her head bobbling with certainty. "I mean, sure. Why not? This is a no-brainer with all the work

Becky and I have coming up with the Harvest Hoedown. I can take Jimmy's old room at the end of the hallway."

Ted's brow furrowed, and he tilted his head, silenced by her teasing.

Robyn giggled, moving forward to kiss him on the lips. She swooned with her arms draped around his neck, and looked into his eyes.

"But I'd rather sleep with you, handsome."

# Chapter Fourteen

## TEDDY

The Harvest Hoedown was less than twenty-four hours away, the farm teeming with extra help getting the party setup ready. James stacked wood next to a trailer holding a colossal barbecue grill parked on the outskirts of the party perimeter, a tall pipe already pilfering plumes of fragrant, meaty smoke into the air. Big John, a local and award-winning barbecue master, was hired for the festivities, his blue-ribbon chicken and brisket a crowd favorite. Ted's mouth watered just thinking about eating it. The sun overhead blazed with late summer and early fall splendor, the air holding the scent of hickory and pine, meat and sweet honey.

Hank grinned from ear to ear, focused on aiming a set of rented lights toward the stage setup, the back of his shirt soaked with perspiration. Walter spotted him on the ladder from below, his expression in a scowl as if he had better things to do.

Ted heard a peel of girlish giggles and turned toward the red barn. Becky and Robyn were putting the finishing touches on corn stalk and grapevine decorations on either side of the big doors. The girls pulled sunflowers from a large bucket, interspersing the yellow blooms into the vine and corn shocks. The warm touches of décor captured the spirit of the festival. Carefully situated hay bales were also part of the decorations, the festive atmosphere really starting to come together.

Robyn noticed him right away and offered a little wave as her cheeks flushed with a wide smile. Nodding at her from across the graveled party space, Ted ambled toward her. The woman was a Godsend, the nights she stayed on the farm filling a cavernous void in his spirit. Waking up with her lying across his chest made him forget the long, lonely road he'd traversed without her by his side, his sordid past labeled a felon nothing but a blip in time in the grand scheme of things.

But the memories they shared filtered through his mind like pictures in a frame—when they were summer young, and the small town of Langston Falls was his whole world where love included Robyn, the girl next door. How he wished he could go back to those days when they were on the cusp of chasing their dreams. Where independence was a highway taking them to the city where they planned to start their adult lives together. Or so he thought.

Looking at Robyn now, with her golden hair fluttering in the hot breeze and her calf muscles flexing underneath her frayed jean shorts as she worked, Ted was struck with an idea. Perhaps his freedom was found on the family farm after all; the years of pining and searching for a life outside the fence posts nothing more than wasted youth. All these years, he'd wished he could go back to those days. But now, he felt a peculiar sense he was finally right where he was meant to be.

"Hey," Robyn breathlessly uttered, coming up next to him. "You done for the day?" She held her hand above her brow, shading her green eyes from the sun's glare. Ted nodded.

"Hey, big brother!" Becky hollered.

"Hey, Becks," he answered. "Can I steal her away for a few minutes?" Ted slung his arm across Robyn's shoulders.

"Sure. We're pretty much done here anyway, and I've gotta do a live shot for my blog in a few minutes. Fans love to see all of this in action. I'll see you later, Robyn."

"See ya, Becky. Don't worry about the mess here. I'll take care of it."

"You sure?"

"Absolutely. Good work."

"Same to you. The corn stalks were a brilliant idea. I love them!"

Robyn laughed. "Me too. Knock 'em dead in your live shoot."

"I will."

Ted and Robyn meandered into the cool shade of the barn, away from the workers. "I can help you clean up and any other chores you still have left for the setup."

Robyn linked her fingers with his near her shoulder. "If you're offering, that'd be great. We still have to assemble the portable dance floor outside in front of the stage and put out some more tables, chairs, and hay bales for seating. Charlotte's got the mason jar flower arrangements ready to go. I have to head over to Langston Petals and pick them up in a bit. But everything is coming along like clockwork."

"You've been busy," he chuckled.

"I have been."

Black café chairs were turned upside down on numerous round tables in the barn interior. Edison-style string lights were strung through the refurbished rafters, and a long bar ran parallel to the wall where stalls stood years earlier. The barn had been turned into a tasting room for the family winery where visitors could place their wine orders at the main bar area. Experienced staff was always ready to help during business hours, offering wine by the bottle, glass, or as a Wine Flight where one could choose any four Bennett Wines, and enjoy a smaller sized glass of each.

During the spring and summer weekends, the farm hosted a variety of local food trucks on the property to accompany the wine tastings. For the cooler months, tourists were welcome to bring their own snacks and picnics. Or they could get a seasonal to-go pack of local cheese, artisan crackers, homemade jams, and specialty desserts put together by his sister, Becky, and her team. The entire space held the faint aroma of sweet fruit among the earthiness of the farm and the barbecue smoke filtering in through the open barn door, the family-friendly establishment a popular tourist spot in the mountain town.

"Before we get to work, can you take a break?" Ted asked.

He watched Robyn press her teeth into her lower lip and look over her shoulder at the barn entrance as if assessing the situation. When she eagerly nodded, he pulled her by the hand toward the back of the barn where the ladder to the hayloft was anchored against the wall. Quickly, she climbed the ladder, and he followed, palming her round butt cheek with one hand. In their youth, they'd done this on numerous occasions. The déjà vu moment was uncanny and titillating.

"Teddy," she chortled.

Safe and secluded in the confines of the loft, Ted smirked and slowly crawled across bales toward Robyn with only one thing on his mind. She squealed when he pounced, easing her onto a mound of stray hay in the corner. They were hidden from the entrance, surrounded by stacked bales, the smell sweet and robust, tickling his nostrils.

Looking up at him, Robyn swept his long hair back from his cheeks, holding his face in her hand. "Hello, lover."

"Hello." Licking his lips, he shifted in the dry hay and pressed his mouth against hers. She welcomed him, the rush of lust from her swirling tongue filling him instantly.

Ted leaned back on his haunches, anxious to unbuckle his jeans.

"Here?" she asked, leaning back on her elbows watching him. Her expression held amusement; her eyes turned darker and twinkling with mischief.

Ted panted, fumbling with his zipper. "Yes, I gotta have you. This used to be one of our favorite spots, remember?"

"Yeah, back in high school. But that was when it was just you and me. Teddy, there are dozens of people downstairs, including your family, working below us… "

"And I'm gonna work you under me." Freeing his raging boner from his jeans, he nodded at Robyn. "Come on. A little quickie never hurt anyone."

Robyn unzipped her jean shorts and pulled them down, taking her panties with them. "You're insatiable," she giggled.

Ted teased her wet opening with his fingers before fumbling in his pants pocket for a condom.

"I love it you're prepared," she said.

Ripping the foil packet, he was quick with his actions and sheathed himself as she waited. "I'm a regular Boy Scout. I'm always prepared to have you."

Robyn gasped when he plundered her, riding her hard. He wasn't kidding when he said it'd be quick. The pale gold hay was pliable and soft beneath them, the sounds of thrusts and grunts echoing into the old rafters in a haze of barn dust.

"Lift up your shirt," he stuttered. Sweat trickled down his cheeks into his beard, his arm muscles bulging with brute strength.

Robyn obeyed his command and lifted her shirt, exposing her sports bra underneath.

He pressed his hot mouth to her chest and managed to free one of her breasts from the tight fabric, suckling her pert nipple between his lips.

"Oh, Teddy," she moaned and writhed beneath him.

And that's all it took, his orgasm ripping through him like a lightning bolt. His release was pure ecstasy; his body turned rigid with unfathomable pleasure.

"*Fuck*," he hissed.

Each and every time he made love to Robyn brought him to the very edge of desire. If he could bottle this undeniable passion he felt for the woman lying beneath him, he could set the world on fire. There wasn't a day, an hour, a moment when he didn't want her so bad he'd go back on everything he believed just to be with her. But even with his newfound freedom and his dick deep in her tight heat, he was scared she would still forget about him.

"Hey." Robyn's voice cut through his thoughts and brought him back to earth. "Are you okay?"

Ted breathed heavily, his arms aching from keeping his body from squashing her. "Yeah. Incredible. You're amazing, Robyn."

Her smile was brilliant, her hair scattered all around her with bits of hay pieces caught in her tresses. "Glad I could be of service."

Ted realized the pleasure was all for him and felt guilty

for a split second before he pulled out, rolled the condom off, and folded it into a tissue he'd brought along. He tossed the mound on top of his pants to discard later. He had the right mind to take care of her pleasure, angling his head between her thighs.

"What are you doing?" she panted.

Ted looked beyond her soft mound and across her flat tummy, offering her a wicked grin. "Getting you off." He flicked the tip of his tongue across her swollen nub, instantly causing her body to tense. "Hold still, beautiful." Pushing her thighs wider apart, he grinned at her one last time before he feasted, lapping and licking her wet folds with the prowess of a skilled lover.

Her fingers found their way into his hair, and she yanked and yelped as he helped her cross over into the pleasure chasm, his face pressed tight between her legs.

"*Teddy!*" she shrieked.

Clamping his mouth over her entrance, he continued to suck as she bucked underneath him. His mouth stilled, and he watched in awe as her body moved in a wave of delicious ecstasy. Stroking her pubic area, he relished the power he had over her, floored by what she'd just experienced.

"How do you feel now?" his voice groveled as he rested his chin on her bare thigh.

She leaned back on trembling elbows and looked down at him, her mouth slack and her face peppered with beads of perspiration. "I can't feel my toes."

Before he could respond with a flirty retort, the door to the loft banged open against the wooden floorboards as someone clambered into the space.

"*Shit,*" he whispered tersely, immediately tossing Robyn her shorts and grabbing his jeans thrown by the wayside.

"Robyn?" They heard Walt's voice echo.

Hidden behind a stack of bales, Teddy put his finger over his mouth and shook his head as he stuffed the tissue holding the used condom into his pocket. Robyn pulled her top down, covering her chest, and quickly zipped her shorts, sticking her tongue out at him. When she stood up, Ted grimaced.

"Hey, Walt. You looking for me?"

Ted remained out of sight, peering up at Robyn, who acted innocent. He playfully tugged on the frayed edges of her shorts, and she swatted at him out of Walt's line of vision.

"Teddy, I know you're in here too. Might as well come out."

Ted rolled his eyes before he slowly stood. Pieces of hay stuck to his sweaty chest and clung to his hair. There wasn't time to put his shirt on.

"Really, guys? Fucking in the hayloft with all of us working right below?" Walt admonished.

"Watch your mouth, Walter. What do you want?"

Walt clenched his jaw, his steely gaze fixated on Robyn. "There's a fella here looking for you. Thought you'd want to know."

"Oh?"

"Yeah. Said he came from Atlanta to surprise you, so… surprise." Walt's mouth turned up at the corners into a wicked grin before he shook his head, turned, and left them alone.

"Shit," Robyn mumbled, hurriedly smoothing her shirt. She ran her hands through her thoroughly fucked hair peppered with random pieces of hay. "Help me, Teddy."

Picking out wayward pieces of dry hay from her golden tresses, he frowned. "Were you expecting someone?"

"Not exactly. But it can only be one person."

Ted furrowed his brow with unease. "Who?"

"Anderson."

"Anderson?"

"The, um… boyfriend I told you about. Well, ex-boyfriend. He was supposed to let me know when he was back in Atlanta. I haven't heard from him in a while because he's been in California for work. Showing up here out of the blue isn't like him."

Ted watched Robyn brush more bits from her clothing, her features flushed with lingering color from their literal romp in the proverbial hay. Or was she blushing thinking about her ex-boyfriend? Gripping her by the arm, he stopped her from leaving the loft.

"Hey," he started.

"I've gotta go, Teddy. I don't want him to catch us up here together in the loft." Her green eyes were wide with trepidation. Was she nervous seeing Anderson again?

"You broke it off with him, didn't you? He knows we're back together, right?"

His question was answered instantly when Robyn hung her head. Releasing his hold on her arm, he took a dejected step back. "Are you kidding me right now?"

Robyn tilted her chin in the air and looked him square in the eye. "I didn't want to break up with him over the phone, okay? I told him when he got back from LA to call me, and we could get together in person to talk about some things."

"Jesus, Robyn."

Reaching for his hand, she linked her fingers through his. "I'm going to tell him now, okay? Please, don't worry. I've got this under control."

Ted clenched his jaw to keep from saying anything else.

He offered a quick nod, the rolled-up tissue burning a hole in his pocket.

"Just... stay up here for a few more minutes before you come down, or else he might put two and two together. And please, put your shirt back on. I owe him an explanation, especially after he drove all this way from Atlanta." She stood on her tiptoes and gave him a quick peck on the lips, her fingers drifting across the heaving dips and valleys of his rigid abs.

"I'll call you soon."

Ted watched the love of his life scramble down the ladder out of sight. Blowing out a deep exhale of hot air, he lowered himself onto a bale of hay and gripped the back of his neck. The old barn walls started to close in on him, and he felt like he was in prison all over again.

# Chapter Fifteen

## ROBYN

Robyn shielded her eyes as she stepped out of the barn, panning the area for Anderson. He wasn't hard to notice, his pale pink Polo shirt pristine among the sweaty work crew of the hoedown setup. His expensive aviator sunglasses glinted in the afternoon sun, his dark hair perfectly combed back from his face. The man wore loafers peeking out from under his pleated dress pants, making him look like a Yacht-Rock groupie. The city-slicker stuck out like a sore thumb, holding court with a couple of young ladies from the setup team. Leave it to Anderson to draw the girls like bees to honey.

When he noticed her, he threw his hand up in a wave, his million-dollar smile beaming with what looked like gladness. Robyn could swear she saw his perfect teeth flash like diamonds in a spotlight.

"Hey, babe! Long time no see." Anderson swiped the glasses from his face, giving her a quick peck on the cheek. The two girls he'd been conversing with left them alone, giggling in their wake.

Before Robyn could respond, Anderson was quick with a snide remark. "Girl, you reek! What've you been doing all day? Cleaning stalls?" He shook his head, his scrunched expression comical.

"I've been working, Anderson. You would've known had you communicated with me you were coming to Langston Falls today."

"Oh, come on. I'm just playing around. I wanted to surprise you. Surprise!"

Robyn looked over her shoulder and noticed Ted exit the barn, his long hair fluttering in the breeze. His shirt was back on, and his lips pressed into a grim line as he leaned against the red boards of the structure. Was he nonchalantly surveying her reunion with Anderson?

"Hey, earth to Robyn. What's in your hair?" He pulled a large piece of hay from her earlier romp, grimacing at the find and letting it fall between his fingers.

Robyn didn't miss a beat. "I've been putting together some decorations, including corn stalks and, yes, real hay." She started to walk toward the parking lot, glad he fell into step next to her. "Why don't you go on back to my place, and I'll let the team know I'm heading out for a while so we can catch up? Sound good?"

Anderson chuckled and nodded. "As long as you take a shower first. Seriously, I don't know what kind of pleasure you get being on this farm. It's dirty and disgusting, totally beneath you."

Robyn felt heat move through her instantly, the pleasure she received minutes earlier beneath Teddy seeping into the fabric of her panties. She decided his comment wasn't worth a reply. "I need to grab a few things. I'll be right behind you."

"Okay, okay." Anderson lowered his sunglasses over his

eyes and continued toward his over-the-top Land Rover. "I brought a good bottle of wine I can open while we catch up. None of that country-crap you're always drinking. Don't be too long."

Robyn plastered a fake smile on her face and watched Anderson back out of the parking space, offering him a polite wave before taking off. She didn't know what she ever saw in him, his constant barbs regarding her appearance, work, and the kind of wine she enjoyed piercing her heart with remorse. Walking toward the barn, she fixated her gaze on another man—the man she always dreamt about in the deepest recesses of her heart.

"Teddy," she started.

He didn't say anything and forlornly shoved his hands into the front pockets of his jeans.

"I love you. I just need to take care of this, okay?"

His nose twitched as he bowed his head. "You go do what you gotta do. Don't let me stand in your way."

Robyn placed her hands on her hips and cocked her head. "What's that supposed to mean?"

Their eyes locked, something intense and honest passing between them. He stepped toward her, pressing his hot lips against her forehead.

"Nothing. I'll see you later."

The dejected look on his handsome face instantly filled her with regret, and she watched him walk away.

———

"Now that's more like it. You don't smell like sweat and… barn anymore," Anderson commented.

He sat on the couch looking like a proud peacock in his stupid pink shirt. When he crossed his foot over his opposite knee, his usual preppy look lacked socks, his shiny loafers and skinny ankles making Robyn cringe. She'd much rather have Teddy Bennett in jeans and cowboy boots any day of the week.

Rubbing a towel through her wet hair, she sat across from Anderson in her grandmother's rocking chair and flicked her chin toward the stem-less wine glass in his hand. "I see you've already started happy hour."

"I have. Help yourself to a glass." He took a sip of expensive chardonnay, his brow hitching with a flirty gaze as he remained comfortable in his seat. Anderson wasn't known for his chivalry, his lack of catering to her needs a source of vexation since they started dating. Robyn usually shrugged it off, but it was grating her nerves right now. And the last thing she needed was for him to get shit-faced and have to stay over at her place. Ted would come unglued for sure.

"No thanks." Her shoulders slumped in a sigh. "Anderson, we need to talk."

"Uh-oh," his voice lilted as he sat upright. "What's on your mind?"

Robyn licked her lips, unsure how to officially break things off with him. "We had some fun, Anderson. I mean, these last few months have been... enjoyable when we've made an effort to be together."

Anderson set his wine glass on the side table, his frown apparent. "You know I've been busy with my career, babe. It is what it is."

Robyn huffed. "I've been busy, too, you know. And I've... changed."

"What do you mean you've changed? What's changed since we last saw each other?"

She shook her head. "I've been busy with some new...

projects. And because we've rarely been together, I've moved on. You said it yourself; we hardly have time for each other."

"Well, that's because you choose to live in this God-forsaken small town, in a tiny house in the country away from civilization. I hope these new projects include studying for the bar exam."

Robyn stared at Anderson blankly, the words coming out of his mouth a certain reality check in her spirit. When she didn't answer him, he rolled his eyes.

"You can't tell me you're actually happy living here in Langston-fucking-Falls working in a flower shop? I mean, come on, Robyn. You're so much better than this. Come and move in with me in Atlanta. You can get back to your real work. And you'll be near your father. Let's cut the crap here. Make your lawyer-dad proud and finish what you set out to do. Start living your life."

Robyn seethed and abruptly stood. "I *am* living my life —here, in Langston Falls! And leave my father out of this."

Anderson rose from his seat and slowly closed the gap between them. "Babe, you're more than a small-town, country-bumpkin. You have so much potential. I know this —your father knows this." He picked up her hand and held it against his mouth, kissing her skin. His beady eyes bore a hole into hers. "Come to Atlanta with me. Take the fucking bar exam and be with me, Robyn."

She remained rigid in her stance, removing her hand from his. She was careful with her chosen words, trying her best to be as honest as possible.

"You don't wanna be with me, Anderson. I gave away my heart a long time ago—my whole heart. You shouldn't want to be with me."

"But what if I do? Admit it—you've always wanted to

live in the city and become a bad-ass lawyer like your dad. And I sure as hell wouldn't mind having you on my arm."

"Like what, arm-candy?" She seethed.

"Well, as long as you're showered and dressed appropriately," he teased. "I mean, case in point. What exactly are you wearing right now?"

Robyn looked down at herself. The tight tee-shirt she wore accentuated her bosom, and her frayed Daisy Dukes were comfortable against her tanned thighs. "Why do you always care so much about what I'm wearing? I'm at home, Anderson. *My* home. I can wear whatever I want—"

"I was kidding. You can't even take a joke anymore," he interrupted, throwing up his hands in a truce.

Her jaw clenched with fury. How dare Anderson judge her choices and make plans for her? This was her life to decide—and she had no plans to leave, not with Teddy back in town. Standing tall, she was resolute with her reply.

"It's over, Anderson. It's been over for a long time. We've grown apart. I don't have anything more to give you. We both have different dreams and goals for our lives."

"Uh-huh. And I suppose your dream is to schlep flowers to the locals for the rest of your life?"

"Maybe it is for now. I don't know. But I'm happy where I'm at, and that's okay."

Robyn wasn't about to tell him she was over-the-moon ecstatic having the love of her life back in town. If she told Anderson the truth, there'd be hell to pay. The man was a master manipulator, a handy trait in his career acquiring wealth and prestige. He was a guy who usually got what he wanted—but not anymore. Not with her. The pissed-off vibe in the room not getting his way with her was the last straw.

Anderson shook his head and grabbed his wine off the

side table, taking a hefty swig. "You're gonna regret this one day. When you've gained forty pounds from squeezing out a couple of redneck kids and can't fit into your shorts anymore, and your blue-collar husband hollers for another beer while he's watching TV and scratching his balls— you'll remember this moment when you had a chance: a chance to go after your *real* dreams with a good-looking guy who could give you the fucking world."

"My world is here, in Langston Falls," she growled, standing her ground. "We don't even love each other, Anderson."

He scoffed at her comment. "What's love got to do with it?" Keeping his distance, he puffed his pink-covered chest with bravado. The word "love" out in the open seemed to shut him down. "Fine. Have it your way. I've got plenty of other girls waiting in the wings."

"Oh, you're rich!" she volleyed back. "Admit it, Anderson. You've been cheating on me all along, haven't you?"

Anderson finished off his wine and banged the empty tumbler on the table. He was lucky the glass didn't shatter. "A man's gotta do what a man's gotta do, babe. You said it yourself; we've grown apart. We hardly ever see each other. And for the record, your absence really didn't make my heart grow fonder, especially after catching a whiff of you today out on the farm."

"*Get out!*" she shouted.

"Ooo, I love it when you get all feisty like this. You're a little country hellion, aren't you? No wonder you love being out here in the middle of nowhere, so you can howl at the moon." He mimicked a coyote howling which really set her off.

"Anderson, that's enough. Please stop!"

"Lighten up, babe. You sure you don't want one last

quickie before I hit the road? For old time's sake? So you can remember what you'll miss out on for years to come?"

Visions of Anderson and his less-than-stellar sexual moves and lack of reciprocation sealed his fate. The guy wasn't even a very good kisser.

"I said, *get out!*" Her hand shook as she pointed toward the front door.

"Have it your way. It's your loss." He walked right by her in a whoosh of expensive cologne and opened the door. "Here's one last tip for you, sweetheart: lay off the barbecue at that hoedown thing you got coming up tomorrow. Your stomach is starting to pooch out. Not attractive."

"*Ohh!*" she screamed, shoving him over the threshold onto the front stoop and slamming the door behind him.

Pacing angrily, she peeked out the window and waited until he drove off. When the red taillights of his car crested the hill, she made her way into the kitchen, picked up the expensive bottle of wine he'd brought, and poured the contents down the drain. This gave her much satisfaction.

"I hope this cost you a pretty penny, dick-weed," she seethed. She tossed the now empty bottle into the recycle bin in a crash of shattered glass for dramatic effect. Panting, she pulled another bottle of wine from her cupboard.

The Bennett Farms Aged Cabernet was the family's bestseller, one she was saving for a special occasion. No time like the present, right? She was officially free from Anderson's cocky deadweight. Although, his last comment made her cringe, and she consciously palmed her flat tummy for a beat.

"This is more like it," she said to herself, uncorking the familiar bottle.

Lifting the cork to her nose and inhaling deeply, she smiled when the subtle notes of oak and vanilla hit her senses. Taking a long pull directly from the bottle, she closed her eyes and allowed the velvety smoothness to enter her system. She licked her wine-drenched lips before raising the bottle triumphantly into the air.

"Cheers to true love," she said out loud. Another gulp from the bottle, and her gumption waned. She eyed her cell phone on the counter before dialing Ted's number. When it went straight to voicemail, she sighed, intent on leaving him a message.

"Hey, handsome. The Anderson situation took a little time, but it is over. Finished. Kaput. He just left." She paused, her final whisper full of longing. "I'm on my way. And I can't wait to kiss you."

# Chapter Sixteen

## TEDDY

On the day of the Harvest Hoedown, the weather was perfect, the shifting shades of sunset painting the sky in large swaths of warm colors as far as the eye could see. The backdrop of the North Georgia Mountains made for a breathtaking view from Ted's seat outside the barn, his leg shaking with excitement as he awaited Hank's band to start their first set on the trailer stage. The turnout for the event was huge, locals and tourists coming out in droves, enjoying the slightly cooler breeze among the barbecue and wine.

Ted sipped from a bottle of water, taking in the crowd. No one looked familiar to him, and folks left him alone as he waited for Robyn to come back from the ladies' room. They'd talked into the wee hours of the morning, and he admitted he was hurt by her not coming clean about her ex. The conversation was tense, but she assured him the whole thing was officially over. She was finally his and made a promise to never hurt him again. His only regret was not discussing her discarded dreams, wanting to know the real reason she hadn't become a lawyer. But there'd be time for that later. Tonight was all about celebrating the farm and all it had to offer, and the mega-talent of his little brother.

Bright lights clamped to steel pipes and trusses came on, the stage in front of him illuminated as a noticeable gasp rippled through the audience. Ted sat up to get a better look, the pride he felt for Hank hard to contain.

"Looks like they're about ready to start," Robyn beamed. She swiped her short skirt with her hands across her ass before sitting next to him. "Are you ready to be blown away?"

Ted eyed Robyn with a grin, the orbs of the bright lights noticeable in her smiling, green gaze. She crossed her bare legs at the knee, her worn cowboy boots in swirls of baby blue and tan leather looking mighty fine on her sexy legs.

"I can't wait," he said. "I've been looking forward to this for a very long time."

Robyn nodded as if she understood. Looping her arm around his bicep, she leaned her head against his shoulder. "The whole event has been wonderful, from the barbecue to the wine tasting, to the square dancing and now Hank's band. You should be proud of your siblings, especially Becky, who came up with the idea a few years ago."

"I am proud—of my entire family. It was hard imagining this night without seeing it with my own eyes."

She turned and pinned him with a look he was familiar with—one part confident, the other part sensitive. The intense feeling of this night was something he wanted to recall perfectly when it was all over.

"And let's not forget about you and everything you've done to make it great," he added.

Robyn shook her head as if delighted by his remark. "I'm a hired hand, Teddy. I'm nothing special in the grand scheme of things."

"Are you kidding me? You're the icing on my cake." He winked, inducing a massive grin from her before his father walked out on stage. "It's show time."

Roy Bennett wore jeans, a crisp button-down shirt, cowboy boots, and a black Stetson hat. He looked every bit the patriarch of a successful winery and farm. He grinned in the glow of a focused spotlight, tipping his hat toward the audience in a welcome.

"Good evening. I'm Roy Bennett of the Bennett Christmas Tree Farm and Winery."

The excited crowd clapped and whistled, Ted joining in with a shit-eating grin. His father was a rock star in this town. His chest swelled with Bennett pride, knowing he was living his second chance in real-time. Glancing at Robyn, his emotions surged. She looked right at him and seemed to sense the sentimental moment. Nodding, she kissed him on his bearded cheek, calming him down. He hadn't been this excited since he learned he was about to be released from the Georgia State Penitentiary.

"I hope y'all have enjoyed this evening and the great barbecue Big John prepared for the festivities. As a matter of fact, let's give ol' Big John a hearty round of applause." Roy slapped his hands together, coercing John up onto the stage. The audience was on their feet as Big John waved his thick fingers in the air, his apron stained with sauce and charcoal soot.

"There's plenty more barbecue if you haven't had your fill." Roy waited for a beat until the audience quieted. "Tonight is all about celebrating the bounty of our harvest as we look forward to the Christmas season. The Harvest Hoedown is an annual event my beautiful daughter, Rebecca Bennett, started a few years ago. And right now, I'd like to bring her out onto the stage to introduce the band."

Roy looked stage left and reached his hand toward Becky, passing the microphone off to her.

"She looks so cute tonight in her gingham dress and cowboy boots," Robyn said toward Ted's ear. All he could do was nod, mesmerized by the grown-up version of his baby sister.

"Hey, y'all," Becky waved as a few men in the crowd whistled. Ted sat up a little straighter and looked around, his protective nature rearing its big brother head.

"Easy cowboy, they're harmless and just admiring a pretty lady," Robyn reassured, patting him on the arm.

"Yeah, my little *sister*," he grumbled.

Becky didn't seem phased in the least, her confidence commendable. "Like my daddy said, the Harvest Hoedown is an annual event for all of us in Langston Falls. I hope y'all enjoyed the barbecue, the earlier square dancing by our experienced caller, and the special spiked cider made with our wine. And thank you for dressing up in your "country best." I've loved seeing all the cowboy boots, bandanas, hats, flannel shirts, and flashy belt buckles. Y'all look real good in the photo ops by our historic Red Barn."

Ted leaned into Robyn. "She's a natural up there. I can't believe her confidence."

"She's like that in all her videos, too. She's a tried-and-true Bennett, like her big brother."

Gratitude rushed through Ted like the Langston River flowing over the famous falls his hometown was named for. Robyn was correct—Becky was a Bennett through and through, her gumption beguiling. How he wished he could have watched her in her formative years, growing into the woman she was today.

"But we've saved the best for last," Becky continued. "I know y'all have been waiting for this. It gives me great pleasure to introduce the entertainment for tonight—give it up for my brother, Hank Bennett, and the Bonafide Band!"

Hank strutted out onto the stage with an acoustic guitar slung over his shoulder, his messy curls and megawatt smile across his chiseled face on full display. He paused by his baby sister and kissed her on the cheek as the crowd went wild, the drummer kicking off the beat to the first song.

Ted held his breath, his wide eyes taking it all in. He was overwhelmed by the spectacle, mesmerized by his brother doused in bright light. Hank commanded the stage, sending the audience into a tizzy with the upbeat, catchy first song about a hard-working cowboy partying with the boys. He looked like a country music mega-star, the crowd hanging on to his every lyric. His lean physique was highlighted in the bright lights, his blue jeans, black t-shirt, and boots matching his bandmates. He was handsome and in total control. The pride Ted felt was overwhelming.

Hank finished the first song to a roar of applause. Taking the mic off the stand, he paced back and forth, grinning from ear to ear, his youthfulness and excited demeanor infectious as he waited for the crowd to settle down.

"Wow, what a night! A guy could sure get used to this." Laughter permeated the outside venue, the twinkling stars of twilight adding to the magical mix.

"I've been writing songs for a while now, many of them up in the loft of the historic barn right over there." Hank pointed to the structure. Ted turned and eyed Robyn with a smirk. It seemed like a lot of magic happened in the family barn.

"Some of my songs are especially near and dear to my heart, especially this next tune. My big brother is behind the music of this one, and he's sitting right there on the front row."

Ted tensed as Hank pointed him out, all heads turning to look at him.

"This brave man has inspired many songs over the years. Teddy, you have the biggest heart for your family and hometown, and I want you to know ..." His voice cracked with emotion. "... I love you, brother."

Ted nervously ran a hand down his bearded chin as Robyn leaned in and gave him a strong side hug. He thought his heart might burst with elation.

"Did you know about this?" he mumbled through his fingers.

"Mmm-hmmm," she replied.

Hank's chest rose with a deep intake of air. "Ever since I was a young boy, Teddy always believed I'd sing a song in front of an audience one day. He'd say, "Hank-ster, mark my words; you're gonna make it!" And lo and behold, my brother was on to something. Me and the Bonafide Band have been on the road from time to time, playing our music for all who will listen. In fact, we're fixin' to head to Nashville in the coming months and get some of our original music recorded."

The crowd clapped and whistled, and a female voice rang out, "I love you, Hank!"

"I love you, too, darlin'," he waved. "Thanks for being here, all of you—especially, my big brother, Ted. I'd like to dedicate this next song to him. It's a song I wrote with him in mind, and it's called, 'Brotherly Love.'"

A hush fell over the audience, and Ted watched Hank's hands pick and strum the guitar effortlessly in a hauntingly beautiful melody. His voice pierced the night as he sang about a gentle man who taught him life lessons, about a brother who had unending pride for his family, and how he remained steadfast through his darkest hours. Tears streamed down Ted's face as he watched and listened to his baby brother serenade him. The vulnerability and transparency he evoked were precious at that moment. This is what made him love him with every fiber of his being. Hank was honest, sensitive, and creative, his song and the dedication a healing salve on Ted's battered spirit.

Hank strummed the last chord and let it reverberate, allowing it to end in a whisper before he looked up and nodded. The crowd went wild, standing on their feet and slapping their hands hard. Ted was laughing and crying simultaneously, overwhelmed by the gesture. His brother had to wait several seconds for the noise to pipe down, the smile on his face infectious as he looked down at the front row and winked at him.

"Thank you," Ted mouthed, the gamut of his emotions surprising him. The smile Hank offered was heartfelt, all the pain and anguish Ted felt during the years he spent behind bars falling to the wayside. But his happiness was short-lived—

"Ted Bennett?"

Ted looked over his shoulder, his eyes going wide at the sight of Janelle Kirby. The woman had aged significantly since the last time he laid eyes on her in the courtroom. The band started another song, Hank urging the audience to stay on their feet and clap along.

"Mrs. Kirby," Ted shouted over the music.

She nodded and displayed remorse in her expression. "I know you're enjoying your brother's band. But could I have two seconds with you, please?"

Robyn did a double-take, recognizing the woman in a millisecond and coming to Ted's defense. "Mrs. Kirby now is not the time—"

"It's okay, Robyn. I can spare a few minutes."

She clutched him by the arm. "You sure? You want me to come with you?"

"No, I'm fine. I'll be right back." Bending low, Ted nodded at Mrs. Kirby across his seatback and pointed toward the red barn. He met the woman at the entrance, the rest of his family in the audience too caught up in the energetic song and Hank's talent to notice.

Shuffling his cowboy boots in the dirt, Ted found it hard to look Mrs. Kirby in the eye, the undeniable guilt and sorrow he felt toward her bubbling to the surface. A flashback of that horrible night came to the forefront of his mind, and he grimaced.

# Chapter Seventeen

## TEDDY

Six Years Ago

Ted agreed to be the designated driver. It was only fair, especially after the previous weekend when his buddy, Max, held the unpopular job. In a town as small as Langston Falls where everybody knew your business, one had to be careful driving around late at night, especially with all the Barney Fife deputies on the prowl.

The party was on the outskirts of town, Ted and Robyn hanging out with their college friends. Ted had been sipping on water all night, watching his girl get tipsy on cheap wine coolers, rocking out with her girlfriends to the music playing loudly over a portable speaker. When her cheeks turned pink, and she wrapped her limp arms around his neck, he knew she was feeling no pain.

"Teddy, Susan said we're running low on beer for the guys. It isn't even midnight yet. Do you think we could go get some more? Pretty please?" Robyn batted her dark eyelashes at him, her sexy features against the bonfire light causing his jeans to swell.

"Sure. Let me round up Max and Ethan, and we'll get it done."

"Have I ever told you you're my hero?" she slurred, handing him a wad of cash Susan must've collected from the beer drinkers.

"No. But you know I'll always take care of my girl," he replied, cupping her face with his hands and giving her a long, hard kiss.

"Mmmmm," she moaned. "I wanna come with you. You can send the boys in to get the beer while we make out in the truck bed, like we used to back in high school."

Ted chuckled. "Sounds fun." He lifted her long hair away from her ear, nipping at her skin. "Come on."

"Be back in a few, Suzy-Q," she tittered, waving to her friend.

With one arm wrapped around Robyn's waist, Ted pulled the keys to his dad's pickup truck from his pocket, bummed his Jeep was still in the shop. He looked around the crowd for Max and Ethan, spotting them a few yards away from the fire sipping from red plastic cups. Since childhood, the threesome had been best friends, their bond tight, like his brothers. Ted approached and overheard them talking about their glory days playing football with a few other fellas.

Grabbing Max by the elbow, Ted pulled him aside. "Hey, we need to do a quick beer run. I'll drive, and you and Ethan grab a case. There's a corner market not too far down the street."

Max's eyes widened with glee. "That's the mart Joe Kirby works at now. Yeah, I'll go." He turned to Ethan.

"Come on, E, we're going on a beer run where Joe is working."

"Cool," Ethan said. "Let's go."

Ted and Robyn waited in the truck cab, the idling motor humming with a deep throttle. Max told him to wait because he needed to get his wallet from his car in case Joe decided to be a prick and demand identification. Of course, Ethan tagged along, the two a regular Frick and Frack when they were together.

With his arm resting across the open window ledge, and Robyn resting her head on his shoulder, Ted urged the guys faster as they finally made their way to the truck. "Come on boys, let's get moving. I don't have all night."

"Alright, alright already," Max appeased. He opened the smaller door to the back of the extended cab and climbed in. The foursome took off to the nearest quickie mart, where their friend, Joe Kirby, worked the night shift.

Ted glanced at the pair in the rearview mirror. The two chuckled, Max's lips pressed together to thwart off a smile.

"What?" Ted grinned, curious as to what he was up to.

"Nothing."

Ethan suddenly busted out laughing, Max joining him. They were obviously keeping something from them.

"What are y'all doing?" Robyn grinned, shifting her body to look at them in the back seat.

"Yeah, what's going on?" Ted asked again, eyeing the black top in front of him. "Come on, let us in on it."

Max leaned forward and rested his chin on the seatback. When Ted turned to eye him, he was taken aback by the black ski mask covering his face.

"Really, Max? You're gonna scare Joe while he's working?"

"That's so mean," Robyn frowned.

Ethan was quick to pull a similar mask over his head, the two looking incredibly stupid. "Why not? I think we can livin' Joe's night up with a little scare, don't you think?"

"Yeah. He deserves it after the time he egged my mom's house during junior-senior wars," Max added, laughing obnoxiously in his inebriated state. Ted made a mental note to swipe his car keys and give him a ride home after the party.

"Guys, that was way back in high school. Can't you let it go?" Ted shook his head. Were his friends always this dumb?

"Just keepin' Joe on his toes. You know we're harmless. It's not like we're gonna get him fired. Besides, he's always going on and on about how bored he is working the night shift. Believe me, he'll get a kick out of this."

Ted rolled his eyes as he turned the truck into the mini-mart lot, intentionally parking in the shadows to appease his friends with their childish prank. "Well, go on then. Get out, scare Joe, and don't forget the damn beer. You still got the money, right Max?"

Max lifted the ski mask, his wide grin comical. "Yep. It's in my pocket. We won't be long. Keep the truck running for our getaway." He wiggled his eyebrows, causing Ethan to snort-laugh, and Robyn to giggle. The two bumbled out of the truck and pulled the masks snug over their faces. Ted nodded and watched his friends creep along the wall like snipers until they entered the mart out of sight.

He chuckled, "What a bunch of morons."

But they were his dearest friends, their bond from their small-town elementary school through the local college sealed forever. Hell, he was sure they'd be standing at the altar with him someday soon, wearing black tuxes as he watched Robyn walk down the aisle toward him.

"Come here, beautiful."

Robyn scooted closer to his side and pressed her warm lips to his, her breath sweet from the alcohol.

She was the one, and he planned on asking her to marry him before she became too immersed in her law school studies. He was so fucking proud of her, graduating magna cum laude from their college class with her undergraduate degree in English. Since he'd graduated with a business degree, he needed to figure out his next steps, too. His mother told him to take a break first and enjoy the fruits of his collegiate labor.

Pulling back from their lip-lock, Ted smiled. "Are you getting excited about Colorado?" The trip was a generous graduation present from their families and one he looked forward to. Maybe he could propose to her there?

Before she could answer, a distinctive pop startled them both. Craning his head to look toward the highway behind him, he thought it was a passing vehicle backfiring in the dark night.

"What was that?" Robyn asked.

"I don't know."

Max and Ethan suddenly high-tailed it out the front doors of the mart. Ted was distracted and confused because they were empty-handed.

"What the hell are you two doing? Where's the beer?" Ted shouted.

Max screamed, "Floor it, Ted. Get us outta here!"

"Oh my God, what happened?" Robyn shrieked.

Ted didn't think twice, the panic in Max's voice putting him into drive. The tires screeched as Ted peeled out of the parking lot, anger and confusion mounting.

"What the hell is going on?" Ted looked at the pair in the rearview mirror, both of them huddled in the backseat.

That's when he noticed a gun in Max's hand, glinting in the headlights of a passing car.

"What the fuck, Max? Is that a real gun?"

Robyn jerked her head to look at Max, the fear in her voice real. "Why do you have a gun, Max?"

By this time, Ethan was sobbing, rocking back and forth against the seat. Ted slammed on the brakes, causing the two to fumble forward without their seatbelts. Angling his body to look at them, he screamed at the pair. "*What did you do?*"

Max's eyes held a faraway look, shock setting in. "We… we wanted to prank Joe. We wore the masks, and I… held up this gun to scare him." His hand shook, holding the weapon. "It wasn't loaded. It wasn't supposed to go off. Oh. My. God."

Ethan wailed louder as Max dropped the gun on the front passenger seat between Robyn and Ted like it was a venomous snake. Robyn pressed herself against the door as Ted stared at the sinister weapon, the truth sinking in.

Max shot Joe Kirby.

Yanking the gear shift, he put the truck into drive and floored it, nearly tipping the vehicle over as he turned around using the small shoulder of the road.

"What are you doing?" Robyn shouted.

"I'm going back. We need to make sure Joe is okay."

Max gripped Ted's shoulder with force. "I fucking shot him in the face, Ted. Do you understand? Joe is dead. I killed him. *I killed Joe…*"

Ted swallowed hard, the urge to wail like Ethan in the backseat nearly shutting him down. Joe Kirby was dead? What the actual *fuck*? Max and Ethan were only supposed to scare their friend wearing masks into the place. Why did Max decide to bring a gun into the equation?

"Where did you get the gun, Max?" Ted asked through gritted teeth. His knuckles turned white from his grip on the steering wheel. When Max didn't respond, Ted shouted, *"Where did you get the gun?"*

"It's mine. I keep it in my car. I have a concealed carry permit I got when I turned eighteen," he screamed back. "I didn't think it was loaded. It wasn't supposed to be loaded." Max pressed his palms to his face, his body shaking in anguish.

The tires squealed as Ted pulled right up to the front door of the mini-mart. There were no other vehicles in sight, the night sky streaking with a flash of heat lightning. Ted turned toward Robyn. "Call 9-1-1 and stay put. I'm going in."

"Don't do it, Teddy," Ethan sobbed. His wet face was beet-red. "You can never un-see him like that."

Ted threw open the truck door, not even bothering to close it, his swift steps carrying him over the threshold of the establishment. The door dinged as he entered, his heart beating wildly. The air was still, and he immediately spotted Joe's black work shoes sticking out from behind the checkout counter. Holding his breath, he slowly angled his head to look around the blood-splattered partition.

"Joe?" His voice warbled with fear. "You okay, buddy?"

When his eyes landed on poor Joe and the remnants of his destroyed face, he clamped his hand over his mouth in a cry of distress. Shaking his head, he couldn't believe what he was seeing. Poor Joe was dead, the metallic smell of the dark pool of blood surrounding his lifeless body infiltrating Ted's system. Collapsing to his knees, his body was wracked with uncontrollable sobbing. He reached forward and gripped one of Joe's shoes, begging God to bring him back to life; that it was all an accident—an innocent prank gone horribly wrong.

The wailing sound of a police car pierced the air with a high pitch, the blue and red flashing lights bouncing off the store's interior walls. Ted could hardly see through the haze of his tears, images of the two policemen with guns drawn nothing but fluid shadows. He responded quickly to their commands, laying flat on the ground with his hands behind his head. The cold sting of handcuffs clamped shut around his wrists, and the two officers yanked him to his feet, one of them reading him his Miranda rights.

"You have the right to remain silent. Anything you say can and will be used against you in a court of law. You have the right to talk to an attorney and have him present with you while you are being questioned…"

Ted pressed his eyes shut, Robyn's beautiful face coming to mind. She was only following his instructions to call the police, and now they'd arrived, thinking he was the one who shot Joe. He couldn't think straight, only that he had to get back to her—to feel her protective arms around him and help him get out of this mess. Her father was a lawyer. Yes —her father, Mr. Morgan, could get him out of this. He was sure the man would work on his behalf and explain to these officers he was an innocent bystander, he and his foolish friends on a beer run to Joe's place of work. Surely, Mr. Morgan could save him, convincing the powers that be it was all an unfortunate accident.

But as soon as he stepped out into the night and saw even more police cars converging on the scene, his blood ran cold. He watched Robyn being handcuffed and forced through the opening to the secured backseat of one squad car, while his friends, Max and Ethan were already inside another. Ethan looked like he was still sobbing, and Max held Ted's gaze mouthing the words, "I'm sorry."

Cuffed and locked inside a separate car away from his friends and girlfriend, he was surrounded by iron bars, his Colorado proposal dreams imploding in a record scratch bringing him back to reality.

Life as he knew it was officially over.

# Chapter Eighteen

## TEDDY

Ted finally looked Mrs. Kirby in the eye, caught off guard by her soft, smiling features. He kept his distance, her unexpected kind tone making him wary of a possible ulterior motive. Some of the wait staff worked around them, cleaning off the interior tables of the barn to the sounds of Hank's singing voice flying high into the rafters. The vast open-air space seemed to close in on Ted like a dark cloud.

"Uh, how are you, Mrs. Kirby? Are you, um, enjoying the Harvest Hoedown tonight?" His voice came out in a timid mumble as he tried to start some small talk. For the life of him, he couldn't imagine what she wanted after all these years.

"I am, Ted. What your family has done with the farm is remarkable, especially the winery. You must be glad to be home with them."

"Yes, ma'am. Very much." He eagerly nodded, his heart thumping.

The woman hesitated, her smile fading. Her big brown eyes glistened looking up at him, the orbs of the Edison-style string lights dotting her weathered features with light. Ted's heart ached for Joe's mom. In their youth, the woman was always accommodating when they all hung out at her house on numerous occasions. Back then, she was a single mom raising Joe and his younger brother, Glen, on a small apple farm. He always felt sorry for her caring for her boys on her own while he had both parents raising him and his siblings. It never seemed fair to him, fair being an understatement.

Many times during the hearings, Ted noticed Mrs. Kirby in the courtroom. A white-lace handkerchief was always pressed to her mouth as she listened to the unfathomable details about her son's demise, Glen always by her side and comforting her during the process. Even though Ted knew he was innocent, he still felt liable—that he should've had the right mind to stop Max and Ethan before they followed through with their tragic prank. But it happened—and there was nothing he could ever do to bring Joe back.

Mrs. Kirby inhaled a deep breath, Ted anticipating a strong lecture. "I'm so sorry you had to go to jail for all those years."

Ted took a step back, unsure how to reply. "Excuse me?"

"I know you had nothing to do with Joe's death. I know it was a terrible accident."

"Mrs. Kirby, I…"

"Please, let me finish."

Ted nodded, pressing his lips together. She walked toward the back of the barn, and he followed, listening to every word.

"I was there at the hearings. I listened to the entire story every time each one of you was on the witness stand in your individual trials. I pored over the police reports, and I spoke with all the young adults at the party you were at before you left on the beer run."

Ted swallowed hard, his entire body trembling with nerves. When she stopped in her tracks and looked up at him with the saddest eyes he'd ever seen, he wanted to reach out and hug her. But he continued to keep his distance.

"It wasn't until I saw the surveillance footage a few weeks ago—" Her voice cracked with emotion, and she shook her head.

"Wait... what surveillance footage?" Ted was taken aback. He'd been told the cameras at the mini-mart weren't working on the night of Joe's death.

Taking a moment to contain her feelings, Mrs. Kirby stood tall and looked him right in the eye. "You turned your truck around and came back. You prayed over my boy. I watched you. Your shock was evident. You didn't mean for him to get shot. You didn't know Max had a gun." Stretching her thin arm toward him, she pressed her wrinkled hand against his shoulder. "Ted, you didn't deserve the sentence you received. It was harsh and cruel. And... and I'm so sorry."

"I'm sorry, too," he whispered. Something sincere and profound passed between him and Joe's grieving mother. Ted knew right away what it was—forgiveness.

All the things he thought he'd figured out behind bars, he was learning again, in real-time. He'd struggled to get to the heart of the matter, Joe's ashes already scattered across his favorite fishing spot near Langston Falls. Ted needed to put this all behind him, the anger he'd been carrying eating him up inside. For Mrs. Kirby to offer him forgiveness was a game-changer. So was the surveillance footage.

"*Ma?*"

Ted and Mrs. Kirby turned their heads simultaneously to see a large man coming toward them. Mrs. Kirby immediately put herself between them, holding her hand up for him to stop.

"Glen, please. I needed to say my peace."

"Glen?" Ted muttered incredulously. His eyes went wide taking in the burly younger brother of Joe, only Glen wasn't a kid anymore—he was a grown-up beast.

"Don't you speak to me," he spat, bumping up against his mom.

"Hey, man. I don't want any trouble. Your mother—"

"I don't care if my mother wanted to talk to you. You stay away from her, you fucking murderer!"

Ted was taken aback by Glen's vicious tone and accusation.

"Glen, honey. Let's go back out and enjoy the music. Please. I'm finished here," she pleaded.

Glen kept his focus on Ted and stood his ground. "I can't believe they let you out. I can't believe you get to live your life free to do... whatever the hell you want to do," he shouted. His eyes were black as night, his hands fisted by his sides. "Get the fuck out of my sight before I tear you to shreds."

"Glen, please!" Mrs. Kirby begged.

Ted did a double-take when he noticed Walt in his peripheral vision, Robyn clinging to his arm. He could swear he saw smoke coming out of his brother's flared nostrils, his posture ready to attack.

"Like I said, I don't want any trouble, Glen. I'm going, right now, out of your sight." Ted held up his hands in surrender and turned to exit through the back of the barn.

He thought he was in the clear, but then he heard Mrs. Kirby shriek. Before he could turn around, he was blindsided, struck in the back of the head. The unexpected blow made him tumble forward onto his knees. Looking up, half expecting to see Glen's fists rain down on him, he was shocked when his eyes landed on Walt holding him back in a chokehold. His brother's bicep flexed and curled around the man's throat, cutting off his airway.

"You mess with the bull; you get the horns," Walt seethed.

Robyn scurried over to Ted and helped him up. "You can't fight him, Teddy. You'll go back to jail if you fight him."

"Come on!" Glen shouted, egging him on, struggling to get free. "You fucking *killer*!"

Ted curled his fingers into fists and was tempted but stopped when he noticed Mrs. Kirby cowering near the bar, shaking her head. She didn't deserve this—any of it. By this time, his brother James and a few other festival workers trotted into the barn. The concerned looks on their faces made Ted pause, and was that Sam McNeil, his parole officer, by James' side? *Holy shit…*

"Guys, knock it off. I mean it," Sam announced with authority. She flashed a badge in front of Glen, her clout impressive.

"Ms. McNeil, I didn't do anything. I didn't know they were here," Ted tried to explain. He pressed his palm over his head where Glen bludgeoned him, a sure headache coming on.

Sam approached him as Hank's music continued to play in the background. "Let's get you inside the main house away from all these spectators, okay?" She turned and spoke directly to Glen, who was still being held back by Walt. "Are we going to have a problem if Mr. Bennett releases you?"

Glen fumed with hatred, glaring at Sam and shaking his

head. She wasn't fazed, keeping her posture in a wide stance and her eyes glued to his face.

"Walter, let go of Mr. Kirby nice and easy," she instructed.

Walt nodded and eased back, Glen freeing himself and stepping away in a huff. He spat on the ground—and then he swung, not at Walt but at Sam. Everything happened in an instant. Robyn screamed as Sam was knocked out cold, her petite body falling like a sack of potatoes into a heap on the barn floor.

"*Samantha!*" James shouted, coming to her aid.

Glen turned his attention to Walt, the two of them going at each other, swinging with force. James grabbed Sam by the wrist and dragged her body away from the mayhem as Ted saw red and went into protection mode. He bowed up and headed straight into the fistfight without a second thought. His adrenaline kicked up a notch, his strength ten-fold as he shoved his younger brother out of the way. His knuckles made contact with Glen's jaw, the pain in his hand instant. The man reciprocated with several blows to Ted's face before he grabbed his neck in a choke hold. Ted's airflow constricted for a beat as he struggled to free himself. In a split second, he kneed Glen in the groin, shutting the fight down instantly. The big guy crumpled to the dirt, writhing in pain as he cupped the outside of his jeans.

"You... you *son-of-a-bitch!*" he yelped.

Ted wiped blood from his lip and towered over the big bully. There was evil in Glen's expression as he looked up at him.

"You shouldn't have done that. I'm pressing charges," he heaved. "You're going back to jail, you stupid prick! I've got you right where I want you." His ensuing laugh held wickedness.

Ted shook his head, the thought of more jail time making him sick to his stomach. Robyn reached for him, and he waved her off, sprinting toward the barn exit. He pushed his way through the forming crowd, his head throbbing and his emotions erupting. His legs moved faster and faster as he ran across the open meadow toward the road, the word "jail" echoing in his mind and filling him with dread.

Cars were parked bumper to bumper along the fence line, Hank's vocals soaring into the night. Ted glanced over his shoulder, the bright stage lights illuminating his brother for the huge crowd to see. Too bad he'd missed most of it. He ground his teeth and pushed himself harder, his boots slipping once or twice across the graveled road.

This was never going to end. There would always be someone like Glen Kirby blaming him for Joe's death— wanting to hurt him or his family for what he'd been a part of, even though he was innocent. Hadn't he paid his penance? Hadn't he paid the price for being at the wrong place at the wrong time?

His lungs burned and sweat poured from his brow, trickling into his beard. After running for more than a mile, he slowed his pace along the tall grasses by the country road-side, the full moon casting slanted rays across the pastures on either side of him. He could make out the giant oak tree on the family land, a silhouette forming in front of him. If he could just make his way to the tree, he could rest and figure out his next steps. The gate moaned on rusted hinges as he opened it. A few more yards through the high, yellow grasses, and he was there, the tombstones of his ancestors a welcome relief. Hiding in the shadows next to his mother's marker, he sat down on the hard earth, willing himself to breathe easier.

He shouldn't have gone into the barn with Mrs. Kirby alone, not without Robyn or Sam as a chaperone. God, he hoped Sam was okay. At least she wasn't a witness to his fists colliding with Glen's ugly face. Perhaps she wouldn't carry his ass back to jail after all? And he knew James, Robyn, and Walt were in the barn taking care of her. And what about his father and Becky? Maybe they were clueless, still enjoying Hank's concert from the wings, singing along to every song.

As Ted's heart steadied, he closed his eyes, thankful for the peace and quiet of the night. Resting his elbows on his bent knees, he cupped his aching head. He thought of all the bad luck and the heartache he went through—how he lost his family and Robyn for years and how he had to learn to live without them during those agonizing years in prison. And now, there were no guarantees. His life was uncertain, his yearning undefined. He wasn't forgiven. Nope, it was quite the opposite. There were people all around him, filled with rage. How in the hell was he ever going to survive? This nightmare was never going to end.

A thought crossed Ted's mind, but could he get away with it? Maybe if he disappeared, he could start a new life —a new beginning, away from his mistakes and the misery he caused his family. The thought of going back to jail made his head spin. He'd never survive, not again.

Ted's head shot up when he heard footsteps stomping through the grass coming closer. Squinting in the darkness, he tried to make out the figure looming toward him.

"Teddy?"

It was Walt, his shirt ripped across his shoulder, and his lip bloody and swollen.

"Go home, Walter."

Walt was out of breath from trailing him, his head cocked to the side, looking down at his pitiful figure in the night. "No way."

Ted gripped the back of his neck and sighed. "Is Sam okay?"

"James and Robyn are with her. She was only out for a few seconds. She begged me to come and find you." He plopped right next to Ted.

Ted pressed his eyes shut, his worst nightmare coming true. "Walt, I'm not going back to jail. I can't go back to jail…"

Walt grabbed him by the arm, the moonlight through the tree casting shadows across his concerned features. "Glen's the one who's going to jail. He struck an officer of the law."

Ted furrowed his brow. "You mean, Sam?

"Yes! You think she's gonna let him get away with it? No way."

Ted struggled to get his thoughts straight, the ache in his head not helping matters.

"I know what you're thinking," Walt mumbled under his breath.

"What am I thinking, Walter?"

"You're trying to come up with a game plan to run away —to start over somewhere where no one knows who you are or what you've been through. You can't do that, Teddy. Running from the law would only make things worse."

Ted knew his brother was right. Slumping in his seated position, he suddenly felt like he was a million years old. The previous adrenaline pumping through his veins dissipated with every new realization, leaving him cold and empty.

"Besides, you could never leave Robyn behind. She's your soul mate, Teddy. You two belong together."

Ted jerked his head to look at Walt straight on, the smile on his brother's handsome, battered face cockeyed from his admission. "I know, I know. I come across as not liking her —I've even blamed her for everything that happened to you. But I promise I'm done with it now. I can see it so clearly, the way you two act around each other since she's been staying at the farm. You belong together. And I think if you disappeared, she'd probably shrivel up and die, as would I."

His brother was right. He could never leave Robyn or his family behind.

Walt rose to his feet and offered Ted his hand. "Come on. Let's go home and see where things are at. I promise it's gonna be okay. I'll always have your back."

Ted gripped his brother's hand and stood on shaky legs, his head woozy from the fight and the surge of emotions. He was thankful for his brother's loyalty. The two started for the fence line.

"Sam McNeil is a good person from what little interaction I've had with her," Walt said.

"Yeah, about that. Why was she here tonight? Was she checking up on me? Making sure I didn't indulge in a little festival cider-wine?" Ted asked.

Walt sniggered in the darkness. "Nope. Our brother James invited her to the event tonight. Even though they can't officially go on any dates because it's a conflict of interest with her being your parole officer, it hasn't stopped them from flirting."

Ted stopped in his tracks. "Are you shittin' me?"

"It's true, Teddy. James was gonna talk to you about it. But I guess now that you know they're interested in each other, things might turn out differently for you. Do you know what this means?"

"What?" Ted questioned.

Walt patted him on the back. "The odds are finally in your favor, bro."

The relief in his brother's tone made Ted pause. Perhaps he was on to something.

# Chapter Nineteen

## ROBYN

Robyn stood by the front window of the main house, staring out into the darkness. She stroked Delia's yellow head as the big dog panted by her side. Visions of Ted battered and bruised somewhere out in the woods made her heart ache for him. Glancing over her shoulder, two county officers lingered in the kitchen where Becky served them coffee and chatted nervously about the weather, biding time. She watched James cater to Sam, who sat in a kitchen chair pressing a plastic bag filled with ice to her eye. The entire scene was surreal, Robyn doing her best to remain calm.

Glen Kirby's heinous act of striking a woman would forever haunt Robyn, and his brutal attack on Teddy and his brother, Walt, was unforgivable. When the cops showed up, she was quick to defend the Bennett brothers, Glen taken away in handcuffs and read his rights for police brutality. The man spewed obscenities, his angry words regarding Ted and his overt parole violation attacking him landing on deaf ears. The officers were more concerned for Sam, that one of their own was injured. They hauled Glen off to the local jail in front of his poor mother and all of the festival attendees to see. For now, Ted had dodged a bullet.

Glen Kirby should've never been allowed on the Bennett property, word on the street saying he'd been looking for an opportunity to confront Ted since he was released from jail—to finally take out his anger on one of the three men he held responsible for his brother's death. Robyn should've been more alert. She should've kept Ted in a more private area of the event, not front and center for the entire crowd to see. And poor Hank thought he was honoring his big brother by dedicating his incredible original song to him. Little did he know, he placed a bull's eye on Teddy's back for all the locals to see, including Glen Kirby.

"Hey, are you alright?" Becky asked, coming up beside Robyn.

Robyn shook her head. "I want Teddy to be okay. I wish he'd come home. The not knowing is killing me."

Becky nodded as if she understood. "I know. But Walt is out there looking for him. If anyone can find Teddy, it's Walt."

Robyn cocked her head to look at Becky. Ted's younger sister was such a pretty woman. Her big brown eyes and features were similar to his, and her smile was calming and sincere like their late mother. "I sure hope so. God, Becky, I'm so glad you weren't in the barn when it all went down. It was awful." She nodded toward James and Sam. "And poor Samantha didn't see it coming. Glen knocked her out with one punch."

Becky palmed Robyn's back. "But she's okay, see? James is taking good care of her, and the police hauled Glen away. He'll be sorry for punching a woman, especially an officer of the law. It's a felony."

"Yeah, but won't this be adding fuel to the fire? I mean, I get it. Glen is still angry after all these years. His only brother is dead. But for him to take it out on Ted and Sam —it's just not right."

"I know," Becky agreed. "Did you know Ethan is being released next month? Sam told me. Poor Max still has another ten to fifteen years to go."

Robyn grimaced, the memory of the trial haunting her for years. She'd gotten off without so much as a ticket, Ted taking a plea deal pleading guilty in order to get her charges dismissed. If she'd had a record, she could've never gone to law school, and Teddy knew it. He told her he'd do anything for her, sacrificing his life so she could have hers. But in the end, she became so disenchanted with the entire legal system, she felt there was no justice in the world. How could she go on with her life and dreams when Teddy was confined and living in a cage? This is why she never finished what she'd started. This is why she couldn't move on, the thought of Ted taking the fall and in a jail cell consuming her with unmitigated guilt.

Robyn sighed as Delia nudged her hand with her snout. "I wish there was something more we could do. Having those officers waiting around to question Ted isn't helping matters. It's... unnerving." She rubbed her wrist with a hand, the ghost feeling of handcuffs long ago rattling her spirit.

They were interrupted by Roy and Hank coming through the back door, the youngest Bennett brother anxiously looking around the room.

"Is he here? Is Teddy okay?" Hank asked before he noticed Sam. Kneeling to be eye-level with her, he squeezed her knee. "Shit, Sam. I heard what happened. Are you okay?"

Sam offered a weak smile and patted Hank on the hand. "I'm fine, Hank. And don't worry, Walt is out looking for Ted."

Hank frowned, his eyes tracing her face. "I can't believe Glen hit you. I mean, what kind of creep goes around hitting women?"

Sam shook her head. "Believe it or not, Hank, I've been through worse. Unfortunately, this is sometimes part of my job description."

"Getting attacked by a man? It should never happen," Roy chimed in. "James, grab the cold pack from the freezer. You know, the one my chiropractor gave me for my shoulder."

"The ice in this bag is working fine, Mr. Bennett. I don't need y'all fussing over me."

"Damn straight, I'm gonna fuss over you. This happened on my property, on my watch, during what was supposed to be a joyful event. I'm so sorry you had to go through this."

James handed off the thin, malleable cold pack to Sam. "Here you go." Roy whistled when she pulled the plastic bag filled with melting ice off her face and traded it with James.

"Oh, darlin', I'm afraid you're gonna have a pretty impressive shiner. He popped you good."

Sam touched the tender skin around her eye and winced.

Becky joined the conversation, her voice soft and consoling. "Don't worry, Sam. A little makeup will cover the black and blue right up."

The swollen skin around Sam's eye was already turning purple. James picked up Sam's free hand and brought it to his mouth, kissing her knuckles. The display of affection was unexpected yet comforting under the circumstances. Robyn thought the pair made a really nice couple.

Jaxson barked as the screen door in the kitchen opened, and Walt entered. Teddy was not too far behind him, both brothers looking battered and bruised. The kitchen erupted into a frenzy of relieved family members and excited dogs.

"Teddy!" Robyn rushed to his side, her gaze running the length of his tall stature, ensuring he was still in one piece. Ted pulled her into a hug, his manly muskiness familiar and comforting. "Are you hurt? Are you okay?" she asked, clinging to his torso.

"I'm fine. Just a few bumps and scrapes. I'm sorry I ran off and worried you."

Pulling back from him, she scowled, noticing the dried blood in his whiskers near his mouth, his lip split from a punch to the face. "It's okay. I would've run off, too. Let me get you cleaned up," she said. As she started toward the kitchen sink, Ted gripped her by the wrist and wouldn't let go. She acquiesced and nestled back into his arms.

The household became a flurry of activity, the officers' presence unnerving as Sam asked Ted and Walt to have a seat near her so she could get an official statement from them. Becky catered to the duo, bringing them bottled water and kitchen towels. Robyn stood behind Ted's chair, her hand pressed against his shoulder as he wiped his face. The thought of Teddy potentially being hauled off to jail again was at the forefront of her mind, her stomach churning with unease.

"I'm going to need a statement from you first, Walt. I need to know what exactly happened from the very beginning. Do you think you can be non-biased and just tell me the facts? This is critical to your brother's parole position."

Walt eyed Ted who sat across from him, his jaw

clenched with purpose. "I'll tell you what happened. Glen Kirby tried to start a fight with Ted, but I stopped him. You walked in when I had him in a chokehold, keeping him from attacking my brother." Walt's words were short and clipped as if he were trying to keep his own anger in check. "And then you instructed me to let Glen go nice and easy, and all hell broke loose."

Sam nodded, settling the ice pack she'd been keeping pressed against her face onto the kitchen table, her black eye swelling and getting darker by the minute. "And what exactly do you mean when you say, 'and all hell broke loose?'"

Walt glanced at Ted for a beat before he continued. "Well… you were knocked out, and then I started pounding Glen with my fists." He held up his hands to show her the redness and bruising across his knuckles. "Just ask James. He was there, too."

All eyes turned to James, who sat next to Sam. His face flushed, and he held up his hands with innocence. "Guys, I already told Samantha I didn't see anything because I was too busy getting her out of harm's way. I have no idea who hit who or what went down."

Hank shook his head and muttered something to his father, the looks on their faces filled with concern.

Sam turned her attention to Ted. "And what did you do while your brother was pounding Glen?"

Everyone in the room, including the officers, focused on Ted. Robyn held her breath. She squeezed his shoulder as he glanced up at her. When their eyes met, she subtly shook her head, begging him without words not to say anything incriminating. The room became so quiet you could hear a pin drop.

Ted cleared his throat. "I, uh… I did what any brother would do in the situation."

"Teddy, don't…" Robyn whispered, leaning closer to his ear, her heart galloping.

"Go on," Sam encouraged. "Tell me the truth, Ted. Tell me what you did."

Ted seemed to look at each person in the room, lingering on his father's face before dropping the bomb. "I defended my brother and you. I struck Glen Kirby in the face with my fist, and then I kneed him in the groin."

Audible sighs and moans were heard after his confession, Robyn pressing her eyes shut and fearing the worst. Ted continued to hold his head high.

Sam wearily stood, her expression hard to read. "Ted, I'm afraid I'm going to have to take you to the precinct and fill out some official paperwork. Glen Kirby wants to press charges against you." She turned toward Roy, the grim look on his face making Robyn want to weep. "Mr. Bennett, I trust you to accompany your son with the officers tonight."

"Yes, ma'am," he uttered.

"Tonight?" Robyn blurted. "But—"

"Robyn," Ted interrupted. He stood and put his arm around her, his warmth and strength viable to her existence.

Robyn wasn't having it. "Can't you see he's hurt, Sam? Can't he… at least take a shower and clean up before you take him away again?" Tears pricked the corners of her eyes, and she willed herself to keep it together in front of everyone. Ted turned her body to face him, his magnificent presence filled with unexpected calmness.

"Don't fall apart on me, baby. I need you to be strong—please, be strong," he implored.

Robyn blinked several times, looking into the depths of his kind, innocent eyes. Ted was a shining light even in the worst circumstances. He was always like that—a man grateful for his family. He was a simple man who enjoyed simple things in life, like the early morning mountain mist, a sexy chat lingering over coffee, the chance to love everyone around him. Her heart thumped, resolution pulsing through her veins. Her nod was slight as he pulled her forward into his warmth.

Sam slowly crossed the room and came right up to Robyn and Ted, her remorseful expression morphing into confidence. "Self-defense is not a crime. And defending others, including me is not a crime. But you may need a parole hearing to prove it was defense. I'll do my best, but you must know, if a violation report has to be filed, it doesn't look good to the parole board."

Ted remained steadfast. "I understand."

Sam nodded, her gaze apologetic toward Robyn.

James approached and mumbled, "I'm sorry, Teddy."

"I know."

The vibe in the room felt heavy like they were at a funeral or a wake, Ted's potential second incarceration on the horizon. Robyn felt gutted; the wind completely knocked out of her sails.

"Why don't you take ten minutes and clean yourself up. Robyn, you can help him. I'll let the sheriff know we'll be at the station soon."

Ted nodded, and they started toward the hallway. Every family member hugged Teddy, telling him to think positive and all was not lost. Walt waited his turn, looking around before speaking closely to Ted's ear so she could overhear.

"I changed my mind. If you want, I can get you out of here, Teddy. You just say the word."

Ted smiled, the brotherly love between the two apparent. "Like you said, Walt. Everything will be okay."

"You sure?" The wild look in Walt's eyes indicated he'd do just about anything for him.

"I'm sure." He fingered the ripped sleeve of his brother's shirt. "You need to get cleaned up, too. Looks like you lost a fight with a bobcat," he chuckled. The remark added some levity into the dark mood.

Walt smiled for a beat before his tone turned serious. "I don't lose. I get even."

Ted shook his head, grabbing his brother and hugging him with force. "Don't be an idiot," he muttered.

Robyn held Ted's hand as they climbed the stairs, her emotions teetering on edge. How was she ever going to let him go again? The uncertainty of what was at stake was a hard pill to swallow, and she wasn't sure how to navigate her feelings. When he closed the door to his bedroom, his fingers pushed into the sides of her hair like a comb, his gaze full of love and acceptance. Her heart fell to her feet. This felt eerily similar to the time they said goodbye six years ago.

"I love you, Robyn. I love you so much. This is nothing but a bump in the road. We'll get through this, okay?"

Tears immediately sluiced down her face as she nodded between his hands. His lips crashed against hers, the kiss full of desperation and longing. Oh, how she ached for him to truly be free. Unfortunately, there was nothing more she could do to help him.

Her entire world was this man—and for now, she was grateful to love him in the moment.

# Chapter Twenty

## TEDDY

Ted sat next to his father in the back seat of the police car. The two didn't say a word as the officer drove along the winding country roads through the thick night toward town. The sky appeared black, the light of the constellations snuffed out by the clouds. The atmosphere paralleled Ted's mood. He was numb and indifferent—pissed off, yet calm, cool, and collected, a dichotomy for sure. From deep within, his heart turned darker, the situation eliminating what little hope he'd held on to by the tips of his fingers.

If he had it to do over again, he'd still knock the smirk right off Glen Kirby's face in a heartbeat. How dare the prick waltz onto his family's property and cause a scene, and in front of his own mother? Who does that? Leaning his head back, he exhaled a long sigh through his nose, willing himself to keep it together.

"You did the right thing, son," his dad muttered in the shadows.

Angling his head to get a better view of his father's profile, Ted suddenly felt sorry for the aging man sitting beside him. Hadn't the Bennett family patriarch been through enough already? And every single time something bad happened, all fingers pointed at Ted.

"You hear me?" Roy said a little louder. "You did the right thing protecting Ms. McNeil. Any jackass in a court of law will agree. Sam is one of them—one of their own. If they can't see you were protecting her, then we have a much bigger problem on our hands."

"Like the harsh sentencing, Judge Danforth handed down to me the first time? I don't think I'll be coming home any time soon, Dad." Ted didn't mean for his voice to come across with so much resentment in his tone. He watched his father run his hands through his hair with exasperation.

"Now, let's not jump to any conclusions, okay? Judge Danforth isn't the one deciding the outcome of tonight. It's Samantha and the local sheriff. I know Sheriff Jenkins. He's been on the Langston Falls force for about three years now. He's a good fella. Fair."

Ted didn't say anything, his thoughts jumbled with possible outcomes. There was a chance he'd be put back in jail for a parole violation. Then again, the charges could be dropped because he was defending an officer of the law, who was also a woman. The odds were fifty-fifty. He could live with that. But there was something more pressing on his mind—something he needed to say to his father just in case things didn't go his way.

"Dad, I want to marry Robyn. I want her to be my wife." Ted wasn't sure why he chose this moment to fill his dad in on his intentions. But his words were finally out in the open, lingering in the backseat of the cop car like a fine mist.

Roy nodded in the dimness. "I know you do, Teddy. You two are meant to be. We all know that."

"I don't think you understand. Whatever happens at the station tonight, no matter the outcome, I'll get through it without any complaints. You have my word. But as soon as I get out, when I'm able to go home again, I want to ask her to marry me. And I want to have the wedding on the farm as soon as possible."

Roy cleared his throat. "I'm pretty sure a wedding can be arranged. But Teddy, aren't you forgetting something?"

Ted furrowed his brow. "What, Dad?"

"Don't you need to ask Robyn first?"

Ted was silenced for a beat before his dad started laughing, the robust sound deep and resonant in his throat. Ted couldn't help himself and joined in. The old saying, "father knows best," was true to form, Roy Bennett's practicality stopping Ted from getting ahead of himself.

Roy wiped under his eyes with the sleeve of his shirt. "Oh, Teddy. Let's get this bullshit out of the way, and then we can talk more about your future with Robyn. One thing at a time, okay?"

"Okay," Ted chuckled.

A few minutes later, the police car rolled into town. Ted gazed out the window, his eyes tracing the historic brick buildings of the downtown area. When the car passed right in front of the quaint flower shop where Robyn worked, his lips pulled upward in a slight grin. The powerful memory of when he first saw her after being apart for six years filled him with melancholy. The visceral feel of that particular day was something he recalled perfectly: The shop's exotic scent of flowers. The pink nail polish on her toes peeking out from the tips of her sandals. The warmth of her touch, zapping him with an electrical current rendering him speechless. And her emerald eyes staring back at him in wonder. He could get lost in those eyes forever—and forever was his goal. But once again, he was in the unfortunate situation where he had power over nothing. The only certainty in his life was his love for Robyn constantly thrumming through his being. For now, he'd have to go back to his old habits—the ones he learned while he was in prison: keep breathing, and stay alive.

His brother, James, pulled up next to the cop car, and Ted watched as he gallantly opened the door for Sam. He was happy his brother was finally interested in someone, even if that person was his parole officer. They still hadn't had a chance to talk about it, and Ted was antsy for details about how they hooked up.

Roy mumbled a polite "thanks" to the officer who opened his door to let him out. Ted reciprocated with a curt nod, sliding out from the backseat. At least he wasn't in handcuffs and voluntarily escorted inside.

Sam walked closely next to him. "Let me do all the talking, okay, Ted? Sheriff Jenkins knows what went down, but when he sees what Glen did to me with his own eyes, I think we can get around the messiness of an assault charge which could lead to filing a parole violation." The black and blue evidence around her swollen eye was a sinister reminder of why they were at the police station.

"Whatever you think is best, Ms. McNeil," he replied. Ted eyed James, who pursed his lips into a tight smile, his stance protective next to Sam.

The inside of the station was like stepping into a television crime drama set from the 1980s. There were several oversized desks laden with piles of paperwork, the obtrusive, large furniture lined up in rows with computer and telephone cords snaking over the sides. Worn chairs with ripped, mauve-colored seatbacks lined one of the walls, and the dingy linoleum floor was the faded color of pea soup.

The stale air held a burnt coffee scent mixed with body odor, the olfactory combination making Ted grimace.

From behind a glass partition of a large corner office, a middle-aged man in full uniform talking on a landline waved them in. Sam paused, encouraging Roy and James to have a seat in the waiting area while she and Ted took care of business.

"Hopefully, this won't take too long," she said with a slight smile, her gaze lingering on James for a beat. Sam swept her arm out in front of her, encouraging Ted to go into the office first. Nervous, he kept his eyes downcast as he listened to the phone conversation.

"I know, Mrs. Baumgartner. But the show is over, and folks are heading home now. The noise ordinance hasn't been broken." He glanced at his wristwatch. "In fact, there's still another thirty-five minutes before you can officially call in a complaint." He listened and nodded, rolling his eyes for Ted and Sam to see.

Ted knew he was talking to his neighbor, Mrs. Deloris Baumgartner. His father mentioned the elderly lady wasn't a fan of the Bennett Farm festivals as of late, the bright stage lights and loud music apparently causing her old hound dogs to howl. Ted thought it was pretty funny, imagining Mrs. Baumgartner pressing her hands over her ears, begging the canines to shut up.

Sheriff Jenkins appeased the woman and said his good-bye, hanging up the phone. "Sorry about that. We average a couple of calls per week from Deloris. It's always something," he chuckled. When he turned his attention to Sam, he put his hands on his gun belt fastened around his hips, and frowned. "I cannot believe Glen Kirby did this to you, Sam. Are you positive you're okay? Sure you don't need any medical attention?"

Sam waved him off. "I'm fine, really."

"Please, y'all have a seat."

Ted and Sam sat in worn wooden chairs directly across from Sheriff Jenkins. At least his office was a little less stinky and organized. The man pulled a sheet of paper out from a file and handed it to Sam. "Glen Kirby's been arrested for assault against you, Sam. But I should warn you, he's adamant he wants to press charges against Ted."

Sam scanned the paper and shook her head. "Can't you use prosecutorial discretion being the sheriff and not press charges against Mr. Bennett? It was self-defense. I mean, look at me, Sheriff. Ted honestly perceived fear as Mr. Kirby assaulted me and came to my aid. The guy knocked me unconscious."

Sheriff Jenkins scrubbed a hand across the five o'clock shadow smattering his jaw. "I understand, but there are limitations that apply when defending others. The accused, which is you, Mr. Bennett, must have reasonable grounds for your perceived fear to establish this defense."

Both Sam and the sheriff looked right at Ted, making him self-conscious. He cleared his throat, careful with his words. "With all due respect, Sheriff Jenkins, what would you have done if you were in my shoes?"

The sheriff's shoulders rose in a deep sigh before he answered. "I would've clocked that son-of-a-bitch out in one punch."

"So, you'll drop the charges?" Sam asked with eagerness.

"Now, hold on. It's not that simple, and you know it. I'm afraid I'm going to have to hold Mr. Bennett for a little bit until I can get some legal advice."

"But Sheriff Jenkins…" Sam argued.

"A couple of hours in the holding cell isn't gonna kill you, is it, Mr. Bennett?"

Ted licked his lips, the thought of spending time locked up turning his blood cold. "No, sir," he mumbled.

The three stood as Sheriff Jenkins punched in a number on his desk phone. "I promise, we'll have a solution in the next few hours. With it being the weekend and all, I'm having difficulty getting in touch with the District Attorney."

As Sheriff Jenkins summoned one of his deputies, Sam clutched Ted by the arms, her forehead wrinkled with worry. "I've got some strings I can pull, too. Just... sit tight for now. I'll do my best."

Pulling his wallet and cell phone from his pocket, he handed the items off to her. "Will you please give these to my dad to hold on to for me?"

"Sure thing." She smiled, taking them from his hands. When she looked up at him, he swore he could see a shimmer of tears in her eyes. "I'm so sorry, Ted."

Ted nodded before he obediently followed a deputy the sheriff summoned through a back door, bypassing his father and brother. Their footsteps echoed in the vacant hallway, the deputy's keys jangling from a large circle clipped to his gun belt as he unlocked a thick, metal door. On the other side, boisterous male voices were heard as they approached a huge area surrounded by metal bars, the holding cell containing several men.

His jaw clenched with fury. How did this happen? How did he end up here again? He knew the drill. They kept you in this holding cell while they prepared your official paperwork. When they were finished, they cuffed you and took you into another room to get fingerprinted and photographed, the mug shot released for the entire world to see. He'd then be strip-searched and have to hand over his clothes and boots to the authorities, dressing in a bright orange jumpsuit.

"It's been a busy Friday night in Langston Falls," the deputy smirked. He pulled the circle of keys from his belt again and unlocked the large cell. "Make yourself at home." He eyed him with a sinister smile playing on his lips.

Ted shuffled inside, the sound of the door slamming shut making him cringe. He stayed positioned by the entrance, willing himself to remain calm and wait patiently for Sam's return. He watched the deputy pause by the metal door. Something was off with him.

"Hey, thanks dude," a gruff voice shouted from inside the cell.

Confused, Ted kept his back turned, not wanting to initiate conversation with the stranger. Ted frowned as he watched the deputy salute and disappear through the door. The riffraff in the holding tank was probably nothing but a bunch of weekend drunks or petty thieves. He didn't want to start any trouble.

"Hey, you." The voice was loud and gruff as the man approached. Ted angled his head to catch a glimpse of the antagonizer, his mouth dropping open when he realized who it was.

Glen Kirby.

Ted knew the small town of Langston Falls, Georgia didn't have adequate space for weekend offenders, thus the overcrowded holding cell. But to put him in the same area as the guy who punched a fellow officer? The same guy who pressed assault and battery charges against him? It suddenly dawned on him this was deliberate, the deputy in cahoots with Glen. This nightmare was unfathomable.

"Look, Glen, I don't want any more trouble tonight."

Two other burly men puffed their chests out and stood prominently on either side of Glen Kirby like a bunch of redneck bodyguards. The ridiculousness of their actions reminded Ted of a bad mafia movie.

"You're a fucking murderer, you stupid prick. And you're gonna pay." Glen's eyes were slits, his anger causing his face to flush as he pushed up the sleeves of his shirt.

"*Guard?*" Ted shouted through the bars, his pulse quickening. He glanced at the corners of the holding cell and waved at the cameras. Glen's eyes followed where he was looking, and he laughed.

"You think those cameras are actually working, pretty boy?" He reached out and boldly flicked Ted's long hair.

"Glen, you don't want to do this," he said evenly. His back pressed against the hard steel, his knuckles turning white from his grip on the metal bars containing him so he wouldn't throw the first punch.

Glen sneered. "Oh, but you know I do." His face twisted with an evil expression as he came closer. The two were in a stand-off—until Glen reared his thick arm back and slugged Ted in the jaw. His head slammed across the bars, and he saw stars. One of Glen's minions grabbed a fistful of his hair and dragged him into the center of the room, throwing him down to the floor.

"*Glen!* Please, I'm begging you. Don't do this!"

Glen towered over him and nodded. "Pick him back up, boys."

Ted was pulled to his feet, his arms flush against his back. He was tempted to kick Glen in the groin again with the tip of his pointy cowboy boot. But the thought of going back to prison and losing Robyn all over again was too much to bear. Before he could follow through with the notion of defending himself, Glen slugged him hard in the stomach, making him hunch over in immediate pain.

"Show me his ugly face," he seethed.

Yanking his head back by the hair, the brute exposed Ted's face. He eyed the other cowardly men standing nearby, no one saying a word or coming to his defense. When his gaze landed back on Glen, he beseeched him one last time, the taste of blood lingering on his split lip.

"Listen to me, Glen. I promise I won't press any charges if you let me go. Let's stop this once and for all, okay? This needs to stop."

Glen looked like he was mulling over Ted's request for a few seconds, but then he shook his head and came closer. His hot breath grazed Ted's ear when he spoke, his ominous word final.

"*Murderer.*"

Ted tensed, anticipating the forthcoming blows, ready to accept the bludgeoning. In the back of his mind, he knew the only way he might escape a possible parole violation was to not fight back—to allow these bullies to beat him senseless. Maybe then, the court might find favor for him and let him go home again.

The first hit to his face caused him to see stars. The next blows were more aggressive and severe, his head slamming into metal over and over again. The ensuing tunnel vision descended fast and furious…

And his entire world went black.

# Chapter Twenty-One

ROBYN

Robyn squinted against the bright glimmers bouncing off the pond's surface as she lay across the rough boards of the dock in the sun. She watched Ted splash in the water, his thick muscled arms arching in a freestyle stroke coming toward her. Smiling, she rested her chin on the tops of her hands, content in the moment. The air was thick with humidity, the blazing sun sure to redden the skin across her shoulders.

Ted gripped the edge of the dock and grinned at her, water sluicing down his clean-shaven face, his short hair matted to his head. Wait... *what?*

Robyn furrowed her brow, unsure of what was happening. As she sat up, Ted took a deep breath and submerged himself below the surface of the murky pond water. Dangling her legs over the dock ledge, she stared at the bubbles rising and gurgling to the surface, anxious for him to pop out of the water again. But seconds passed, and then minutes—the distant, ominous sound of a crow echoing across the adjacent meadow.

"*Teddy*?" she hollered. The bubbles stopped, and she felt her blood run cold. "*Teddy*!"

Flinging her body into the pond, her heated skin stung against the chill of the water, her arms and legs flailing...

---

Robyn was startled out of the dream, her heart thundering. Blinking several times, she realized she was still in the Bennett's family room, lying on the couch. It was a dream, thank God. Delia pressed her cold, wet snout against Robyn's hand and whined.

"It's okay, girl," she comforted. If only it was Teddy comforting her.

Robyn slowly sat up and rubbed her eyes. Becky, Hank, and Walt remained seated at the kitchen table playing cards, several coffee cups and empty plates scattered about from their earlier homemade pie raid. Becky seemed to notice her and frowned.

"You okay, Robyn?" she asked from across the room. Her brothers turned simultaneously, their handsome gazes similar to Teddy's.

"Um... yeah. I must have dozed off." She wasn't about to tell them about her dream—or maybe it was a nightmare. The high school version of Teddy in the dream confused her. "Any word?"

"No," Walt answered, hanging his head. "I thought for sure we'd know something by now."

"What time is it?" Robyn stroked Delia's head, concerned they hadn't received any news.

"It's after midnight. You want me to make another pot of coffee? You hungry?" Leave it to smiling Becky to remain the consummate hostess.

Robyn stood and stretched her arms above her head before she leaned over and grabbed her cowboy boots she'd parked next to the couch. "No, thank you. I think I'll go on up to Ted's room and change out of these festival clothes."

"Good idea," Becky agreed.

"When you come back down, join us, and we can start a game of Rummy," Hank chimed in. His enthusiasm and authentic charm made her smile.

"Okay, but if you remember, I kicked your butt last time," she teased, pointing her finger at him.

They all laughed at the memory, Hank shrugging. "I don't know. It's been a while. I've gotten better. Girls against boys, just like the old days?"

Robyn looked at each Bennett sibling and nodded. "Okay." Hank whooped as she headed toward the hallway with boots in hand. "I won't be long."

Scrambling up the stairs, her earlier dream was nothing more than a faded memory, scattered pictures from their youth. Thankful for the diversion of cards and the competitive nature of Ted's family, she was quick with her actions. She changed out of her clothes into a pair of yoga pants and one of Teddy's oversized t-shirts. In the bathroom, she splashed cold water across her face and patted her skin with a fluffy towel. Staring at her reflection in the mirror, she pulled her hair back into a tight ponytail and ran a soft tissue under her eyes. She looked tired and haggard from the evening, anxious for Ted to come home where they could finally snuggle and fall asleep in each other's arms.

A soft knock on the bedroom door diverted her attention. Robyn shook her head, amused, thinking it was one of the brothers egging her to get a move on so they could start the card game.

"I'm coming," she hollered, draping the towel back over

a rack. Opening the door, she was shocked to find Becky on the other side. Her sweet face was distorted from crying.

"What is it? What happened?" Robyn could barely get the words out, hidden fears rising to the surface. Becky flung herself into Robyn's arms and sobbed. She stroked her hair, afraid to move—afraid to hear the latest, awful news she was sure was coming.

"G... Glen. He... he hurt Teddy," Becky managed to utter between fits.

Robyn pulled back from her, holding her shoulders firmly in her hands. Searching Becky's eyes, she offered a quick prayer to the heavens before she stoically proceeded with her barrage of sentences. "What do you mean? We all know Glen hurt Teddy. And Teddy fought back. That's why he's at the police station, to get everything straightened out."

"No, you don't understand," Becky wailed. "Glen was there... at the station. They put them... in the same holding cell. Glen... *beat* him." The young woman was overcome with emotion and buried her head against Robyn's shoulder.

Robyn was numb, trying to process the news. She wrapped her arms around Becky's quaking body as she tried to steady herself. There was a good chance she might pass out, her breathing staggered and thin. But she wouldn't allow herself to fall apart. No, she couldn't go there—she had to be strong; she had to be there for Teddy.

Robyn inhaled a deep breath and backed away from Becky. Her eyes traced the bedroom, searching for her athletic shoes and a sweatshirt.

"What are you doing?" Becky asked, wiping her eyes with the heel of her hand.

"Go," Robyn commanded. "Get your shoes on. Find a

sweater or a long-sleeved shirt. Hospitals tend to be cold, especially at night."

Becky nodded aggressively and ran out of the bedroom. Every molecule and cell in Robyn's body hummed with a surge of adrenaline, propelling her to get a move on. But when she stood up after tying her shoes, she remained standing in one place, her feet stuck to the floorboards like glue. An image of Teddy going under the water from her earlier dream flashed through her conscious, making her pause. Was it a premonition? Was he about to disappear from her life forever? Pressing her eyes shut, she shook her head.

"No," she uttered with resolution. "You're okay. You're gonna be okay, Teddy. You have to be."

She opened her eyes and turned slowly in a circle, taking in every aspect of Ted's room, her chest heaving with emotion. The urge to collapse into the fetal position on the bed and sob into the pillow was genuine. She wanted to cry just as hard as the first time, years ago, when Teddy sacrificed himself for her and was hauled off to prison. The crazy thing was, she felt even sadder now, mortified he'd been hurt—beaten in a cage like an animal. Unlike the tears she cried back then, these were fueled by a broken heart, without anger or regret to dilute them. Her sweet Teddy was injured, and she blamed herself again. This was all her fault, just like it was six years ago.

For a millisecond, she thought about packing her bags and heading to Atlanta into the safe arms of her father, far away from the horror. She considered herself bad luck. Perhaps her absence could change the outcome of these latest events. But her thoughts were short-lived, the primal instinct to protect and defend her man filling her with intention.

Grabbing her purse and a hoodie from Teddy's drawer, she bolted out of the bedroom, running as if his life depended on it.

———

They rode in Walt's pickup truck in silence, Becky clinging to Robyn in the tiny backseat. Hank sat up front in the passenger seat, his head turned as if he were looking out the window. But there was nothing but blackness outside, the promise and light of a new day still several hours away. The truck tires hummed along the pavement, the white noise soothing under the circumstances. Robyn noticed Walt glance her way in the rearview mirror, his jaw clenched in a formidable frown.

Earlier, when she came downstairs, she was met with three of Ted's very distraught siblings. The big dogs cowered in the corner, Walt's angry outbursts understandable.

"I'm going to kill that son-of-a-bitch with my bare hands," he seethed, flinging a coffee cup against the kitchen cupboards in a dramatic crash of ceramic.

"No, you're not," Becky wailed. "Don't stoop to his level, Walter. You're not like him. You're *nothing* like him."

Hank came to his sister's aid, pulling her into his sturdy arms. "Walt, you need to get a grip, man. You're not helping matters."

"Oh, yeah?" He fisted his hand in Hank's face. "What the fuck, Hank? Dad said they were on their way to Langston Hospital. Teddy was found unconscious, practically beaten to death." His words induced another audible cry from Becky pressed into Hank's chest. He had no response, soothing his baby sister with his hug.

Robyn approached Walt with boldness and gripped him by the arm. His head jerked to look right at her, his pupils wild and dark. When she didn't say a word and allowed him to see her tear-stained face, his shoulders slumped in defeat. He bowed his head, the tension dissipating from beneath her touch.

"We need to go, Walt. He's going to need us all there. Do you think you can drive?" she calmly asked, swiping her fingers across her wet face.

Walt's jaw tensed, her question seeming to give him direction. "Of course I can drive. Let's go."

The lampposts gave off a ghostly glow in the fogginess of the late night. The truck passed the closed businesses and went through the one traffic signal in the community, the yellow-flashing caution light bright against the dreary blackness of night. They continued, passing the police station, all eyes lingering on the unassuming building for a few seconds.

Robyn swallowed hard, trying not to imagine Teddy outnumbered by a bunch of thugs in the holding cell an hour earlier. She knew without a doubt he tried to diffuse the situation with a calm demeanor, doing his best not to antagonize Glen Kirby and get into more trouble. But if Glen had cronies, it would've been impossible for Ted to try and defend himself. The thought made her sick to her stomach.

Walt pulled into the large lot of Langston Hospital and parked. All four got out of the truck and quickly headed toward the emergency room entrance. Robyn overheard Hank encourage Walt to keep it together. Walt didn't respond, his imposing figure continuing in a determined march to get to their destination. As soon as the automatic

KG FLETCHER

doors opened, Becky spotted her father and ran into his arms.

"*Daddy!*"

James and Samantha stood nearby, the looks on their faces hard to read. Robyn hung back and watched the scene unfold, Roy Bennett, offering hugs and words of comfort to his children. When he spotted Robyn by the door, he waved her over. Holding her head high, she was determined not to fall apart in front of the family patriarch. Roy pulled her into his arms, his sigh heavy.

"Teddy's a fighter," he reassured.

"I know," she whimpered, her face buried in the crook of his neck. He smelled like pine and coffee, his crisp white festival shirt from earlier now wrinkled and untucked from his black jeans. He held her to his chest so tightly she could feel his heartbeat. The man was obviously disheveled, the news of Teddy and the brawl upsetting.

"Can I see him?" she asked.

Roy pulled back from her, the sadness in his blue-gray eyes something that would haunt her for years to come. Her vision blurred, and she struggled for her next breath as the words out of Roy Bennett's mouth rocked her to her core.

"He's in bad shape, darlin'. We have to wait." His voice wavered with emotion, the gentle man trying hard to hold it together.

"And we have to pray."

# Chapter Twenty-Two

## ROBYN

On the night of the brutal beating, Ted was airlifted to Grady Memorial Hospital in Atlanta, the fifth largest public hospital in the nation. The busy level one trauma unit kept him alive for those first twenty-four hours. That was a week ago, and he was still in critical condition because of the injuries he sustained at the hands of Glen Kirby and his bully accomplices.

Someone dropped the ball on that fateful night. By the time the other deputies of the Langston Falls precinct finally realized what was happening and heard the shouts and hollers of the other riled up men in the holding cell, Ted was already beaten unconscious. The family learned there had been a miscommunication among the night staff, the deputy escorting Ted to the cell a cousin of Glen Kirby's. Glen was supposed to be held in another cell, away from the general population. That Ted was intentionally placed in such a dangerous situation had repercussions. The deputy was placed on administrative leave, and Sam McNeil advised the family to file charges. But Roy was adamant they concentrate on getting Ted the medical help he needed before they moved forward with any kind of indictment.

The team of doctors at Grady agreed Ted had one thing going for him; he was bigger than average and more solidly built than a regular guy. He was strong but outnumbered, able to sustain the kicks and punches to his head and body until he was sucker-punched and knocked out cold. Crumpled on the dirty cell floor, the heinous crime continued, the brutes breaking his ankle, and puncturing his lung when one of his ribs broke from blunt force trauma. His poor face was beaten so severely his eyes swelled shut. Once Ted was airlifted to the hospital, the situation turned dire, and he was put into a medically induced coma, giving his brain time to heal after enduring countless severe blows to his head. The neurologist in the intensive care unit assured the family he would bring Ted out of the coma as soon as possible, but only when the swelling receded.

Images of Teddy filtered through Robyn's mind. The first time she was allowed to see him in the hospital was an incredibly emotional day. She and Becky stood together looking into his trauma room through a glass window. The sight of him unconscious with all the tubes and wires connected to the machines keeping him alive made her cling to his sister for support. Her soft sobs were uncontrollable as they both wondered how someone larger than life could end up so broken.

It was hard to shut her mind off, the guilt she continually felt consuming her in angst. On the night of the festival, she should've had Roy or the other Bennett brothers accompany Ted into the barn while he chatted with Mrs. Kirby. Or better yet, six years ago she should've never coerced him into going on a beer run with Max and Ethan.

"Crap," Robyn muttered under her breath. Swiping at a rogue tear dribbling down her face, she tried to shake off her negative thoughts and concentrate on her driving. She didn't want to fall apart in front of Ted's family, her unanswered prayers filling her with dread. She had to get out the hospital for a break and drove aimlessly around the vicinity.

The downtown Atlanta area was congested. Gripping the steering wheel a little tighter, she edged her way onto Peachtree Street, having no idea where she was going. She needed to get away for a little while and thought about visiting the Martin Luther King, Jr. National Historic Park nearby. But she was thirsty and needed caffeine. Maybe she could find a Starbucks drive-thru and then take a break with her coffee and visit the park? The weather was moody though, with a slight chance of rain in the forecast. Maybe an afternoon at the Georgia Aquarium might be better? But looking down at her layered look of yoga pants, a t-shirt, and a hoodie made her realize she wasn't dressed to play tourist.

Traffic was abysmal, but she didn't care. She relished the alone time in the quiet interior of her car, needing a breather from the entire Bennett clan camped out in a private waiting room back at the hospital. When they weren't all glumly waiting for hourly updates regarding Teddy's condition, Roy and his brood bunked with family friends near the downtown connector. Robyn stayed with her father in his luxurious high-rise condo near Mercedes-Benz Stadium. His comfortable home held a view of Centennial Olympic Park and the latest tourist attraction; an impressive twenty-story Ferris wheel. She'd always wanted to take a ride on the attraction, knowing the panoramic views of downtown were impressive. But her father's talk of her relocating to Atlanta for good, away from all the Bennetts, was too much. She was emotionally drained.

Idling at a traffic light, Robyn's eyes traced the cityscape, and she inhaled sharply. The familiar Georgia Pacific Tower loomed ahead, the stair-like pink granite design staggering to the ground. Biting her lower lip, she remembered all the times she parked in the underground lot and took the elevator to the fifty-first floor where Anderson worked. Wouldn't he be surprised if she showed up out of the blue with a cordial hello? But why would she? Things were over between them, and she hadn't heard a word from him since the day before the festival when he walked out of her house in a flash of pink Polo. Anyway, he was probably out of town, wheeling and dealing his next contract, flirting with the latest Barbie-doll he could get his hands on.

Robyn was semi-familiar with the area and knew of a coffee shop on the block near the lobby of Anderson's building. She used to frequent the café when she'd wait for Anderson to get off work during her visits to the city, the delicious lattes a consolation of sorts because he was always late. Decision made, she pulled the Jeep into the dark underbelly of the office building and parked in a visitor's space near the entrance. Hopping out of her car, she was surprised to see a security guard walking toward her. Swallowing hard, she angled her chin in the air doing her best to come across as somewhat professional. But her clothing was anything but.

"Good morning," the cheerful man greeted.

"Good morning."

"You're gonna need an authorization pass to park in the space. Who's your contact?"

Robyn blinked back at the officer, Anderson's name

coming out of her mouth before she could retract it. "Anderson Albright? He's a friend of mine."

"And your name?"

"Robyn. Robyn Morgan of Langston Falls."

The officer nodded and looked at the clipboard he held in his hands. His scowl was immediate. "I'm sorry. There doesn't seem to be a Robyn Morgan on the authorization list. Could've been an oversight. Let me contact Mr. Albright and grant you access." He started toward the security office.

"Wait," she pleaded. The officer turned around. "Anderson doesn't know I'm here. We used to date, and I, um… I used to meet him at the café down the street. I'm… visiting and recognized the Georgia Pacific Tower. Listen, all I want to do is grab a quick cup of coffee. Can I park here for a minute? I won't be long, I promise."

The officer listened to her babble before he smiled. "I'm afraid I don't have the authority to grant you access without Mr. Albright's approval. Gotta play by the rules. If he knows you're in town, I'm sure he wouldn't mind if you parked here. Let me make a quick call on your behalf."

Robyn watched the man enter the small guard shack and pick up a phone. God, did she really want to bring Anderson into this? There was still time for her to make a getaway. But when the officer seemed to laugh at something Anderson said over the phone, she continued to wait, curious about what he said.

"You're in luck. Mr. Albright is in the building and said he'd be delighted to grant you access to park your car."

"Delighted," she repeated skeptically. "Okay."

He handed her a visitor's tag. "Just hang it on your rearview mirror, and you're good to go. And enjoy your latte," he winked.

"Thanks."

Robyn shuffled back to her car and quickly hung the tag in place, thankful Anderson came through for her. Locking the doors, she waved at the officer before she trudged up the cement stairs and exited onto the city sidewalk. The cool shadows of the towering skyscraper made her shiver.

A few minutes later, she was seated and sipping from a steaming mug, the warm essence of caffeine infiltrating her senses. This is what she needed: a moment to herself. A moment to relax and figure out her next steps. Since the night Teddy was attacked, she wracked her brain thinking of a way she could help him—anything to get her mind on a solution rather than the problem. Unfortunately, she'd convinced herself *she* was the problem.

Her eyes caught a flash of expensive teal fabric out the window, Anderson's imploring gaze above his immaculate suit catching hers. His wave seemed friendly enough as he opened the café door gallantly, allowing another customer to exit before he came inside. Robyn smoothed her hair back from her face and sat a little taller, Anderson's presence not that unexpected. If only she'd planned a better outfit today and maybe a smidge of makeup to thwart of his impending jabs.

"You look like death on a cracker," he joked, sliding into the booth on the opposite side. He held the same cocky attitude toward her when they were dating. Some things never changed.

Robyn wasn't sure what triggered her tears. Was it the sight of a familiar face or the word 'death' hanging in the air? Whatever it was, she pressed her hands over her eyes and started sobbing. Anderson was quick on his feet, sliding onto her bench seat and enfolding her in his arms. He whispered words of comfort into her ear.

"Shhh, what is it? Tell me, Robyn. I'm here for you." He offered her his perfectly ironed handkerchief from the breast pocket of his suit. She shooed it away, pressing a paper napkin to her face.

"What are you doing here?" he asked.

It was a fair question, but she wasn't sure how to explain. "I... I'm here with the Bennett family."

Anderson pulled back from her, tucking a stray hair over her ear. Tipping her chin, so she looked him right in the eye, he seemed confused. "If you're here with the Bennett family, why are you all alone in this café? Do I sense a little trouble in paradise?"

Robyn inhaled a deep breath, her brow furrowing in response to his wayward comment. "No... it's nothing like that. Teddy... he was... airlifted to Grady Hospital last week."

The look of shock on Anderson's face was immediate. "Damn. Tell me what happened. I've got all day for you." He waved over the waitress and ordered a black coffee, never leaving Robyn's side.

She wiped her nose, thankful for his friendship after all they'd been through. "You really can be a decent man when you try."

"I know," he joked, jutting his chest out with grandeur. "It's what draws all the pretty ladies." He comically wiggled his eyebrows, adding wittiness to the situation. "Now, fill me in on what happened to poor Teddy. I'm all ears, ready to listen. That's what friends do. We can be friends, can't we?"

Friends? The thought was a foreign concept to Robyn. But here he was, taking time out of his busy schedule and coming to her aid. She should at least try. If anything, he was an ally during her time of need. She decided to let bygones be bygones and leaned against his shoulder for comfort.

"This might take a while," she warned. "Are you sure I'm not keeping you from anything? Anyone?"

Anderson smirked. "She can wait."

# Chapter Twenty-Three

## ROBYN

"Hey, Matlock."

Robyn's father greeted her with the familiar childhood nickname, his suit jacket hanging over the kitchen chair where he sat. The pet name all started when she was a young girl, right after her mother died in a terrible car accident. Her father took a sabbatical from his law firm and they numbly watched reruns together of the American legal drama series *Matlock* on television for weeks. She was fascinated by the lead actor, Andy Griffith, who played cantankerous attorney, Ben Matlock, the fictional lawyer exposing perpetrators in dramatic trials, usually after visiting crime scenes and discovering overlooked clues. Robyn was at an impressionable age, fascinated by the legal entertainment, and boldly told her father she wanted to prosecute bad guys just like the actor did on TV. But now the nickname stung a little, and she couldn't bring herself to ask him to stop calling her that. Instead, she responded like normal.

"Hey, Dad."

"Any news today?" He shuffled a stack of legal papers into a tidy pile, his signature mug of coffee parked nearby.

"Nope."

"No news is good news, I suppose."

Robyn watched her father loosen his tie, the early evening sky through the high-rise window morphing from muddled grays to dark blue hues against the skyline. She wearily sat across from him, glad to be home after her emotional day at the coffee house and hospital.

Earlier, Anderson listened to her every word, offering sympathy for what she and the Bennett family were going through. When they parted ways, he requested she give him periodic updates, genuinely concerned for Teddy's outcome. Her ex's attitude toward her was refreshing, and she promised to keep him in the loop. Of course, he made jokes about her appearance, his off-hand remarks reminding her of why they never made it as a couple to begin with, not that it mattered anymore. But she was glad they could remain friends, grateful he was there for her.

"Are you working on a big case?" she asked her dad.

"Several. Trying to stay organized."

Robyn nodded. "I can fix you an early dinner if you want." She'd hardly spent any time with her father. And she hated her current situation; moping and depressed most days wearing the same yoga pants, jeans, and sweatshirts she'd hurriedly packed a week before.

"No, sweetie. I'm good. I had a late lunch." He took a long sip from the mug she'd given him for Christmas last year. A cartoon image of a baby Yoda smiled back at her, the phrase, 'Yoda best lawyer' etched underneath.

The doorbell rang, Robyn scowling with unease. "Are you expecting someone?"

"Yes. Samantha McNeil," he replied, rising from his seat and disappearing toward the front door.

"Sam?" she muttered to herself. Sam hadn't mentioned any scheduled visit before she'd left the hospital.

Her dad reentered a minute later with Sam by his side. Robyn offered a silent smile, Sam grinning back at her with friendliness. The two often chatted when she had time to stop by the hospital to check in with the family. Teddy's parole officer often lent an ear to her angst regarding Ted's future. Robyn tried to get Sam to tell her outright if he would have to go back to jail once he was healed because of the fight in the red barn. But her allegiance to officer-client privilege was admirable under the circumstances.

"Hey, Robyn," she greeted with cheer.

"Hey. Can I get you anything? Water? Coffee?"

"No, thank you. I'll only be a few minutes. I know it's getting close to dinnertime." She paused. "I need to talk to you."

Robyn frowned, her eyes darting to her cell phone on the kitchen table. She hadn't received any texts while at the café, and none of the Bennetts had recently called or left a voicemail. She turned rigid in her seat, her mouth pressed into a grim line. She glanced at her father, who held a poker face. If he knew something she didn't, he wasn't giving anything away. Her mind swirled with all kinds of news, all of which was bad—very bad. Did Roy call Sam, afraid to tell Robyn outright Teddy had taken a turn for the worst? Was he officially deemed brain-dead, or God forbid, had he actually passed away?

Robyn felt hot tears prick the edges of her eyes. God, hadn't she cried enough in one day? Her hands trembled with unmitigated fear. When her father reached across the table and offered his open palm, she gripped his fingers, anchoring herself to his lifeline, ready to hear Sam's words.

"We need to prepare a legal motion to get Ted's probation terminated as soon as possible. I've come across convincing evidence since he was nearly beaten to death." Sam didn't mince words; her tawny eyes fixated on hers.

"I... I don't understand," Robyn stuttered. She pulled back from her father's hand. "Dad, do you know anything about this?"

His expression softened, and he tilted his head, the slow smile spreading across his face bewildering. "Yes. Officer McNeil called me earlier with the news. Hear her out."

Robyn inhaled a deep, cleansing breath and nodded. "Okay. Go on," she whispered. Her skin prickled with nerves, a small ember of hope igniting in her chest.

Sam's smile held reassurance as she clasped her hands together on the table. "Surveillance footage of the night Joe Kirby was killed has surfaced."

"*What?*"

Sam nodded excitedly. "Because the surveillance existed and was not presented in Ted's trial, this is blatant prosecutorial misconduct. The prosecution can't hide exculpatory evidence. But sometimes it happens. And unfortunately, it happened to Ted."

"Oh my God, what does this mean?" Robyn's heart pounded.

"If the video had been released to the defense and seen by the jury, I have no doubt Ted would've been acquitted."

Robyn choked on a sob, this extraordinary turn of events hard to believe. Still, the unfortunate outcome of Ted's case robbed him years of his life because of the plea deal he took, his sacrifice deliberate and all for her.

"Even if the prosecutor didn't act intentionally, a judge

can declare a mistrial since the error rendered the proceeding fundamentally unfair to Ted. This has been an unmitigated tragedy that must be set right. Once we get the wheels in motion, Ted will be acquitted and have no more parole or community service moving forward. His record would be wiped clean. He'd be done."

"He'd be a free man, Matlock."

Robyn was taken aback by her father's use of the word 'free.' That's all Teddy ever talked about since he came home—freedom. Teddy had been through hell with the grueling trial, and the harsh sentence Judge Danforth handed down. There was a denied appeal, five years behind bars, another year in a halfway house, probation, and community service. And now out of nowhere, surveillance footage suddenly appears, the proof they needed since the very beginning. Enough was enough.

"The easiest thing we can do now is file a complaint with the State Bar of Georgia and present the surveillance evidence. I'm already on it," her father said.

"Yes, with your father's help representing Ted again, and with the new evidence, I think we can make a convincing argument about why Ted needs to be acquitted, especially after everything that's happened recently," Sam added. "It will be up to the judge's discretion assigned to the case. But I think Ted's chances are pretty high because he's already paid restitution serving jail time, and he came to the aid of an officer, me, during a fight. Ted has suffered enough, the injustice pretty clear cut after what's happened to him. A continued probation sentence would only have a negative effect on him physically and mentally. And we certainly don't want that."

Robyn hung on to every word coming out of Sam's

mouth. "So, how does this work? You said we file a complaint?"

"Yes." Mr. Morgan nodded, the two girls looking his way. "I'll notify the district attorney of our petition, and once all the paperwork has been filed, the court will set a date for a virtual hearing, at which time I'll be able to argue the case for acquittal. The prosecutor has the option to oppose the motion, but I don't believe that will happen in this case. Once both sides have been heard, the judge will make a final decision."

"Okay. Will Ted have to appear in court again?" Robyn asked.

Sam jumped in with her findings, pulling a pad of notes from her purse. "I don't think so. This is all done nowadays through technology, emails, and phone calls. Once we get things rolling, I think that's it. When he's acquitted, he'd be done, and he'll never have to report to me again, unless he wants to tell me funny stories about his brother, James," she joked.

Robyn giggled. She genuinely liked Sam, even if she was Ted's parole officer. And if Ted was acquitted, Sam and James could make a go of it as a real couple without her getting into any trouble.

"What about Mrs. Kirby? Could she oppose this? Does she have a say?"

"Absolutely not," Sam reassured. "Believe it or not, Mrs. Kirby is the one who told me about the surveillance video. Apparently she told Ted about it too, on the night of the Harvest Hoedown."

"Teddy knew about this? Wh… why didn't he say anything?"

"He didn't have time," her dad replied. "After the

Hoedown fight and being carted off to jail again where he was beaten, there just wasn't any time."

Robyn was overwhelmed with the fire-hose blast of information, the mere mention of that night filling her with sorrow. She was impressed with her father's willingness to do right by Ted. She was also floored by Sam's due diligence but wondered what her motive was.

"Why are you doing this, Sam?"

Sam dipped her head, her profile pretty and her cheeks blotting with color. "I knew the second I met Ted, his family, and you that y'all were special. And something never felt right about Ted's case. I don't usually get this involved with my parolees, but after getting to know James and learning more about Ted's story and studying his file, I couldn't look the other way."

"Judge Danforth made an example out of Ted; we all know that," Mr. Morgan added. "Everyone in the courtroom was floored by Ted's harsh sentencing, especially after taking a plea deal to keep your record clean. I'd never seen anything like it in all my years of practice. The jury deemed Ted an accessory to the crime, especially after he drove away from the scene. He was labeled, 'the getaway driver.' But Ted came back after he knew what happened, and now we have viable proof with the surveillance footage."

Sam nodded. "You and Ted knew your friends were up to something that night, but you never saw the gun until after the fact. Both of you never voluntarily participated in Ethan and Max's prank gone wrong."

Mr. Morgan sighed. "Unfortunately, y'all were at the wrong place at the wrong time, Ted's punishment excessively severe."

Sam concurred. "Yes. It was a terrible outcome for Ted. An unreasonable sentence for a crime he didn't commit."

"Detestable," Robyn snarled. She still couldn't wrap her head around such a harsh punishment. "But why didn't you tell me sooner, Sam? I could've been helping you somehow."

Sam leaned closer, gripping Robyn's wrist with gentleness. "I didn't want to add any more stress to what you're already going through while Ted recovers in the hospital. I mean, the research was easy, and then I talked to your dad a couple of times."

Robyn glanced at her father, who nodded.

Sam continued with earnest. "After bringing my findings to your dad, we both agreed we have a darn good chance to get the conviction set aside." She hesitated. "But you should know, there is another caveat to all this."

"What?" Robyn held her breath.

"You asked me if Ted would have to appear in court again, and I told you no. But I take it back. He may have to appear not for himself but for another reason altogether."

Robyn's heart fell to her stomach, her angst turning up a notch. She instantly knew the reason. "Glen Kirby."

Sam nodded.

Her father shifted in his chair, the low voice he used in the courtroom gaining Robyn's attention. "Mrs. Kirby brought her son, Glen, to the Harvest Hoedown. Glen will be held accountable, culpable for any damages moving forward if the Bennett family decides they want to proceed with their own charges. If there's a trial, Ted may be subpoenaed as a witness as to what went down the night in the barn. If charges are filed against Glen Kirby, we have to be prepared for potential push-back or a possible delay regarding the conviction complaint filed with the State Bar of Georgia."

"Does Roy know about any of this?" Robyn asked.

"I've told Roy I'll do my best to keep Ted out of jail for a possible parole violation. But remember, until we can get the conviction set aside, he's still technically on parole. Absurd but true. But Roy doesn't know about the surveillance evidence yet," Sam explained. "I wanted to talk to you, first. And if you ask me, I think we have one hell of a chance with this."

Robyn smiled for the first time all day, her dad and Sam reciprocating. Somehow, she always believed there was a way to free Teddy early, or in this case, in the eleventh hour. She never imagined it would take over six years and a brutal beating before the nightmare might finally end. Teddy could be a free man with no record at all if things finally went their way. He just needed to pull through and get better. To see the look of joy on his healed face was everything she ever wished for.

The legs of a chair scrapped across the tiled floor as Sam stood and rested her hands on her hips. "Well then, it looks like we've got some work to do. You up for it, Matlock?"

Robyn snickered quietly at the nickname coming out of Sam's mouth. For some odd reason, she wasn't bothered by it anymore. She stood right next to her, determined to see this through.

"Absolutely."

# Chapter Twenty-Four

## TEDDY

Ted heard the voices again, familiar and emotional whispers urging him to wake up. But he was awake, wasn't he? He just couldn't speak, his throat constricted, and the pain... God, the unfathomable pain. Flashbacks of his life filtered in and out of his consciousness, many of the memories lighthearted and full of love—so much love.

He fell into a deep sleep, where warmth penetrated his being, the sound of his mother's laughter filling the air. He was running after her in slow motion through the fields beyond the red barn, where the late-blooming wildflowers of Indian summer peppered the earth in an explosion of color. Every so often, his mother turned to see him gaining on her, the smile on her face dimpled and beautiful. She reached back, their fingertips brushing for a fleeting moment before she surged several yards ahead of him. He grew tired and frustrated, mad he couldn't catch her in their little game. Stopping, he sulked among the tall, spindly flowers, the magnificent North Georgia Mountains rising up beyond the horizon. The air around him hushed and stilled.

"*Mama*?" he hollered, hoping she would stop. His voice echoed in his ears.

She paused and turned around, her smile replaced with a poignant expression. A gentle breeze blew her hair back from her face, orbs of sunlight causing her skin to glow. He noticed a ringlet of flowers on her head, a craft she and Becky loved to partake in. Placing both hands over her heart with tenderness, his mother's wedding ring glinted in the light. Ted slowly blinked against the brightness, and when he opened his eyes again, she was gone…

---

Ted moaned, his mouth unusually parched. The primal need for a sip of water was on the forefront of his mind.

"Teddy?" he heard his father say.

It took everything in Ted's power to force his eyelids open; the images surrounding him shadowed and hazy until his eyes adjusted to the overhead lights, and he was able to focus.

"Dad?" His voice was—what the hell happened to his voice? His throat felt like it was layered with sandpaper, raw and dehydrated.

"I'm here, son. We're all here."

Ted groaned. "Water?"

His father spoke quietly to someone else in the room, the face of a very pretty lady coming into his view. Her expression was kind, her dark eyes warm and compassionate. Tendrils of curly brown hair framed her features, and the clothes she wore were plain and powder blue.

"Welcome back, Mr. Bennett. My name is Lacy, your attending nurse. I'm gonna raise your bed a little bit so you can take a few sips of water." The tone of her voice soothed him as he lay perfectly still. The bed moved slowly, the mechanical components humming as the mattresses lifted, giving him a better view to take in his surroundings, his body aching and his mind groggy. His father was the only other person in the sterile white room, patiently staying out of Lacy's way.

"There we are." The bed stopped, and Ted sighed. The pretty lady brought a large cup up to his mouth, gently positioning a straw to his lips. "Just a few sips. I don't want you to overdo it on your first try, okay?"

Ted attempted a nod, but the ache in his head and neck were too debilitating. His lips trembled as he opened his mouth, the first sip of water sliding down his throat cool and refreshing.

"It's… good," he croaked in-between swallows.

"Yes, it is," Lacy smiled.

He watched with disappointment as she set the cup down on a nearby table, not able to vocalize he wasn't quite finished. That's when he noticed all the machines surrounding the bed and scowled.

His father came closer and bent low, kissing him with fondness on the cheek. "Teddy, I'm so glad you're awake."

Ted frowned. "What happened?"

Roy glanced at Lacy, the nurse nodding. She patted Ted on the arm. "I'll let your dad fill you in while I go and get the doctor. He's gonna be mighty happy to see you're finally awake." The door closed with a thump as Roy pulled a chair closer to the bed and sat.

"I… thought you said… everyone was here?" Ted's words came out slow, the very act of speaking laborious and difficult.

With his father in close proximity, his appearance was concerning. He looked tired, the wrinkles around his eyes pronounced from the fluorescent lighting in the room. "They're all here in the waiting room. Do you remember anything?"

Ted raised his hand to stroke his beard, but there was nothing but stubble across his cheeks. Fingering the sides of his head, he was confused by the feel of gauzy fabric.

"Son, you've been in a coma for over a week. The doctors had to stitch up a few places on your head and face. But you're on your way to a full recovery." His tone was upbeat.

"A... coma?" His foggy brain couldn't quite compute the word.

"Yes. What's the last thing you remember before you woke up a few minutes ago?"

"I... I was with Mom."

His father paled, moving closer. "Go on."

Ted licked his lips, the images fresh in his mind. "We were in the meadow. You know, the one near the big oak, where she's buried? I was... running after her. But she was too fast."

Roy nodded. "What else?"

Ted concentrated on his breathing—in and out, in and out.

"She... stopped. And then she pressed her hands over her heart. It was like... she told me she loved me but didn't want me to follow her anymore." Ted paused, taking a few deep breaths. "Does that make any sense?"

His dad pressed his calloused hand over his and squeezed. "It wasn't your time, son."

"My... time?" he questioned.

Roy changed the subject. "Do you remember anything else?"

Ted closed his eyes, doing his best to ponder his recent

past. A flash of something crossed his mind—an image of Hank. His younger brother was singing on a stage, the bright lights and loud music echoing through Ted's senses.

"I remember... Hank-ster. He was... singing?"

"That's right. His band performed at the Harvest Hoedown. Can you recall anything about that night?" Roy seemed to hold his breath.

Ted furrowed his brow, another image coming to mind. His chest rose in a sharp air intake, flashes of sexy long legs in blue and tan leather cowboy boots coming to mind.

"Robyn?"

Roy nodded. "Yes. She's here."

"She is?" Ted edged his way to the side of the bed, the tube snaking out of his arm pulling taught.

Roy came to his aid, urging him to lay back. "You're too weak, Teddy. You go on and lay back down. I'll bring her to you. How does that sound?"

The exertion from his actions made him dizzy, and he was thankful for his father's offer. "Okay," he exhaled.

The pain in his ribcage was excruciating, and he wondered what other places on his body had suffered. He still wasn't sure how he got hurt or why he was in a hospital room; his recollection jumbled in cloudy bits and pieces. His father mentioned the Harvest Hoedown, snippets from the night hard to decipher. There was Hank and his music, Robyn and her boots, but what else? Wracking his brain, he suddenly remembered barbeque, the visceral memory of hickory smoke infiltrating his nose instantly. And... square-dancing? Yes. He attempted to square-dance with Robyn in a big group on the dance floor—the same floor they assembled the day before. There was laughter. So much laughter. And then what?

With his eyes pressed shut, he felt himself fading, the

edges of his mind going dark. His body felt light as a feather as he drifted into a deep sleep.

His arm tingled, the back-and-forth movement of fingers drawing tiny circles against his skin causing him to stir. Inhaling a deep breath, he opened his eyes, his gaze immediately landing on Robyn, who sat mere inches beside him. She was so beautiful—an angel in disguise. Could she hear his heart thrumming in double time being so near? His natural instinct was to reach out and touch her. But his efforts were thwarted by his condition.

The corners of his mouth turned up into a tired smile as he stared at her. "Hi, gorgeous," he mustered.

"Hi." Her green eyes sparkled like precious jewels, and tears coursed down her cheeks. Her loving expression and close presence filled him with hope.

"Please, don't cry." He followed Robyn's gaze across the room and noticed his father sitting in the corner.

"Hey, Teddy," he waved. "How are you feeling, buddy?"

Ted sighed, the ache in his weary body depleted of energy. "Not too good, Dad. I'm thirsty again."

Roy stood and came over to where Robyn was sitting. With the press of a button, the bed began to slowly rise, bringing Ted into an upright position again. "Lacy instructed me to only give you a few sips, Teddy. Robyn can help you."

Ted felt powerless, his body betraying him. He wanted to fold Robyn into his arms and kiss her hard on the mouth. But he could barely keep his eyes open. She held the straw to his lips, and he sipped, their eyes locked in an intense stare of longing. There wasn't a stitch of makeup on her face, and her golden hair was braided to the side. She reminded him of when they were in high school—young and fresh-faced, innocent and stunning. But there was something else, too: a shadow of worry clouding her features.

Rolling his hand over with his palm facing up, he was thankful when she placed her small hand into his. He squeezed her fingers. "How long has it been, Robyn?"

She squeezed back. "Over a week."

"Tell me… everything."

Concern etched her features, and she looked at Roy again, who gave her the go-ahead with a quick nod. "You can tell him, darlin'."

Robyn's voice was calm and quiet. Ted listened intently to every single word coming out of her lush mouth. Everything she told him was familiar, details about the Harvest Hoedown like puzzle pieces being put together to form the story in its entirety. When she mentioned Mrs. Kirby, Ted tensed, heat flushing his face. Robyn must have sensed his reaction because she stopped and gently cupped his cheek.

"Is it too much? Do you need me to stop? How about another sip of water?"

"No. I… I remember now. There was a fight."

Roy stood behind Robyn and placed his hand on her shoulder. "That's right. Glen Kirby was the instigator, remember?"

Ted closed his eyes, the enormity of his circumstances weighing heavy on his heart. He knew Glen was at fault, but so was he. None of this would've happened if his boot hadn't made contact with Glen's groin at the hoedown. Better yet, none of this would have transpired if he hadn't gone on that beer run so long ago. His hand fisted at his side, remembering when his knuckles slammed into the man's face.

"I'm going back to jail, aren't I?"

"Not necessarily," Robyn soothed. There was a thread of solace woven between her words, the broad smile blossoming across her face unexpected. "We have a plan, Teddy. A plan to get you acquitted."

"What?" He looked at his father, who nodded.

"Robyn's dad filed the motion. You've been through enough, Teddy. You've paid your penance."

"But... how is this even... possible?" he asked in stuttered words.

Robyn could hardly contain her excitement. "Sam found out about surveillance video not admitted in the trial."

Ted had a flashback of Mrs. Kirby talking about the video the night of the hoedown. "Yes... I remember. Mrs. Kirby mentioned it the night I saw her. I was... going to tell you about it but things got out of hand."

His dad leaned low, his voice warbled with emotion. "Well, we're on it now. Do you know what this means? No more parole, no more community service. You can work at the winery again. Hell, you can even have a glass of Bennett Farms Cabernet if you want," he chuckled.

Ted allowed the words to sink in. "I'll finally be... free?"

Robyn nodded vigorously, her answer breathy and heartfelt. "Yes."

His head started to throb, the overload of information too much to process. "I have... so many questions."

"Don't worry about it now. You need to concentrate on getting better so you can come back home where you belong." His father seemed resolute.

Ted mulled the word around in his head again.

*Free.*

Could he dare believe freedom was even possible? His energy waned, thinking about turning the page on this horror story. He held on to the faintest glimmer of hope his happily-ever-after was within reach, his emotions startling and hovering in his periphery.

Ted was overcome, choking back his feelings and reaching for both of them. As they held hands, a new sense of optimism washed over him, the release of his pent-up worry a catharsis. Never in a million years did he expect to be purged from this burden. Liberation dared to spill into his chest, pooling and trickling all over him. And through it all, he'd somehow managed to stay alive.

An image came to his mind, the dream he had earlier a prophecy. He understood the message now, his dear mother urging him to stay behind. And now, here he was—on the cusp of becoming a free man with the love of his life by his side.

And he knew exactly what he had to do. He had to keep breathing in and out. He had to feed his body, sleep when he was tired, and recover from his injuries. He had to stay alive—because the sun would rise again tomorrow.

And that's when the real work and healing would begin.

# Chapter Twenty-Five

## ROBYN

"Hold still," Robyn giggled, combing Ted's short hair in place. She was tender in her actions, careful near the area where a four-inch scar peaked out from underneath his recent haircut. Ted continued running his hands down her sides each time she lifted her arms until she settled across his lap. He winced ever so slightly.

"I can't finish with you tickling me," she admonished with a flirty smile.

Ted grabbed her chin, puckering her lips and pulling her forward into a kiss. "Mmmmm," he moaned.

Robyn pulled back and marveled at his clean-shaven face. She was still getting used to his cropped hair and the absence of his whiskers since he was discharged from the hospital a few weeks earlier and recovering at Bennett Farms. But his fresh appearance wasn't the only thing she was coming to terms with. She eyed the cane leaned against the porch rail of the main house, the device aiding Teddy as he continued to heal from his broken ankle.

Through a series of events in the few weeks since he'd

been released from the hospital, Ted's probation termination was pending, in limbo because of a subpoena. Sure enough, he was ordered to appear in court to testify in Glen Kirby's assault trial brought on by charges filed by Sheriff Jenkins. The trial was a formality, holding up the motion to set aside his conviction, keeping Ted from being free and clear of his probation and community service hours. Although the prosecutor did not oppose the motion when the original paperwork was filed, the assigned judge wanted to wait until after Glen's trial to offer a final verdict.

"Are you sure I'm not hurting you, sitting on your lap?" Robyn asked.

Ted shook his head, his dark eyes soft and alluring. "No. I like having you this close to me. You're very kissable." He palmed her cheek and pecked her mouth again, sweeping her long hair over her shoulder.

The front door opened, and Jaxson and Delia bolted outside in a flash of yellow and sable fur. Their nails clicked across the weathered boards of the porch as they leapt onto the grass and cantered across the lawn. James and Sam came behind the big dogs, stopping to greet Ted and Robyn.

"Y'all ready?" James asked. He was dressed in a suit, the navy color matching Sam's pretty dress.

Robyn wrapped her arms protectively around Teddy's neck as she continued to sit on his lap, pressing her face against his smooth cheek. The two of them looked up at the couple with appreciation, Sam a regular visitor to Bennett Farms.

"Totally ready, right Teddy?" Robyn kissed his cheek and was about to stand when he pulled her back snugly into his arms.

"Don't get up," he murmured, his warm breath tickling the shell of her ear. "Not yet."

Hank burst onto the porch, his tie halfway knotted, pleading with James to help him. "I don't know how to tie this thing. Help!"

James chuckled and angled his brother to better view the silk garment around his neck. "Cross the wide end over the thin end first, Hank. Like this." He was quick with his fingers, knotting the tie perfectly under his brother's chin.

Hank looked uncomfortable, sticking a finger between the tie and the fabric of his white button-down shirt, trying to get some slack. "Geez, Jimmy. You got it too tight."

"It's perfect, Hank. You're just not used to it," he laughed.

Robyn watched the scene unfold, content to be in Teddy's strong arms. "You boys look handsome in suits and ties," she offered. "Y'all clean up real nice."

Hank turned and offered a boyish grin, his wavy hair hanging over one eye. The poor guy wasn't used to the corporate apparel, his usual attire tight tees, tighter blue jeans, and cowboy boots. "Thanks, Robyn."

Walt, Becky, and Roy were the last ones to come out of the house, the entire family dressed in their Sunday best. Roy held his signature black hat in one hand and held the door open for Becky. Ted's sister wore a floral long-sleeved dress, her hair pulled back into a tight bun at the nape of her neck. Roy seemed to notice Robyn sitting on Ted's lap and frowned. She immediately stood and fetched Ted's cane, helping him to his feet.

"You got it?" she asked.

"I've got it," he smiled, his hand gripping the top of the thick stick. He still had weeks of physical therapy to endure, his ribs finally on the mend after the terrible beating he suffered. His ankle was healing nicely, out of the cast and in a cumbersome black boot for extra protection.

Robyn sighed, the sight of Teddy in his gray suit leaving her speechless. Even with the prominent scar across his head and another one branded under his right eye, he was still the most handsome man she had ever laid eyes on. His short hair appeared darker, and his lips fuller without all the whiskers. Standing on her tiptoes, she gave him a quick peck. "Come on, I'll help you down the steps."

Walt quickly came to his brother's aid, his suit fitting his toned body like a glove. "I've got him, Robyn."

She took a step back and watched the brotherly love in real-time. Walt held onto Ted by the elbow and patiently helped him down the stairs, one step at a time to the pathway leading them to their cars. The change in Walter was remarkable since Ted came home from the hospital. He was always around to help in any way. Walt took his brother to physical therapy three times a week, challenging him to push himself and always encouraging him with his efforts to get stronger—better. Robyn had to admit, she held a soft spot in her heart for Walt now, their previous disdain replaced with genuine respect.

Sam approached Robyn and smiled. "This is it. Today is the day."

"The day of reckoning," Robyn humorously quipped, trying to keep it together.

Sam nodded. "Seriously, I have a good feeling we'll be celebrating Ted's freedom real soon."

"From your mouth to God's ears," Robyn replied.

James affectionately palmed Sam's lower back. "We'll see you at the courthouse, Robyn."

"See you there."

Walt and Hank managed to get Ted into the Jeep

without too much trouble, Robyn taking the wheel. They could've ridden with James and Sam in her sedan, but Ted was adamant he wanted to ride in the car he shared with Robyn. She knew it made him feel more like himself and was glad no one fussed about it.

"You guys want to ride with us?" she asked his brothers.

Walt shook his head; his tone turned humorous. "No way. Not unless Teddy's driving." His grin was clownish, comically exposing his white teeth. She knew he was teasing and waved him off with an exaggerated eye roll. Hank pushed Walt toward Roy's pickup truck, slapping him across the back and laughing aloud.

The convoy of vehicles picked up dust on the gravel road, passing under the heavy-gauge steel Bennett Farms sign. The gardenia bushes on either side of the entrance to the farm lay dormant in the season, and the tall Georgia pines stood proudly, casting long slanted shadows across the windshield. Robyn gripped the steering wheel and glanced over at Teddy. He seemed lost in thought, staring out the window at the autumnal view of the trees and meadows whizzing by the roadside.

"Hey," she said, gaining his attention.

He looked over at her and smiled, his features chiseled and perfect in the natural light. Ted was different since the altercation, his easy-going countenance reminding her of their high school and college days. She so hoped no setbacks were looming ahead.

"This is all a formality. Remember, my dad said it's unlikely Judge Danforth will be the presiding judge today."

"I know," he replied.

"And you're only giving your side of the story as a witness if you're called to. It's not about you today. And don't forget, my dad will be sitting next to you, as your lawyer, representing you if you need him," she added softly.

Ted reached across the Jeep interior and lightly stroked his fingers down her cheek. "Truth be told, I'd rather have you represent me."

"Yes, Teddy, but I'm not a lawyer."

"But you still could be. You should be."

Robyn didn't answer him right away, her dreams of becoming an attorney still on the back burner. "You know as well as I do, your testimony today will get you on the other side of this. I mean, I know you don't want to testify, but you might have to because you were subpoenaed. I also know you have no intentions of ever filing charges against Glen. And I still don't understand why."

Ted sighed. "I know you don't understand. I don't expect you to. The guilt I feel for what went down that night long ago will never go away. Fast-forward to today, and I don't blame Glen for anything. He misses his brother, Joe. I miss Joe. I would've probably done the same thing if I were in his shoes..."

"You would've beaten the shit out of him?" she interrupted, her blood pressure rising.

"Probably. I don't know..." Ted pinched his lips between his fingers. "I... I can't explain it, Robyn. I just... understand. Can you please let it go? I have."

Robyn was mute, a shot of empathy stinging her heart. Even though she knew she'd never fully understood what was going on in that hard head of Ted's, she had to let her anger go. They were silent, the thrum of the Jeep engine driving over the asphalt road filling the void.

Robyn's thoughts diverted to Glen Kirby. He and his bully cronies would have their day in court. Even though Ted hadn't pressed any charges against the three men who hurt him, Sheriff Jenkins did because it happened to one of his own, Samantha McNeil. It also happened to Ted on his watch at his station. Ted was a victim to a crime on government property; aggravated assault and battery, pure and simple. The penalty for the felony conviction in Georgia included a fine of up to one-hundred thousand dollars, jail time up to twenty years, and full compensation to the victims. Robyn wanted vengeance, but then again, she wanted all of this to be over.

"I love you," Teddy announced.

Robyn blushed. She glanced at Ted, batting her lashes. "You know, I love you, too."

"You've always been there for me through everything."

Robyn nodded, his words conjuring up images of him alone in his jail cell, holding her photo in his hands. He only recently opened up to her about some of the details of his life behind bars, the picture she'd secretly slipped in-between the pages of his Bible a source of comfort for him all those years. He was right. During his darkest hours, she was with him in spirit, the love they shared healing energy —a lifeline they clung to until they could be together again. And here they were, finally on the cusp of the end. Or was it the beginning? It didn't matter, as long as they ended up together.

The parade of cars drove in front of the old courthouse, the limestone building with large columns dating back to the 1800s. Robyn spotted her father on the front steps, his energetic wave instigating a surge of optimism through her being. With the Jeep parked in the side lot, she leaned toward Teddy and tenderly ran her fingertips through his short sideburns. His features turned soft, his lips parting in a slow exhale.

"Do you have any idea the things I want to do with you?" he asked.

Robyn raised her brows as her lower region pooled with heat. It'd been a long time since they fooled around, his recovery coming first. She leaned across the middle console and peppered his mouth with feather-light kisses. "I have a right mind to do a few things of my own with you, too."

Teddy chuckled.

The other Bennett's exited their vehicles, congregating near the liftgate of Roy's pickup truck. Walt made his way to the passenger side of the Jeep, ready to help Ted exit the car in his bulky boot. "We need to get a move on, Teddy…"

Ted ignored his brother on the other side of the door, his fierce gaze pinning Robyn with a look she knew well: one part mad love, the other part perseverant. Without a doubt, she knew Ted Bennett was a man who would never, ever give up.

"Robyn, whatever happens in there, I want you to know… you're all I want."

Robyn traced his lips with her fingers. He grabbed her hand and kissed the tips of her digits, his eyes never leaving hers. "Do you hear me? You're all I've ever needed."

Her heart swelled, thankful for his passion, knowing precisely what he meant. Theirs was a love story that could have ended in tragedy. But with the help of Divine Intervention, her father, Samantha McNeil, and the entire Bennett family, they were on the cusp of unfathomable joy. If all went according to plan inside the courtroom today, she could finally love Teddy freely with all of her heart and soul.

Walt knocked on the window, his brow furrowed with annoyance. "Come on, Ted. You don't want to be late for this." When he tried to open the door, it was locked. "Come on, unlock the door."

Hank came up next to his brother and cupped his hand over his eyes, peering through the tinted windows. "Y'all good in there?"

Ted never broke his gaze with Robyn's as he held her hand pressed against his lips.

"Are you okay, Teddy?" she asked, concerned by his hesitation to exit the vehicle.

His smile rivaled the setting sun over the North Georgia Mountains. "Better than okay. I have you."

She slipped her arms around his neck and pulled him forward into a hug, making sure she was gentle in her actions.

Walt shouted, "Get a room!" as the entire Bennett family surrounded the Jeep with smiling faces.

Ted combed his fingers through the sides of her hair, his mouth connecting with hers in a deep and meaningful kiss. And that's when Robyn knew.

No matter what happened in court, no one could ever keep them apart again.

# Chapter Twenty-Six

## TEDDY

Ted sat next to Robyn's father with his hands fisted in his lap as he tried to tamper his nerves. Sheriff Jenkins sat on the other side of him in full uniform, his fingers drumming on his thigh. Clark Kennedy, the District Attorney, and the lawyer representing the Kirby family sat across the aisle, both formidable men shuffling papers back and forth. Ted glanced over his shoulder at the rest of his family quietly sitting behind him. Next to Walt, Robyn offered a fragile smile, her angelic face filling him with a sure calmness. A colossal wall clock indicated the time, and Ted anxiously rolled his neck around. Glen Kirby was out on bond, he and his mother missing from the equation.

As if sensing Ted's rising anxiety, Mr. Morgan leaned closer to him and whispered, "Don't worry, we can't start this without them. And if Glen doesn't show up at all, he'll be in contempt of court."

A few seconds later, the door opened, and in walked Glen Kirby with his mother by his side. The guy wore a black suit and bold red tie, the scowl on his face broody and mean as if he had something to prove. Ted slowly exhaled the breath he'd been holding, urging himself to remain composed. His mid-section ached from the tension, the residual effect of his broken ribs a reminder of why they were here in the first place.

It was odd being in the same drab courtroom again, the harsh sentencing imposed by Judge Danforth six years ago something he would have nightmares about for the rest of his life. Gritting his teeth, he remained steadfast, knowing he wasn't the one on trial this time. They were here for a different reason: he was a potential witness called to appear in Glen Kirby's aggravated assault and battery case.

Mrs. Kirby glanced at him before she settled next to her son, her words mumbled and nervous toward the attorneys. "I'm so sorry we're late. Please forgive me."

Ted was ready to move on with the hearing, prepared to get the formalities over with so he could go back to his life. The bailiff entered the courtroom from a side door and spoke loudly, indicating things were about to start.

"All rise. The Court of the Second Judicial Circuit, Criminal Division, is now in session, the Honorable Judge Danforth presiding in place of Judge Francis today."

Ted's shocked inhale of breath was audible, his heart free-falling to his feet. An ominous feeling filled his senses. This was not happening. A murmured wave of disturbed, whispered voices rolled through the crowd as a specific sinister word filtered through his head: retaliation.

Everyone stood as the white-haired elderly man with a gruff exterior entered the room and sat behind the bench, his very presence dominant and intimidating. "Please, be seated."

"I thought you said it was a different judge presiding today," Ted whispered tersely to Mr. Morgan.

"I know. It was supposed to be Judge Francis. Something must've happened, and they called Judge Danforth to fill in."

The judge addressed the courtroom with precision. "Good morning, ladies and gentlemen. Calling the case of the People of the State of Georgia versus Glen Franklin Kirby. Are both sides ready?"

"Ready for the People, Your Honor," the District Attorney responded.

"Ready for the Defense, Your Honor," the Kirby lawyer added.

Glen and his lawyer were summoned to the front of the courtroom, where Judge Danforth swore him in. "State your full name, please."

"Glen Franklin Kirby."

"You do solemnly swear that the testimony you shall give in the matter now pending between yourself and the People of the State of Georgia shall be the truth, the whole truth, and nothing but the truth, so help you, God?"

"Yes, sir," Glen mumbled unconvincingly.

"Very good. Let's proceed." The judge looked over his notes and frowned. "Mr. Kirby, you are charged with aggravated assault and battery but have chosen to plead down to a lesser charge of simple assault and battery. And how do you plead?"

Glen stood with cocky sureness, jutting his chin into the air with gusto. "Guilty, your honor."

Judge Danforth glared, swiping his glasses from his face. "You struck an officer of the law, Mr. Kirby. And the officer was a female, Miss Samantha McNeil. I must say, this is a despicable act. Do you find it thrilling to strike a woman?" A hush settled over the courtroom, all eyes trained on Glen.

"No, sir. It was an accident, in the heat of the moment."

"I see. And your behavior continued in the county jail that night, injuring Mr...." The judge's eyes grew wide with recognition. "Mr. Theodore Bennett." The judge paused, searching the front row in the courtroom, his shoulders rising in a deep sigh as he focused on Ted before continuing.

Ted held his breath, praying the judge couldn't hear his heart pounding franticly like a bass drum. Leave it to the small-town police department and judges of Langston Falls to totally mess up his life. Or maybe he was just the unluckiest guy on the planet.

Referring to his notes, the judge continued. "Mr. Kirby, it says here you rendered Mr. Bennett comatose for over a week. Care to enlighten this courtroom regarding your callous behavior? Now's your chance to get your side of the story on record."

Ted watched Glen's hands fist against his sides. "I'm sorry, Your Honor," he whined. "When I saw Ted after all these years on the night of the festival, something snapped inside me. All I could see was the man who murdered my brother..."

Mr. Morgan stood. "Sorry, your honor, I know I'm not a party to this action but for the record, Ted Bennett did *not* murder Glen's brother."

"Sustained," Judge Danforth growled. Putting his glasses back over his eyes, he read from the piece of paper. "Mr. Kirby, did you know Samantha McNeil is Theodore Bennett's parole officer assigned to his case?"

"No, sir, I did not know that."

"I see." Judge Danforth looked Ted's way again, squinting as if figuring out his next calculated move. "Tell me, Mr. Kirby. Did Mr. Bennett provoke you in any way?"

Glen shot Ted an evil look. "No, sir."

"Did Theodore Bennett retaliate after witnessing you strike Miss McNeil?"

Glen perked up. "Yes… yes, he did, sir. Ted punched me in the face and the nuts."

A hushed chuckle erupted from the Bennett brothers, Glen's face turning red. He looked over his shoulder at them, his expression filled with hate.

"I see. And later, in the county jail, you took full advantage of the situation when you were both locked in the same holding cell, didn't you, Mr. Kirby. You wanted revenge against Mr. Bennett?"

"I… I was angry. I miss my brother."

Judge Danforth nodded. "My decision here is final today. No need to draw this one out. I hereby sentence you, Glen Franklin Kirby, to two months of community service and a one-thousand dollar fine. The court also requires financial restitution to Samantha McNeil and Theodore Bennett for all medical bills incurred due to your negligence. You will pay these amounts in full." He slammed his gavel indicating Glen's sentencing was over.

Ted eyed his lawyer, Mr. Morgan, who offered a quick nod. It couldn't be that easy. Was it all over? Hardly.

"Right this way, Mr. Kirby." The bailiff ushered Glen back to his seat.

Judge Danforth cleared his throat. "Regardless of the fact this is not on the docket, Mr. DA, I would like to move forward with a probationer violation hearing as to Mr. Theodore Bennett. We can't have this type of behavior, this taking the law into one's own hand, and by a felon no doubt —not in my district."

"Can he do this?" Ted whispered frantically toward Mr. Morgan.

He shrugged. "Unfortunately, Judges can do anything

they want in their courtrooms. We can report him to judicial standards after the fact."

Like that would help anything. Ted licked his lips, knowing he was about to be drilled by the overtly harsh judge. He stood with wobbly knees when the bailiff motioned for him and his lawyer to approach the bench. He glanced over at Robyn for a quick boost of bravery.

"For the record, your honor, I object to these proceedings, for a lack of notice and due process," Mr. Morgan complained.

"Denied."

Somehow, Judge Danforth could make that word hold all the contempt in the world. Ted steeled himself for what was to come as Mr. Morgan leaned over and asked, "Do you want to testify? Try and explain? It is a risk but your right."

"I do." The last time he was in this courtroom he had stayed silent and allowed the attorneys to handle things. Look where that had gotten him.

"Your honor, I would like to call my client to the stand in his own defense."

Ted walked through the gate separating the audience from the participants. To his surprise, Robyn followed right behind, the bailiff stopping her.

"Sorry ma'am, only officers of the court, attorneys and such in front of the bar."

Teddy took the stand and watched Robyn sit back down on the front row of watchers with obvious trepidation. He was touched by her bravery, and knew full well she was feeling angry and helpless by this turn of events, only wanting to be near him for support.

"State your full name, please."

"Theodore Charles Bennett."

"You do solemnly swear that the evidence you shall give in the matter now pending between yourself and the People of the State of Georgia shall be the truth, the whole truth, and nothing but the truth, so help you, God?"

"Yes, Your Honor." Ted forced himself to take tiny breaths in and out, remaining quiet and submissive until asked a question.

"Mr. Bennett, it has come to my attention that you assaulted Mr. Glen Kirby, which in accordance with Georgia state laws, is a direct violation of your probation."

Samantha stood, inducing a glare full of annoyance from the judge. "Your Honor, Ted Bennett was defending *me*, an officer of the law therefore it's not a probation violation."

The entire courtroom came alive with outbursts from several family members in agreement with Sam's bold objection. Ted looked over at Glen, the man's wicked glare holding him captive. He had the audacity to smirk and used his index finger to slice across his throat. Ted knew right then he was in trouble.

"*Order*! Order in this court, or I'll have Miss McNeil in contempt!" Judge Danforth hollered, slamming his gavel hard. Everyone hushed, the judge's expression showing little to no sympathy. His icy demeanor was concerning, and Ted prepared himself for the worst. Somehow, the tables were turned, and he felt like he was the one on trial all over again.

Judge Danforth continued. "Mr. Bennett, my question is quick and to the point. Did you strike Mr. Glen Kirby while on probation?"

Ted felt every eyeball in the courtroom focused on him, the tension thick with injustice and shock, empathy and compassion. Swallowing hard, he stood tall, ready to face the inevitable and accept his fault.

"Yes, Your Honor. I hit Glen Kirby that night."

A hush settled over the crowd so quiet you could hear a pin drop. Judge Danforth's eyes squinted, his lips in a perpetual frown as he made a decision.

"Due to the circumstances of the evidence and sworn testimony of Theodore Charles Bennett, and the prior testimony of Mr. Glen Kirby, I hereby sentence Mr. Bennett to two weeks in the county jail for parole violation, to begin immediately. Sheriff he is in your custody."

Mr. Morgan stood to object to the farce of a hearing, But Judge Danforth announced, "This court is adjourned." He slammed his gavel with finality, the doomed resonance washing over Ted in a wave of utter shock. The soulless man hurriedly disappeared through the side door before all hell broke loose, the edges of his black robe flicking in a final, despicable wave.

The entire Bennett family was on their feet, vocally challenging the sentence with angry outbursts. The bailiff approached Ted and muttered a polite 'sorry' before turning him around and cuffing his hands behind his lower back in front of his family.

"Shit, Ted. I'm so sorry," Sheriff Jenkins apologized.

"It's not your fault," he appeased.

Mr. Morgan gripped Ted by the arm. "I'll get an appeal started immediately. This isn't the end, Ted. The good news is the motion filed to get you acquitted is in action. Fingers crossed it will go through now that this trial is over."

"Well, there's some good news."

Samantha edged herself closer to him among the hoopla and shook her head. "I can't believe this happened.

This wasn't supposed to go down this way. Judge Danforth doesn't give a shit about justice or officers of the law."

Ted turned mute, his eyes tracing the room for Robyn. He wasn't about to go into the slammer without saying goodbye. That's when he noticed his brother Walt angrily shoving his way through the crowd, his intense glare focused on Glen.

"*Walter, no!*" Ted shouted, jerking himself free from Mr. Morgan and the bailiff.

Glen was clueless, shaking hands with his team, the smug look of satisfaction on his face hard not to notice. Ted limped quickly toward the opposition with his hands handcuffed behind him, putting his body between Glen and his brother. "Don't do it, Walter. I'm begging you. He's not worth it."

Walt was wide-eyed, his face contorted with pain and anguish. "You can't go back to jail, Teddy. I won't let them take you back to jail!"

The bailiff held Ted solidly by the bicep, and Sheriff Jenkins put his hand against Glen's chest, pushing him back. Glen continued egging Walter on with snide remarks. "Come on, Walt, take a stab at me. I dare you! And believe me, I'll be pressing charges against you, too, so you can join your murdering brother behind bars!"

Ted whipped his head around and growled, "Stop it, Glen. Leave Walt out of this."

Roy and Robyn held Walt back by his arms as he surged, pleading for him to calm down.

"He's pushing your buttons, son. He's not worth it," Roy beseeched.

"Please, Walt, look at me!" Ted implored. "*Look at me!*" The veins in Walter's neck pulsed, his face flushed with rage as his eyes pooled with angry tears and finally focused. "It's only two weeks, you hear me? I can do anything for two weeks. I'll be back before you know it."

An obviously frazzled Mrs. Kirby and their lawyer escorted Glen out of the courtroom before Walt could strike, his last, gloating comment sealing Ted's fate. "You'll never have a normal life, Ted Bennett. As long as I live, you can count on it!"

"*Fuck you, Glen!*" Walt roared. "I hope you got a stash of cash to pay for my brother's hospital bills; otherwise, your family farm is ours!"

"You're not getting a dime from me, you stupid prick!" Glen countered.

Ted bumped up against his brother, preventing him from antagonizing Glen any further. The courtroom door slammed shut, and Ted captured his angry brother's attention once again. "Did you hear me, Walt? He's not worth it. I broke a rule with my parole, it's as simple as that. Let it play out so we can be on the other side of this. Two weeks is not the end of the world."

"I wanna kill that son-of-a-bitch," Walt seethed.

"I know. I know," Ted soothed. "But remember, Judge Danforth told Glen he has to pay for my hospital stay. You and I both know he doesn't have the kind of money to put a dent in those bills. He'll be in breach of court. Let this legally play out."

Walt swiped his hand under his nose and sniffled. "Alright. But you just say the word…"

"—Okay," Ted interrupted, doing everything in his handcuffed power to calm his brother down. "When I've got my list of provisions written out, I'll break out, and we can hobo our way across the country in an empty railroad car. Sound good?"

Walt did a double-take before he realized Ted was

joking. His broad shoulders lifted in a deep intake of air as he chuckled. James and Samantha calmly suggested he sit down.

Ted turned to the bailiff. "Can I least say goodbye to my family without the cuffs on?"

The bailiff thought for a second before he nodded. "Sure thing. But only for a minute."

"Thank you very much."

The bailiff unclasped the handcuffs around his wrists, freeing Ted for a few precious moments. Robyn stared at him, the look of shock evident on her face. "Come here, beautiful."

She shuffled into his embrace as Roy instructed the rest of the family to give them space. Ted inhaled the flowery aroma of her hair, memorizing every detail of her surrounding essence.

"You can visit me every day," he murmured, stroking her cheeks with the pads of his thumbs. "The county jail is right in the middle of town. You can come by on your lunch breaks. I'm sure Sheriff Jenkins won't mind. He owes me. It'll be fun."

Robyn forced a laugh from her lips, her warm breath skating across the skin of his neck as she hugged him. "Fun. Right."

Ted pulled back and swiped at a rogue tear slipping from the corner of her eye before palming her cheek. He tried to offer a smile of reassurance, but it morphed into a sad, apologetic display of longing. "I love you."

"I love you, too," she whispered, her voice warbled and on edge. "It's so unfair." A sob escaped her mouth as she flung herself into Ted's arms, holding on for dear life.

But he was the one clinging to her. And when his entire

family gathered around them, he felt their unconditional love—shrouding him with loyalty.

# Chapter Twenty-Seven

## TEDDY

It was hard for Ted to fall back into his old patterns, life behind bars a sort of dream-like state as the time ticked by at a snail's pace. The only positive thing this go-around was having Sheriff Jenkins as an ally, the cop sorrowful how things went down and doing his best to make Ted's two-week stay more comfortable.

"You let me know if you want the TV from my office. I hardly watch it anymore, and it might help pass the time."

Wearing an orange jumpsuit, Ted stood in front of the man and shook his head. "I appreciate it, Sheriff. But it's only two weeks. I don't need to lie around and watch TV."

The Sheriff nodded, resting his hands on his gun belt. He stood in the threshold of the tiny jail cell and looked around. "I'm so sorry, Ted. You don't deserve this."

"Yes, I do. I knew the rules, and I broke them."

"But you were protecting Sam. The judge should've made a concession in this case. Jesus, I'll never understand how this town keeps Danforth in office. He has no heart or soul."

Ted chuckled. "You're right about that. But he must think he's serving the community by doing his job to the best of his abilities. He's like a strict parent coming down hard. Maybe he'll lighten up in his old age."

Sheriff Jenkins laughed out loud. "He's already older than my grandmother's luggage." He paused, his broad chest rising in a deep inhale. "Whatever you need, just ask. Are you gonna be alright?"

"I'll be fine," Ted reassured.

The Sheriff nodded one last time before locking Ted in for the night. Lying back on the thin mattress atop a metal rail in the corner, he interlocked his hands behind his head and stared up at the drab ceiling. The déjà vu moments of confinement crept into his thoughts, and he remembered the first night he was locked up after Joe was killed. He was a young man back then, innocent and naïve, on the cusp of starting his life with Robyn by his side. They didn't have a care in the world—until their lives were turned upside down. He never saw it coming.

Ted cried a lot and prayed a great deal more those first few weeks, hoping his dad or Robyn would come and rescue him, that the whole ordeal was nothing but a horrible mistake. But then the weeks turned into months and the months into years. He reinvented himself behind those bars, closing off his feelings and shutting down his heart. It was better that way.

And now? His battered heart was wide open again, vulnerable and trusting. He could get through another two weeks of confinement—he had to. But moving forward, he needed to be careful. Glen Kirby was a ticking time bomb. It was obvious the guy had it out for Ted and his family. Seeing him provoke Walt in the courtroom was terrifying and utterly unfair to his brother. What if he continued to antagonize Walt while he was incarcerated, to where his brother retaliated and ended up behind bars like him? The thought sickened him. Glen Kirby wasn't worth the trouble, but how could he convince Walt otherwise?

And Robyn. Beautiful, devoted Robyn. What about her? Hadn't he put her through enough already? He was crushed she told him outright she blamed herself for everything that happened to him, the guilt she carried sucking the joy from her life. Fuck, she'd sacrificed her lifelong dreams because of him. He didn't want her carrying this burden anymore. But they were both on a hamster wheel going round and round, the end of this nightmare never really within grasp of stopping. For her to willingly wait yet again for a guy like him, a convicted felon, was beyond his comprehension. God, she deserved so much better—and better was what he had to convince himself he was going to give her when he was finally a free man.

Waking up the following day, it took Ted a few seconds to realize where he was. His back ached from the cheap foam mattress beneath him, his sleep restless and leaving him grumpy. Time wasn't on his side anymore, and he had to wait diligently until the Sheriff or one of his deputies unlocked his cell so he could join the rest of the county jail population for a shower and breakfast. Scrubbing his hand across his jaw, he felt the scar tissue where Glen had pummeled him. Scruff was starting to pepper his skin, and he thought it might be a good idea to grow his beard out again to cover up the mark. A part of him also didn't want to see the reminder every day when he looked in a mirror.

Easing his legs over the side of the bed, he eyed the boot covering his ankle. Being in jail meant he couldn't attend his physical therapy for a couple of weeks. Good thing he remembered most of the exercises his therapist and Walt helped him through. Ripping the Velcro sides of the contraption off, he eased his foot to the floor and started rotating his ankle in easy circles. This was something he could do as he counted down the days to his release. He also wanted to ask Sheriff Jenkins for a pad of paper so he could jot down an idea tickling his senses, one that included a grand gesture for Robyn.

Over the next two weeks, the one constant in the county jail was Robyn's daily visit. She came to see him during her lunch hour, her beautiful smile and easygoing nature keeping him from going stir crazy. She brought him good food prepared by Becks and the latest stories regarding his dad and siblings on the farm. For one incredible hour, Ted was himself, a guy who didn't have a care in the world, content to lavish in the love and meal Robyn provided. If he hadn't been able to see her every twenty-four hours, he wasn't so sure he could've survived, her presence filling his cup to overflowing, enabling him to get through another day.

On the final morning of his two-week sentence, he sat at a table by himself in the common area and observed the other men. A few of them played cards while others lazily watched a game show on television. No one seemed to notice Ted in the wings, and he was fine with it. He made no effort to make friends. It was pointless. Still, he had a slight urge to loudly announce to everyone today was his last day in this Godforsaken place, his punishment almost over. But he still hadn't heard about his acquittal, Robyn reassuring him they would know something soon. He supposed he'd have to continue to report to Sam and figure out his community service hours until then. His freedom was still miles away.

"Sheriff wants to see you." A big lug of a deputy glowered at him, casting a shadow over Ted.

"Ok."

Ted followed the large man through a few doors until he pointed toward an interrogation room. "Wait right in there."

Ted nodded and entered the room, sitting with his hands clasped on a wooden table. A few minutes passed before Sheriff Jenkins and his parole officer, Sam McNeil, entered the room. He immediately stood, his heart hammering.

"Hey, Sam. Good to see you. I haven't seen you since Glen's trial. I hope you have some good news for me." His voice was turned up a notch and laced with excitement. The thought of total, unhindered freedom was a viable possibility, his manifestations coming true.

"You look good, Ted. Sheriff says you've been a model prisoner," Sam said with pride.

Sheriff Jenkins offered a grin. "The best."

Ted looked back and forth between the pair, anxious for them to get to the point. "Well?"

Sam pulled out a chair and sat, urging him to do the same. "Have a seat, Ted."

With Sam sitting across from him, Ted watched as she pulled an envelope from her oversized purse. "Your lawyer, Mr. Morgan, finally got word from the District Attorney yesterday. He sent this overnight and asked me to give it to you in person."

"What is it?"

She handed the envelope off to him. "Like you, I have no idea. But I'm hoping it's the results of our motion to set aside conviction, acquitting you of all charges. Mr. Morgan wanted you to open it first, but before you do, I want you to know we did everything in our power to convince the state bar of our intentions."

"Judge Danforth wasn't a part of the decision, was he?" Ted fretted.

"No. I know for a fact it wasn't Judge Danforth. And for the record, I don't know how that man sleeps at night with how he conducts himself in a courtroom. He hands out severe sentences like he's overseeing the Salem Witch Trials."

Ted gulped, knowing Sam wasn't off base with her harsh criticism. Sheriff Jenkins stood behind Sam and palmed her shoulder. "Calm down, Sam. With Danforth out of the way, and the concrete evidence in those surveillance videos, I have a feeling there's nothing but good news in that envelope."

Sam nodded, embarrassed. "Sorry. I guess I'm ready for this to be behind us, especially for you, Ted. You've been through so much."

"Well, for what it's worth, thanks for going to bat for me."

"You're welcome, Ted." The two of them locked eyes before Sam startled him with an excited girlish squeal. "Well, go on! What are you waiting for? Open it."

Ted's brow furrowed as he carefully ripped open the envelope and unfolded a single piece of paper. One glance was all it took for the breath to leave his lungs in a gasp. His eyes shot to Sam, who was hanging on his every word. "Are you shittin' me?"

"What does it say?" she asked. Ted handed the paper off to her, her expression immediately filled with relief.

"Nope. There's nothing shitty about this, Ted," she humorously confirmed.

Sam handed the paper to Sheriff Jenkins. He looked like the cat who swallowed the canary. "Congratulations Ted. Couldn't have happened to a better guy."

Ted was sure his mouth was twisted into a goofy grin, but he didn't care. "What time is it?"

Sam looked at her wristwatch. "Ten-thirty?"

The legs of his chair scraped the hard cement floor as he stood with earnest, jutting his hand out to take back the official letter. "Can I show this to Robyn when she comes by for lunch?"

"Sure thing," Sheriff Jenkins nodded. "Great timing, too. This is the last day you'll have to eat lunch in this place ever again."

Ted stood tall, the taste of absolute freedom on the tip of his tongue. Nothing could be sweeter—except for Robyn's kisses.

# Chapter Twenty-Eight

## ROBYN

Robyn rested her chin in her hand, her elbow propped on the front counter in the deserted flower shop. The weekday morning dragged on with hardly any customers as she lazily watched her boss work across the room. Charlotte was tucking real autumn leaves around the stump of the fir tree in the sawed-off wine barrel in the corner advertising the Bennett Christmas Tree Farm.

The surge of autumn flavor in the small town of Langston Falls was coming on strong with fall-themed hues. Because Charlotte was well-known for her local and seasonal floras, the shop was filled with bits and pieces of harvest color, some of them from her own cutting garden. Mums, hydrangea, sunflowers, and chrysanthemums decorated the space, the warm shades of orange, reddish-brown, butterscotch, and burgundy expertly displayed in artistic ways to please the senses.

Robyn twirled the long stem of a wayward dark red sunflower in her free hand, her brow furrowing with a question. "Charlotte, have you always had your own cutting garden?"

Charlotte stood tall, clutching several sugar-maple leaves in her gloved hands. She huffed a strand of hair out of her eyes and looked over at her. "Yes, I have. When I was a little girl, I used to help my mother in her flower garden, and she used to help her mother in hers. I guess you could say it runs in the family."

"But why do you bring your own flowers into the shop? I mean, you have stuff flown in here from all over. Why not keep your pretty home-grown flowers to yourself for your own pleasure?"

Charlotte set the leaves down and pulled off her garden gloves by the tips of the fingers. "To me, flowers from my own garden are the most natural reflection of this incredible area where we live—much more than florist flowers I have flown in from around the world, although those are beautiful too. We have so many tourists coming through town. I want to give them a true taste of local North Georgia flavor. And besides, it brings me joy to share from my own garden."

"Hmmm," Robyn contemplated. One side of her mouth jacked up into a grin. "I like that."

Charlotte approached the counter, eyeing Robyn with a sweet smile. "Do you want to take a small bouquet of some of my personal flowers to Ted today to cheer him up?"

Robyn set the sunflower she'd been twirling on the counter, her cheeks heating with awkwardness. Was it obvious she was pining for Teddy yet again? "No... I, uh, just wondered why you go to so much trouble to bring in flowers from your own garden."

Charlotte nodded and picked up the sunflower Robyn abandoned on the counter. "May I?' she asked.

Robyn shrugged. "Sure. It's your flower." She watched Charlotte come around the counter and pick up a pair of trimming shears, cutting off part of the long stem.

"Come closer to me," she requested.

Robyn did as she was told, Charlotte tucking the bloom behind her ear. Tender in her actions, her boss adjusted her hair around the remainder of the stem as Robyn stood perfectly still. "Ralph Waldo Emerson once said, *'Many eyes go through the meadow, but few see the flowers in it.'* Do you have any idea what he meant?"

Robyn shook her head, her eyes wide, and her ears perked with interest.

"Well, here's what I think. It's easy to get caught up in all the noise and daily chaos. We forget to stop and appreciate the beautiful little things all the noise distorts. Sometimes we need to take note and literally stop and smell the roses, or in this case, admire the sunflower." Charlotte adjusted the bloom at Robyn's ear a second time."

"A little flower love might be the thing a person needs to make it through the rest of the day. I know it's always helped me." She walked back around the counter and shoved her gloves back onto her hands. "Sometimes a girl needs to wear flowers in her hair. It's as simple as that."

Robyn nodded, captivated by Charlotte's musings. She'd been so caught up in counting down every minute of each day until Teddy's release from his parole violation, she'd forgotten about the simple joys in her life. Charlotte's bit of sunshine in her cloudy world warmed the cockles of her heart, and she was determined to move forward, celebrating the beauty of each day. The peaceful, bubbling resonance from the small display fountain in the corner was comforting, and the sweet aroma of flowers in Langston Petals a bonus to her employment, Charlotte's pep talk reminding her how lucky she was to work in such a charming atmosphere.

Lifting her hand up to her ear, she gently touched the flower's soft petals, thankful for her boss and wise words. "Thanks, Charlotte. I need to take your advice and wear flowers in my hair more often."

Charlotte continued to arrange the colorful leaves under the fir tree. "Works every time."

Robyn hesitated for a beat. "You know he's coming home tomorrow, right?"

"Teddy?"

"Yeah." She averted her eyes and shuffled a pile of receipts next to the cash register, unsure if she should've made the announcement out loud. What if she jinxed it?

"Maple tree sapling."

"I beg your pardon?" Robyn lifted her gaze, perplexed by Charlotte's sudden tree announcement.

"You're gonna need a maple tree sapling to plant. The symbolic meaning behind the maple tree is endurance and fortitude. It's also a pretty tree with bright green leaves in the summertime and turns fiery, passionate red in the fall. It's the perfect ornamental choice all year long. You could plant it together on your property and remember how you got through this season."

Robyn was struck by Charlotte's words. "Endurance and fortitude, huh?"

"Exactly."

The two women eyed each other, Robyn pursing her lips together to thwart a gigantic smile. Charlotte broke their gaze and waved her off with humor. "Now get back to work, young lady. Your days of moping around here are about to come to an end. And you've got a tree to order and a boyfriend to visit today."

Robyn scurried through town at lunchtime, carrying the picnic basket Becky helped put together that morning. Teddy's favorite ham and cheese sandwich was tucked inside along with various other lunchtime goodies, including a half a dozen homemade chocolate chip cookies to share with Sheriff Jenkins. Robyn made the trek every day to the county jail, having lunch with Teddy in a private holding cell away from prying eyes, one of the perks of having the sheriff on their side.

The foliage was on fire in the autumn season, the blazing red, orange, and yellow hues gorgeous among the tidy row of trees lining Main Street. Robyn clutched her jacket at her throat, the air turning colder with a front moving into the mountain town. She loved this time of the year, especially with the holidays on the horizon. The thought of spending quality time with Teddy and his family during the seasonal celebrations kept her going. That and crossing each day off her office calendar with a big fat marker counting down to Teddy's release.

"Good morning, Miss Morgan," one of the familiar deputies greeted as she entered the front office.

"Good morning."

"What's on the menu for today?"

"Ham and cheese." She grinned.

The deputy nodded. "Sounds good. Pairs nicely with apples."

"Apples?" She had no idea what he was talking about.

The deputy pointed toward the waiting area. Robyn's gaze traced the room and landed on Mrs. Kirby, who sat primly next to a basket of apples. Pressing her lips together, she sighed. She'd been anticipating a word from Mrs. Kirby at some point. That it took till the end of Ted's latest jail sentence for the timid woman to appear wasn't surprising.

"Give me a minute, would you?" she asked the deputy, leaving the picnic basket on the counter.

"Sure thing."

Robyn approached Mrs. Kirby and clasped her hands in front of her jacket. "Hello."

"Hello," she replied cheerfully, patting the vacant seat. "The flower in your hair is lovely."

Robyn lifted her hand to her head and touched the red sunflower she'd all but forgotten about. "Thank you." She sat next to the woman. "What are you doing here?"

"I was in the neighborhood and wanted to make sure Ted received this peck of apples. I have about a dozen acres of apple trees on my land, more than enough to share."

"Oh? What kind are they?" Robyn was determined to make small talk, going along with Mrs. Kirby's apple motivation for showing up at the county jail. But she was sure there was another reason behind the visit.

Mrs. Kirby's face lit up. "These are Mutsu apples and can keep for several months in a cold crisper. They're some of the best apples for pie because they stay firm when cooked."

Robyn picked one up, the yellowish-green skin with an orange blush large in her hand. "Are they always this big?" she asked.

Mrs. Kirby nodded. "Yes. This is a full peck with about twenty-five large apples, plenty for a couple of pies or to enjoy on their own." When their eyes finally met, understanding and forgiveness passed between them.

Robyn set the apple back on top of the pile. "I'll make sure Teddy knows they're from you."

Mrs. Kirby reached for her, squeezing Robyn's wrist.

Her voice warbled with emotion. "Thank you." She stood and shrugged on her coat. "I've enjoyed these apples for many decades. I'm hoping you and Ted's family will enjoy them for years to come."

Robyn frowned, unsure of the hidden meaning behind Mrs. Kirby's statement. "Well, I'm sure we'll enjoy every bite."

The woman nodded, her melancholy smile brief. "I'll leave you to it then. It was nice seeing you. You and Ted take care."

"You do the same, Mrs. Kirby." Robyn watched the woman wave politely at the deputy before she disappeared through the front entrance. Shaking her head, she wondered how Mrs. Kirby got by in the world with only her angry son, Glen, by her side. Her peace offering of local-grown apples was honest and sincere, and yet Robyn still felt sorry for her.

Hoisting the wood basket into her hands, she was dumb-struck by the weight of the fruit and wondered how Mrs. Kirby managed to carry the heavy gift from the parking lot inside. "Do you mind if I leave these here while I visit Ted today?" she asked the deputy on duty.

"Not at all."

Robyn signed in on a clipboard and was given a guest lanyard to wear around her neck. She swiped an apple off the pile and tucked it inside the picnic basket. Holding her wares in the crook of her elbow, she followed the deputy to Sheriff Jenkins' office, her lunchtime schedule never wavering since Ted was locked up for a second time.

"Knock, knock," she said, tapping her knuckles on the glass door.

"Right on time," Sheriff Jenkins greeted with cheer. "What's on the menu the day before release?"

"Ugh, when you say it like that, it sounds like the 'special meal' before a death sentence."

The Sheriff guffawed awkwardly, waving her off. "God, no. I didn't mean it like that."

"I know." She gestured toward the picnic basket on her arm. "It's his favorite, ham and cheese. Oh, and get this. Mrs. Kirby was waiting for me in the lobby with a special bonus."

"What? Why?"

Robyn shook her head. "I'm not sure why, but I think she wanted to give Teddy a peace offering before his release tomorrow to let him know she's on his side."

"A peace offering? What kind?"

"Apples."

Sheriff Jenkins scrubbed a hand across his jaw as if perplexed. "Well, that was nice, I guess."

Robyn shrugged.

"How about we not keep Ted waiting any longer? I know he's anxious to see you today."

Robyn followed the Sheriff down a narrow hallway and watched as he unlocked several doors leading to her man. A narrow window in a metal door at the end of the last hall revealed Ted standing alone in the room. The white-washed walls and metal chairs appeared sterile in the prison environment, the orange jumpsuit he wore glaringly bright. Sheriff Jenkins unlocked the door and palmed it open.

"Take your time and enjoy your lunch."

"Thanks, Sheriff. We will," Robyn replied, crossing the threshold.

Ted added. "I appreciate you, Sheriff Jenkins."

The man smiled and locked them in. It was hard for Robyn to fathom he willingly bent the rules each day so she and Ted could spend lunchtime together.

"Hey, beautiful," Ted greeted with fondness. He took the basket from her arm and set it on the floor before he pulled her in for a hug and kiss. His eyes traced the flower in her hair, his bearded cheeks plumping with a rare smile. "So beautiful."

"Thank you, Teddy," she gushed. "Are you hungry? It's your last picnic behind bars."

"Starving," he nipped at her lips.

Robyn giggled. "Well, you're in luck. I've got plenty of your favorites today, including an apple gifted by Mrs. Kirby herself." Bending low, she plucked the fruit from the basket and presented it to him in the palm of her hand.

Ted's forehead creased as he warily eyed the piece of fruit. "Wow. That's unexpected."

"I know, right? She said something about us enjoying her apples for years to come. What do you think she meant?"

"No clue. And I really don't want to talk about Mrs. Kirby right now." He took the apple from her hands and plopped it back into the basket. "I've got something to show you, too." he pulled a piece of paper from the pocket of his orange jumpsuit.

Robyn's eyes grew wide with trepidation, unsure of what was written between the folds. "Good news or bad news?"

Ted remained stone-faced, handing the paper off. "Read it, and you tell me."

Unfolding the letter with trembling fingers, her eyes went back and forth as she read the contents. When she finished, her mouth gaped, her expression in awe as she looked at Teddy.

He nodded aggressively, his entire mood full of buoyant joy. "It's official. I've been acquitted. By tomorrow, I'll be free and clear. I'm legally faultless."

The paper fell from her fingers as she launched her body into Teddy's arms and peppered his hairy face with kisses and happy giggles. The letter floated to the floor, the top of the page stamped with one word in bold red ink: Dismissed.

# Chapter Twenty-Nine

## TEDDY

Ted didn't want anyone to make a huge fuss when he limped out the front doors of the Langston Falls County Jail as a free man. But leave it to Sheriff Jenkins and his now ex-parole officer, Sam McNeil, to embarrass the hell out of him. Confetti cannons went off, covering him and Robyn in tiny bits of colorful paper, the entire precinct applauding his official release.

"Good luck, Ted. We're all so happy for you," the sheriff said, pumping his hand in a hearty shake.

"Thank you, Sheriff Jenkins. For everything." He turned and eyed Samantha with a grin. "I couldn't have done this without you. You're my official guardian angel."

"Come here, you big Teddy-bear." Sam stood on her tiptoes and hugged him around the neck. "I'll see y'all later at the farm tonight."

"Cool."

With his arm snug around Robyn's waist, the two made their getaway. The bright sunny day was charged with electricity, and excitement. He took in a deep lungful of air, anxious to get back to her place, restless to get her home.

"How do you feel?" Robyn asked, eyeing him from across the interior of their Jeep.

Ted skimmed his knuckles across her cheek, her satiny skin blushing beneath his touch. "I feel... good."

Robyn cleared her throat before she started singing. "*I knew that you would, yeah.*" She surprised him with her peppy vocals as unmitigated joy rushed through his system. They bobbed their heads in unison in a chorus duet of the old James Brown song as they made their way across town.

Truth be told, Ted felt light as a feather, the heavy burden of prison life finally falling from his shoulders—for good. He was an ordinary citizen again, free to come and go as he pleased. The feeling was thrilling and titillating, and he wasn't sure how to act, his heart nearly bursting with happiness. So he sang at the top of his lungs, he and Robyn pulsing to the beat of the impromptu tune as they pulled away from the jail. He would never look back.

"Your family wants us to join them for supper. Are you still up for it?"

Ted nodded excitedly, anxious to see everyone out of the confines of his orange jumpsuit. But first things first, he needed to love on his woman in her home—*their* home. They'd talked about moving back in together when she brought his lunch to the jail every day. Robyn insisted, saying they could pick up right where they left off. Only this time, they were older and wiser, the moments they spent together a gift they never wanted to take for granted again.

"I cleaned out my closet and drawers, so there's plenty of room for your clothes. Becky and Walt helped transfer all your stuff over last week."

Ted watched her as she drove, the autumn leaves

whizzing by her pretty profile against the window a kaleido-scope of color. He didn't think there was ever a time he felt happier. But he knew later in the evening, in front of his dad, and his siblings, his happiness would be ten-fold with what he had planned for Robyn. He'd made a list over the last fourteen days of things he needed for his surprise, his family fulfilling his every desire. His list was detailed and intentional, and he spared no expense, dipping into his savings and depending on his family to come through for him. He also insisted they stay quiet, wanting the night ahead to be a total surprise.

"Leave it to Becks and Walt to always help out. How is Walter these days? He never visited me."

"He's good, Teddy. He told me he didn't want to see you in a jail environment and wanted to wait till you were on the other side. Said he's been real busy, too."

"With the winery?"

"No. He told me he's been working on something but wouldn't give me any other details. I'm sure he'll tell you all about it when you see him tonight."

Ted wondered if Walt was alluding to helping with his planned surprise proposal for Robyn, but he couldn't be sure. His brother and father were instrumental in securing the diamond ring he'd picked out from the local jeweler, the purchase completed in the last few days. Could his broody brother have something else up his sleeve? If he did, Ted sure hoped it didn't involve Glen Kirby.

Robyn turned the car onto the dirt road leading to their little cottage in the country. The Tiffany-blue house with white shutters came into view, the nearby pond glimmering in the sunshine. The homestead was a welcome sight for his weary eyes. With the ignition turned off, she turned toward him, her voice filled with melancholy and absolute love.

"Welcome home, Teddy."

They didn't waste any time, Robyn pulling him by the hand into the bedroom. He tossed his jacket to the wayside and pulled his shirt off, pausing in the doorway, allowing his gaze to drift lazily over her feminine curves. She was a luscious creature and moved with a casual grace that took his breath away. The smooth porcelain skin of her neck arched as she swung her arms up over her head taking off her fuzzy sweater. She then unzipped her jeans, letting them fall to the wooden floors. Heat flooded his core as he realized she was wearing sexy lingerie underneath it all.

"For me?" he smiled seductively.

"Always." Her voice was breathy as she sauntered toward him, her delicate hands unclasping and flinging her lacy bra to the wayside.

Their mouths hovered inches apart, their breath hot and full of lust. His passion for Robyn was so immense he felt like he couldn't contain it—that he might break wide open if he touched her. Every single time they were together was incredible, but this? This was something different.

Ted took a deep breath, filling his lungs with the fertile scent of Robyn and his surroundings that defied description. The view from the bedroom was a feast of harvest color, texture, and daylight. Rustling, fiery red maples and buttery meadows of lanky grass. The shimmering diamond surface of the long oval pond surrounded by dark earth. Beyond the pond, Robyn's grandmother's house and a small shed, crumbling and faded. All breathtaking. All familiar. And in the distance, he could see the magnificent backdrop of the North Georgia Mountains, the solid rock anchoring him to the land and the love of his life standing before him.

"Are you okay? Do you need some rest?" Robyn's voice was laced with concern, gaining Ted's attention. She clutched her hands in a praying position against her bare bosom.

Ted shook his head, moving her arms out of the way and filling his hands with her breasts. Her eyes were wide saucers looking back at him, her plump cherry lips tempting him to suckle.

"Help me get this boot off so I can take off my pants." He limped to the edge of the bed and sat, Robyn kneeling and gentle with her actions.

With the boot off, and his pants pulled from his legs, he revealed his commando disposition underneath. Robyn snickered, kneeling in front of him like a goddamn dream, the tip of her tongue tracing the veins of his penis straight up his center.

"Oh, Robyn." Her name fell from his lips in bated breath as she sucked him long and hard, her throat deep as her tongue and lips surrounded his flesh. He threaded his fingers through her hair and moved to her rhythm, the onset of thick pleasure surging through his core. Her green eyes flicked to his, and the sight of her gazing up at him on her knees between his legs was almost too much.

"On the bed, now," Ted heaved.

She crawled over the top of the covers, her ample ass bouncing in the process. Stretching across her feminine curves to open the nightstand drawer, he wasn't surprised to find a box of condoms neatly tucked inside. Ten seconds later, he rolled one on and tugged at her delicate panties, sliding them down her legs.

"Be careful with your ankle, Teddy," she cautioned.

"It's fine," he exhaled, positioned on his knees.

Robyn's center gaped, her pink folds glistening with wetness. Licking his fingers, he rubbed her clit in a slow circle and watched with delight the way the sunlight danced across her flushed skin. When he eased his throbbing dick inside her, she clung to him.

"I want to tell you something," she panted.

"Can't it wait till after I love on you for a few hours?" he chuckled.

Her smile was replete as she pressed her teeth into her lower lip. "No. I want to tell you now."

Ted stopped. "Don't tell me you're pregnant. Are you? Because I would be over the moon if you were—"

Robyn put her fingers over his mouth to stop him from talking. "I've started studying for the bar exam again."

His grin was wide as he rode her again, leaning closer to kiss her forehead. "Are you serious?" For Robyn to get back on the attorney train was everything he'd hoped for.

"Mmmhumm." She dragged her fingernails through his disheveled hair. "After everything that's happened to you, especially after uncovering the surveillance video, I've decided I want to fight the injustice in the world. My goal is to work for the Innocence Project." Ted stopped again, causing Robyn to giggle. "Don't stop, Teddy."

Ted knew full well what the Innocence Project was, his research in the prison library over the years while incarcerated educating him on the not-for-profit organization working to prevent wrongful convictions and reform the criminal justice system. He was dumbfounded, hovering over Robyn with his mouth agape, his dick inside her shocked still.

"I can work for the organization from anywhere. I won't have to move to Atlanta, or work for a local practice. I can work from here, where we both belong. We can always be together, Teddy—forever."

"Forever," he repeated.

Reaching between his legs, Robyn massaged his balls

bringing his dick back to life, the heat between them ramping up. With his body on her body, he made love to her, the sounds of sex in the air for no one else to hear but them. He moved with ease, loving on his woman, his hips grinding against her. He prefered her on her back looking up at him, so sweet and loyal he wanted to weep with gladness.

"Oh, God, Teddy," she panted. "Don't stop. I'm gonna come soon…"

"I want you to. It's been too long," he growled. They became frantic, driven by a desire they both shared.

"*Teddy.*"

His name crossed her lips before he kissed her hard and long and deep, her tongue thrusting madly into his mouth. He raised and lowered himself, her wetness sliding up and down his shaft faster and faster. His face twisted in ecstasy as he inhaled sharply, the exquisite pain hurting so good. A flash of light streaked across his vision, and his body quaked with release. Every sinewy fiber of his muscles soared in his newfound freedom, his powerful orgasm taking flight as he hovered above his lover. He felt airborne, flying high in the stratosphere of kinetic energy surrounding their naked bodies. Oxygen left his lungs in a slow, sexy exhale, his moan deep and satisfying. Collapsing next to her, he trembled with aftershocks, his energy depleted.

"Wow," was all he could say.

Robyn shifted next to him, her hand caressing his heaving chest. "I know, right?"

Turning to face her, they were nose to nose on top of the crumpled bedding. "I want you every single day for the rest of my life."

Her face lit up with a return smile. "Same."

"And I'm so fucking proud of you."

Her return smile drove cupid's arrow deep into his soul. This wasn't a dream. Ted lay there sweating, his heart fully alive and galloping like a racehorse. It was thoughts of Robyn that often comforted him while he was in prison. Her sweet laughter. The feel of her satiny skin beneath his wandering fingers. Her body tucked next to him as they lay on the bed. And now, here he was wide awake for it all, in real-time, loving his woman.

Pride bubbled up from the deepest center of his being, realizing what they'd been through was finally in the past. He did it. He somehow managed to keep himself alive, forcing himself to breathe even when his life seemed hopeless. Ted was sad he didn't have Robyn in his life for all those years. But he was incredibly grateful she stayed with him in spirit. And now, she was back in his arms for good, ready to finish what she started with him in mind.

An essential question he needed to ask her teased the edges of his mind, a question he was going to propose in front of his entire family later that evening.

And he knew without a doubt exactly what her answer would be.

# Chapter Thirty

## TEDDY

A large rectangular table was assembled in the center of the barn, the small, hired staff serving the Bennett family gathered all around. Tea lights flickered romantically among the pink and white peonies in bud vases peppered across the pale green tablecloth. Ted took in the scene with pleasure, his sister, Becky, smiling at him from across the table. A halo of tiny flowers in her hair matched Robyn's, and Sam's, the three females going overboard with the romantic feel of the evening. He knew Becks was intentional with the gesture, the flowers a nod to their late mother.

The scent of grilled steak permeated the air as Roy Bennett stood at the head of the table and lifted a wineglass into the air. "Before dinner is served tonight, I'd like to propose a toast."

With one arm snuggly settled across Robyn's shoulders, Ted picked up his wineglass with his free hand, holding it in the air like the rest of his family. The quixotic atmosphere was exactly how he pictured it in his mind, the ambiance better than he could have imagined as he relayed his vision in a written request to his family while he was behind bars serving his parole violation.

The swooping strands of Edison-style lighting gave off a soft glow, and the antique place settings with scalloped edges painted in gold were another added detail borrowed from the china cabinet of his mother. The menu was exactly what he wanted, too, the food choices some of Robyn's favorites: fire-grilled steaks and loaded baked potatoes, spinach salad, and Becky's famous garlic rolls. He even requested a special dessert for after his proposal; the ramekins of dense chocolate lava cake ready to be topped with homemade whipped cream and raspberries.

Ted eyed his father with gratefulness, the proud patriarch beaming since his return to the real world. Clearing his throat, Roy nodded. "A toast to our dear Teddy." His eyes misted as he held his glass high into the air, his gaze penetrating and full of sincerity. "May all of your hopes and dreams come true and may the memory of this day become sweeter with each passing year. Welcome home, son."

Glasses clinked all around. "Thanks, Dad." Raising the glass of Bennett Farms Cabernet to his lips, he was about to sip when James tapped a silver spoon against his glass.

"I'd like to add, health and long life to you, Ted. I love you, brother."

"I love you too, Jimmy." Ted's eyebrows raised as the rest of his siblings stood, adding to the toasts. Robyn leaned into him and kissed him on the cheek, giggling with glee. The room held an air of familial love and anticipation for the reason they were all gathered together.

"I'm next," Becky announced. Her cheeks flushed as she angled her chin into the air with purpose. "Never, ever forget what is worth remembering and what is best forgotten."

Ted chuckled. "You can say that again."

"Seriously, I'm glad you're home, Teddy," Becky continued. "And don't forget, *I* love you the most." The entire table erupted in laughter, his sister adorable in her own unique way.

"You're my favorite sister, Becks," he teased.

She rolled her eyes as Hank pulled her in for a side hug. "Ha! I'm your *only* sister, Teddy."

"My turn!" Hank announced.

Ted glowed in the spotlight of kind words, enjoying every sentiment from his family.

"I want to pay tribute to what a great guy you are, Teddy. You've been an inspiration to me with your family loyalty and devotion to Robyn." He motioned his glass toward Robyn and smiled. Ted kissed her temple, his heart overflowing with pure gladness.

"Teddy, your kind and generous heart are things that I, your favorite brother, try to emulate." Hank palmed his chest with his free hand with boastfulness.

"Hey, wait a minute, *I'm* Ted's favorite brother," James cajoled. Samantha patted his cheek as she sat grinning beside him. The two were officially dating now that Sam wasn't Ted's parole officer anymore.

Hank held his palm up. "Simmer down, Jimmy. There's only one way to find out who his favorite brother is." He nodded at Ted, his tone filled with teasing. "Go ahead and tell them, Teddy. It's okay; they need to know. Admit it—*I'm* your favorite brother."

"Uh, I'd like to plead the fifth?" Ted countered, shaking his head.

The table erupted in giddy laugher again as Walter sauntered over to Hank and slapped him on the back. "Do y'all mind if I add a few words to the mix?"

Hank seemed taken aback and nodded, the sibling teasing amped up for the occasion. "Ladies and gentlemen, in an unprecedented move, our normally silent and brooding brother, Walter Bennett, the fairness-obsessed middle child, would like to take a moment. Please give him your undivided attention."

Walt chuckled, playfully rearing back his fist in a mock punch and gently sliding his knuckles across Hank's youthful face. All eyes landed on Walt, his brother pausing as if trying to come up with the perfect toast. When he stared directly at Ted from across the table, something honest passed between them.

"Cheers to you, Teddy. I'm... honored to be your brother, and I want you to know I'll always try and watch out for you and protect you. That goes for you, too, Robyn."

Ted's lips trembled in a sincere smile, a surge of emotions threatening to surface.

"And I'd like to add, may your home always be filled with Bennett Farms wine." He held his glass high into the air. "... and may all your ups and downs be under the covers."

Ted snort-laughed, surprised his brother added some humor at the end of his poignant toast. Roy shook his head and thrust his glass toward everyone, peals of laughter filling the air. "That's enough of that. Let's eat."

The delicious meal flew by among the pleasant chatter and tinkling of dishes. As the small group of servers came around and picked up empty plates, Ted eyed his brother Hank from across the table and nodded, giving him the go-ahead for his big surprise. Hank winked and excused himself.

"Mmmm, dinner was amazing," Robyn gushed, snuggling beside him.

"I know." Ted turned in his seat, his gaze tracing the delicate features of her face. "May I have this dance?"

Robyn's brow furrowed for a few seconds before her eyes turned wide at the sound of acoustic guitar music filtering through the air. Looking around the barn interior, she noticed Hank as he strolled in, strumming his guitar. The haunting melody of Elvis' *Can't Help Falling in Love* echoed into the barn rafters.

When she faced Ted again, he was already standing, offering her his hand. Setting her napkin to the side, she put her hand in his and stood. They walked to an empty area, where Ted pulled her flush against his body. The air was heavy with romance, Hank's music, and the smell of earth. Ted's throat was thick with nerves and euphoria, longing, and excitement. Between his family's sentimental toasts and the roar of his heart pounding in his ears, he was soaring again.

Bringing Robyn's hand to his mouth, he kissed the inside of her wrist and felt her pulse jump against his lips. Ted wasn't sure what he'd done in his life to deserve this night, this second chance with this woman. But he was grateful. He wanted more nights like this. He craved them with an insatiable hunger that couldn't be satisfied. He wanted to make a home with her in their cottage. He wanted Robyn's face to be the last thing he saw each night before he shut his eyes and the first thing he saw when he opened them. He wanted all of her with every fiber of his being. He wanted Robyn Morgan to be his wife.

Ted captured her lips in a soft kiss as Hank sung softly in the background. The lyrics to the utterly romantic song were touching and fitting at the moment.

"Some things are meant to be," he whispered.

This induced a gorgeous smile from Robyn, her lashes fluttering flirtatiously. "I couldn't agree more."

This was Ted's perfect opening. "Marry me?"

Robyn stopped dancing. "What?"

Ted gently disengaged from their dance pose and kneeled awkwardly in front of her, his cumbersome boot scraping against the dirt floor. Dipping his hand into his front pocket, he pulled out a diamond engagement ring, the jewel's facets winking in the soft light.

"Will you marry me?" he asked again, holding the ring up for her to see.

She swallowed hard, her hands pressing against his bearded cheeks. Bending low to his level, she nodded aggressively. "Of course, I'll marry you, Teddy. You're the love of my life."

The room erupted in a resounding cheer of jubilation as Ted slipped the ring on her finger. They stood together, their mouths pressed in a fervent kiss as the family gathered all around them.

"I love you, Robyn," he pronounced, clutching her hand directly over his heart. She was breathtakingly gorgeous looking back at him.

"I'll love you till the end."

Ted was laughing now, his body reacting to the sheer relief of her positive response. As each of his siblings congratulated him with hugs and kisses, words of affirmation, and well wishes, Ted's gaze never left Robyn's, the two of them bonded together like never before.

The old prison poster with the saying, 'Freedom is nothing but a chance to be better' filtered through his mind again, his romantic notions of hope urging him through the door into this next chapter of his life. He couldn't have done it without Robyn and her father, his family, and Sam

McNeil. Like the Langston River falling over the cliffs and toward the sea, some things were meant to be, and he was better for it. Robyn had his heart, his whole life in her hands. She would always be his first and his last love. No matter where he went or what he did, he would never be his true self, his *best* self with anyone but Robyn.

"Congratulations, son." Roy Bennett announced, pulling Ted into his arms for a bear hug.

"Thanks, Dad, for—everything. For tonight. For being there during all those horrible years."

"It's all behind you now. Nothing but good things ahead. I'll always be here for you, you know that," he grinned. "I hope you and Robyn have a long and wonderful marriage together like your mom and I did."

Ted nodded, wishing his mother could've been there to witness this joyous occasion. But he knew without a doubt she was with him in spirit. "I know we'll have a long and wonderful marriage because you and mom showed us how it's done."

Roy hugged him again, his chuckle laced with wistfulness. "Believe me, it was all her doing."

"Ted," Walt interrupted with a slap on the back. "Congratulations, bro."

"Thanks, Walt." They watched their father mosey back toward the group.

"It's been a long time coming, right?" His brother seemed relaxed, almost giddy, which was unusual due to his pensive nature.

"More than long enough if you ask me. Thanks again for going above and beyond with this setup. Tonight was a homerun. Seriously, everything was perfect and exactly how I envisioned."

"Glad I could be a small part." Walt gripped Ted by the

bicep and pulled him away from the group who surrounded Robyn and gushed over her ring. "So, you're all moved in at Robyn's place, right?"

"Our place," Ted reiterated. "Yes. I'm finally home where I belong. I appreciate you getting all my things moved over."

Walt nodded, resting his hands on his hips. "Not a problem."

Ted eyed his brother, confused by the shit-eating grin on his face. "What?"

Walt pressed his teeth into his lower lip, his eyes darting toward their family again before landing on Ted's face. He seemed to hesitate, as if mulling over something before his mouth morphed into an ear-splitting grin. "Nothing. I'm just happy for you." Walt heartily slapped Ted on the back.

"Dessert is served," Becky announced, interrupting their brotherly moment.

Everyone made their way back to their seats, the presentation of individual ramekins of chocolate lava cake topped with whipped cream and raspberries a beautiful sight to behold.

"My favorite!" Robyn clapped her hands, squealing with delight.

Ted pulled out her chair, gallant in his actions. More wine was poured, and a pleasant buzz hummed throughout the space as they indulged in the decadent ending of their celebratory meal.

"I can't believe you pulled this off without me finding out." Robyn's luscious tongue slipped out of her mouth as she licked the back of her spoon, the diamond on her finger winking at him. "Mmmm, life is so sweet."

Ted drank in her beauty, the halo of pretty flowers in her hair wilting in the evening. He took a bite of his dessert, the taste an explosion of deliciousness. Robyn was correct—life couldn't get any sweeter.

Resting his arm across her shoulders, he drank in the happy faces of his family gathered around the table. Like the scrumptious chocolate, he savored this moment: the romantic lighting, the good wine and food, the resonant laughter of his family, and Robyn's devoted, tender touch and smile. His satisfaction ran deep, his days of labored breath behind him. He had survived, and now everything he did was enhanced with great joy.

Ted had traversed high mountains and deep valleys, his arduous journey to get back home leaving him hopeless at times. But now, thank God he was on the other side. His hope had transformed, lingering in the breeze across the golden fields of his homeland, his roots running deep like the lone oak sheltering his mother's grave.

His hard life was saturated with sweet love, his rough edges softening with each intentional breath surrounded by the people he loved most in the world. Ted Bennett had always been a faultless man—but now, he was finally free.

vinci-books.com/shamelesslove

**He wasn't supposed to get close. She wasn't supposed to let him.**

A broody protector. A fiery television producer. A one-night temptation that turns into so much more. But when the snow melts, will distance break them apart? *Shameless Love* is a steamy, small-town romance packed with grumpy/sunshine tension, forced proximity, and sizzling chemistry.

Turn the page for a free preview…

# Shameless Love: Chapter One

WALTER BENNETT

With the radio volume cranked, Walt drummed his fingers across the steering wheel and listened to a classic Garth Brooks tune on a local country station. His work truck picked up dust along the country roads of his hometown, Langston Falls, the truck bed loaded with his belongings, his intention to spend his first night in his new home.

Squinting in the bright sunshine, Walt noticed the trees along the roadside forfeiting the last of their leaves in the late autumn season. Thanksgiving had come and gone, and he wanted to be all moved in before the big family Christmas gathering. It was odd loading up his truck at Bennett Farms, the winery and Christmas tree farm the only home he'd ever known. Walt was the middle child of five kids, including his older brothers James and Ted, his younger brother Hank, and his only sister, Rebecca. He and James had shared the renovated carriage quarters near the main house on the land for many years, their daily work on the family farm something he was proud of. But having a new place to call his own at this stage in his life was thrilling, the anticipation of moving finally filling him with excitement. Located several miles down the road, Walt had plans to transform the run-down Kirby property into something fitting for him.

Once the Kirby family moved out after a quick all-cash sale, Walt had brought his dad, Roy Bennett, to the house for a look-see. On the drive over, Roy used the word "shameless" to describe him. Did he feel guilty? Hell no, not anymore, especially after he learned Glen Kirby hightailed it out of town for good. The only thing Walt felt now was an undeniable satisfaction, his retaliation against a man who did his family wrong finally in his rearview mirror—and he had a right mind to rip that mirror off and never look back.

But shameless wasn't the word he'd use. Nope. There was only one word to describe what he'd pulled off: revenge. Call him what you want. Brazen. Spiteful. Uncharitable. Even hateful. He didn't care anymore. Because the sweet taste of vengeance was delicious, and he had no shame in allowing it to linger on his tongue.

As he and his dad pulled up to the ranch-style house, Walt's excitement was short-lived. Beer bottles and remnants of a huge bonfire littered the front yard. Bits of charred, broken furniture continued to smoke in the ashy pile, and Walt was taken aback when he noticed the sizeable spray-painted word, "killer" spelled out across the front door.

"You want me to call Sheriff Jenkins?" Roy asked, his face pinched with worry. The family patriarch was a fair man, but if you crossed one of his own, there'd be hell to pay.

"No, Dad. I don't want to have any more contact with Glen Kirby ever again. He had his last little hoorah. Good riddance."

"Well, let's take a look at the inside before you decide. If that son-of-a-bitch trashed the interior, you're gonna need to do something about it."

"Like what?" Their cowboy boots crunched across the barren front yard, Walt pausing to kick a broken beer bottle out of their path.

"I don't know. Press charges? File a restraining order? You had the locks changed after the local government put the new ownership on the books, right?'

"Of course, Dad. The recording happened on the day of funding when I handed over my life savings to Mrs. Kirby's real estate agent and lawyer."

They stomped up the worn wooden steps to the front door splattered with blood-red dribbled letters. Walt turned around and scanned the neglected front yard with his hands on his hips. He thought Glen Kirby must have been drunk out of his mind to pull off such a stunt. His dad was right. If things on the inside looked anything like they did on the outside, he'd have to give Sheriff Jenkins a call.

The Bennetts and Kirbys had turned into the fucking Hatfields and McCoys.

"Well, come on then. Let's make sure the inside is okay," Roy muttered.

Walt stuck his shiny key into the new lock and opened the front door to his first home. Pride bubbled up in his chest as he crossed the threshold, overcome with a territorial satisfaction he'd pulled this thing off. He promised Teddy he'd get rid of Glen Kirby outright. Stripping the man of his inheritance by taking over his family's house and land was the ultimate price Walt was willing to pay. Glen had no choice but to hightail it out of Langston Falls for good.

The home's interior was cold, the faint aroma of bleach hard not to notice. Leave it to sweet Mrs. Kirby to clean after the movers loaded up her life. She told Walt she was ready for a new chapter, off to live in Macon, Georgia, to be closer to her sister. After everything that had happened between their two families, Walt was genuinely happy for the woman, glad she could finally move on after the horror she'd been through losing her first son, Joe, and watching her other son, Glen, fall completely apart. Now, if Walt only knew where Glen had landed.

"There's no damage on the inside," Roy announced after scoping out the three empty bedrooms and two bathrooms. His boots clomped across the original hardwood floors as he took in everything. "And she left you the fridge. That's good. One less appliance you're gonna have to buy."

Walt nodded, his eyes tracing the large family room. A big picture window looked out across a small backyard before the fence line of the apple orchard started. A sly smile unfurled from his lips, knowing Glen Kirby would never see this pretty view again.

Roy palmed Walt's shoulder. "This place fits you, son. Congratulations."

Walt inhaled a deep breath, thankful for his father's blessing. "Thanks, Dad."

Walt parked his loaded pickup truck on the dirt driveway, eager to move what little possessions he had into his new home. It only took him a few trips to unpack everything. Slamming the lift-gate shut with satisfaction, he rested his hands on his denim-clad hips and surveyed his property with pride. He'd cleaned up the beer bottles and bonfire remnants and spent two hours scrubbing the red paint off the front door before repainting it a fresh forest green to match the shutters. Brittle leaves littered the drive, and trash he'd collected from Glen's last hurrah sat in a tidy pile by the roadside, ready to be picked up by the local garbage collector.

As Walt started up the front steps, ready to unpack and plant roots, he paused and listened. A chilly breeze rustled through the trees, and the loud caw of a single crow called out in the late afternoon. He gripped the back of his neck, his subconscious tickling his memory with something he'd forgotten in the truck cab.

Stomping back to the vehicle, he opened the door and reached across the floorboard, feeling around for the cool metal of his long-barreled shotgun. The weapon was locked and loaded, just in case. Resting the gun against his shoulder, he secured his truck and headed toward the house. Although his mood was buoyant, his senses stayed on high alert. This was his property now, and he wasn't about to allow a disgruntled guy like Glen leaving him shaking in his boots. Nope. Quite the opposite. If Glen still had a bone to pick with him or any of Walt's family, he'd be ready.

Deep in his thoughts, Walt considered a conversation he'd had with his brother, Ted, during their family Thanksgiving gathering when he'd told him about his home purchase.

"I did Mrs. Kirby a huge favor so she can keep her son, Glen, out of jail."

Ted scowled, his words catching in his throat. "Walt, you didn't…"

"Oh, yes, I did." Walt remembered the feeling of pure satisfaction, the Kirby homestead sale legitimate payback for his brother's astronomical medical bills. But it was more than that.

"You get what you give, Teddy. I warned Glen Kirby; you mess with the bull, you get the horns."

"Revenge, Walter? Really?"

"Karma's a bitch. Glen got what was coming to him." Walt had stood his ground, his demeanor smug, and his tone turned sinister.

Ted became noticeably rattled. "I can't think about this right now—how Glen reacted, how you managed to do this in such a short amount of time... What the hell, Walt? Are you trying to get me killed?"

Walt was taken aback. "What? No! I thought you'd be happy about this. Mrs. Kirby is the one who came to me. She wanted to sell her homestead to me."

Ted nodded like a bobblehead doll. "You do realize you've opened an entire new can of worms—or in this case, a can of whoop-ass."

Ted's words echoed in Walt's subconscious as he held the shotgun a little tighter. What if his brother was right and Walt unintentionally opened up a can of whoop-ass by buying the Kirby property out from under Glen? He was a fool rushing into the notion that Ted's life could somehow be perfect after all he'd been through, especially going into this next chapter with his fiancé, Robyn by his side. Had he ruined it for Teddy by buying the Kirby homestead outright? God, he didn't want to worry about the possibility something terrible might happen again—that someone like Glen Kirby could be waiting in the shadows, ready to strike —prepared to instigate a retaliation of his own. If an outsider came in and stole his family's land out from under them, Walt would go ballistic and do whatever it took to regain it. He realized Glen Kirby probably held the same fervor.

Ted had been through so much, serving five years

behind bars for a crime he didn't commit, and then dealing with the aftermath of Glen's rage. To finally see his big brother happy and healthy again was all Walt ever wanted. But now, his mind roiled with unmitigated fear. How could he have been so careless, subjecting his family to the potential of more danger?

But Walt had already made the deal, the ink on the mortgage papers dry and his belongings already moved inside. The old Kirby homestead, which included a vibrant apple orchard, was paid for with every last dime Walt had scrimped and saved. In turn, the proceeds from the sale were used by Glen Kirby's mom to pay off her son's court-ordered restitution. The proceeds from the sale immediately went to Walt's brother, Ted, to satisfy the ruling.

Glen was ordered to pay for the hospital bills incurred when Ted sustained severe injuries on the night of the Harvest Hoedown. The dollar amount was close to two-hundred and fifty thousand. Ted was incapacitated for over a week, in a coma from massive blunt trauma to his head and body by the hands of Glen Kirby and his bullies. The only way for Mrs. Kirby to keep her son out of jail was to pay Ted's hospital bills in full. And the only way to come up with the amount of money she needed was to sell her home and land, Glen's birthright. Walt had been waiting in the wings for the opportunity, ready to help the lady out— prepared to take Glen's inheritance right out from under him. Touché, cocksucker.

Ted's hospital bills were paid in full, thanks to the sale. And now Walt had a place to call his own. Ted would eventually come around and appreciate the gesture, wouldn't he? There was no other choice, and Walt was more than counting on it.

Later that evening, the can of soup Walt made for

dinner wasn't quite as tasty as the meals his sister, Becky, made back at the farm. She was a shining star in their family, her weekly YouTube cooking show blowing up her social media. Becky shared recipes she made for their family and the farmhands, her pretty smile and easy-going nature in the kitchen garnering tens of thousands of diehard fans. Her show was called *The Farmer's Daughter*, similar to *The Pioneer Woman*, featuring Ree Drummond on the Food Network. Walt wouldn't be surprised if Hollywood came calling someday soon, whisking his baby sister off to La-La Land.

Standing next to the sink, he sipped his soup from a cracked mug and looked out a small window into the dark night. He was thankful he'd installed outdoor light sensors and an interior alarm, not that he was afraid of anything or anyone. Still, he was prepared, and being alone for the first time in his life held a certain aura of caution, his family several miles away and his nearest neighbor beyond the apple orchard. He was used to the loud rhythm of family and dogs, sibling rivalry, and tourists. His work at the winery still mattered, and he would make the short commute each day, looking forward to seeing everyone. But at night, it was a different story. The odd quietness of his new world was definitely an adjustment.

The ping of his cell phone startled him out of his daze. Flipping the phone over, he grinned, realizing it was Becky calling to check up on him.

"Hey, Becks. How's it going?"

"Good. But I miss you!" she giggled.

Walt inhaled sharply, thankful for the loving reprieve. "You know I'm only a hop, skip, and a jump away. And you're welcome to come by and visit anytime. I'll even give you the grand tour."

"Walter, you only moved out today. And besides, I wanted to give you some time to put your stamp on things. You know, make the place your own."

Walt panned the kitchen area, which opened into the large family room. There wasn't a stick of furniture in sight. His neck grew hot; his voice traced with embarrassment. "Well, there isn't much to show you right now anyway. But give me a few weeks, and I'll throw a little party or something—"

"A house-warming party!" she screeched with glee. "Let me help you plan it. Please?"

Walt chuckled, the ache in his being foreign to him.

"Daddy can bring over some of the aged cabernet, you know, the good stuff, so we can christen your place properly. And I'll make those pimento cheese sandwiches and sugar cookies you love so much."

Walt's stomach growled at the mere mention of his sister's delicious food choices. Leave it to Becky to entice him with her cooking talents. Eyeing the cold soup in his mug, he set the container in the chipped farmhouse sink. "I'd love that, Becks."

"And maybe we can ask everyone to bring a bottle of liquor or a cocktail gadget, you know, a 'stock the bar' kind of gift for the new homeowner." Becky was on a roll, the event planner's side of her working on all cylinders.

"Whatever you want to do."

Becky was quiet for a beat. "What if… what if I came over now? I mean, I don't want to interrupt whatever you're doing, and I certainly don't want to be an annoying little sister. But silly me, I made one too many chicken pot pies thinking you'd be joining us for supper, like always."

Walt leaned against the kitchen counter. How was she so in tune with him? A peculiar knot formed in the pit of his stomach. At first, he thought it might be legitimate hunger from working too hard all day and skipping lunch. But then he thought it might be something more. Was it homesickness? He wasn't sure.

"I won't stay long. I'll bring over the pot pie, and you can give me the grand tour you mentioned."

Walt swallowed hard. He nodded before the words left his mouth. "As a matter of fact, I'd love a visitor right about now."

Grab your copy…
**vinci-books.com/shamelesslove**

# Playlist

The Bennetts of Langston Falls

*23* - Sam Hunt
*Home Sweet* - Russell Dickerson
*Freedom Was a Highway* - Jimmie Allen
*Chasing After You* - Ryan Hurd & Maren Morris
*Till You Can't* - Cody Johnson
*Can't Help Falling in Love* - Elvis
*Slow Down Summer* - Thomas Rhett
*American Honey* - Lady A
*Half of my Hometown* – Kelsea Ballerini
*We Were Us* - Keith Urban & Miranda Lambert
*Back to Life* - Rascal Flats
*Leave Before You Love Me* - Jonas Brothers
*Just a Kiss* - Lady A
*Never Till Now* - Ashley Cooke & Brett Young
*The Furthest Thing* - Maren Morris
*Forever For a Little While* - Russell Dickerson
*I Believe* - Jonas Brothers

***Want it Again*** - Thomas Rhett
***Your Body is a Wonderland*** - John Mayer
***I'll Never Love Again*** - Lady GaGa
***Doin This*** - Luke Combs
***What My World Spins Around*** - Jordan Davis
***Somebody*** - Justin Bieber
***XO*** - John Mayer

# About the Author

"The Singing Author," KG Fletcher, lives in her very own frat house in Atlanta, GA, with her husband Ladd and three sons. As a singer/songwriter, she became a recipient of the "Airplay International Award" for "Best New Artist," showcasing original songs at The Bluebird Café in Nashville, TN. She earned her BFA in theater at Valdosta State University and has traveled the world professionally as a singer/actress. She is a two-time Georgia Maggie Award Nominee and currently gets to play rock star as a backup singer in the "Remember When Rock Was Young – the Elton John Experience."

KG is a hopeless romantic. When she's not on the road singing, she's probably at home daydreaming about her swoony book boyfriends or arranging a yummy charcuterie board while sipping red wine and listening to Frank Sinatra. She's also a conference speaker and loves to interact with readers on social media and share about her writing and singing journey.

# Acknowledgments

As always, thank you to my fantastic husband and boys who are my biggest supporters and put up with this Mama constantly working and stressing about deadlines. To my Insta-author friends in the Slow Burn Sisterhood group, thank you for being a safe place to vent and for sharing all the romance. Debbie McCormick, your words of encouragement helped me so much, and I'm honored to be your friend! To my Atlanta Writers critique group, thank you for your valuable feedback on that first pesky chapter. To the best beta readers on the planet, Ladd, Blair, and Craig, thank you for pointing out my strengths and weaknesses and listening to me talk nonstop about the Bennett Family and how much I love them. To my Atlanta bestie, Anne, for introducing me to Linville Falls (the inspiration for Langston Falls) and accompanying me on that EPIC book research trip where we met ninety-one-year-old Jack Wiseman, the patriarch of the Linville Falls Winery. Can we do it again??

Special thanks to Vicky Burkholder, my long-time editor, for making this story shine. And to Lee Taylor, my Developmental Editor, for helping me navigate the courtroom drama and legal lingo. I'm so glad we are friends!

Thank you, Gigi Blume, you are and always will be my author bestie. Mmwah!

For my incredible team of ARC readers and all the bloggers who came on board with this series—THANK YOU for loving romance books as much as I do. Special shout-out to my super-talented romance author friend, Eliza Peake, and her expertise in helping me polish my blurbs. You really are the "blurb whisperer!"

For my critique partner, Carrie, who always has my back, and to all of my readers, thank you for your patience. I know it's been a while since I've released a new book. I'm so lucky to have your support, and I'm forever grateful. I have appreciated all of your kind comments on my social media posts and your private messages indicating your excitement for this new series. I'm so glad we can all escape into the wonderful world of books! The consistent reviews you have posted are virtual hugs I will cherish forever.

I hope you will continue the Bennett Family's journey in Book Two of the series, *Shameless Love*. Get ready for broody Walt and his story!

xoxo
KG